Timeless

Text copyright © 2011 by Alexandra Monir
Jacket art copyright © 2011 by Chad Michael Ward

All rights reserved. Published in the United States by Delacorte Press, an imprint of Random House Children's Books, a division of Random House, Inc., New York.

Delacorte Press is a registered trademark and the colophon is a trademark of Random House, Inc.

Grateful acknowledgment is made to Fain Music Co. and Williamson Music, Inc. for permission to reprint lyrics from "I'll Be Seeing You" by Sammy Fain and Irving Kahal, copyright © 1938 by Williamson Music, Inc. Renewed 1966 by Fain Music Co., and The New Irving Kahal Music Company. International copyright secured. All rights reserved. Reprinted by permission of Fain Music Co. and Williamson Music, Inc.

Visit us on the Web! www.randomhouse.com/teens

Educators and librarians, for a variety of teaching tools, visit us at
www.randomhouse.com/teachers

Library of Congress Cataloging-in-Publication Data
Monir, Alexandra.
Timeless / by Alexandra Monir. — 1st ed.
p. cm.
Summary: Forced to live with her wealthy, estranged grandparents in New York City after her mother dies, sixteen-year-old Michele retreats to her room where she finds a diary that transports her back to 1910—with life-changing consequences.
ISBN 978-0-385-73838-5 (hc) — ISBN 978-0-385-90726-2 (lib. bdg.) —
ISBN 978-0-375-89410-7 (ebook)
[1. Time travel—Fiction. 2. Wealth—Fiction. 3. Social classes—Fiction. 4. Families—Fiction. 5. Love—Fiction. 6. New York (N.Y.)—Fiction. 7. New York (N.Y.)—History—1898–1951—Fiction.] I. Title.
PZ7.M7495Ti 2011
[Fic]—dc22
2010019657

The text of this book is set in 12-point Garamond.

Book design by Angela Carlino

Printed in the United States of America

10 9 8 7 6 5 4 3 2 1

First Edition

Random House Children's Books supports the First Amendment
and celebrates the right to read.

Timeless

ALEXANDRA MONIR

Delacorte Press

DEDICATED TO MY PARENTS,
WHOM I LOVE AND CHERISH
FOR ALL TIME.

Timeless

Michele stood alone in the center of a hall of mirrors. The glass re-
vealed a girl identical to Michele, with the same chestnut hair, ivory
skin, and hazel eyes; even wearing the same outfit of dark denim
jeans and black tank top. But when Michele moved forward, the
girl in the glass remained still. And while Michele's own neck was
bare, the reflection in the mirror wore a strange key hanging from
a gold chain, a key unlike anything Michele had ever seen.

It was a gold skeleton key in a shape similar to a cross, but with
a circular bow at the top. The image of a sundial was carved into
the bow. The key looked weathered and somehow wise, as though it
weren't inanimate, but a living being with over a century's worth
of stories to share. Michele was momentarily seized by an urge to

reach through the glass and touch the curious key. But all she felt was the cool surface of the mirror, and the girl with Michele's face betrayed no notice of her.

"Who are you?" Michele whispered. But the mirror image didn't respond, didn't even appear to have heard. Michele shivered nervously, and squeezed her eyes shut. What was this?

And then, suddenly, the silence was broken. Someone was whistling, a slow melody that created goose bumps on the back of Michele's neck. Her eyes snapped open, and she watched in shock as someone joined the girl in the mirror. Michele's breath caught in her throat. She felt paralyzed, unable to do anything but stare at him through the glass.

His eyes were such a deep blue they seemed to dazzle against his contrasting thick dark hair. Eyes the color of sapphires. And though she could somehow tell that he was around her age, he was dressed like none of the other boys she knew. He wore a crisp white collared shirt under a white silk vest and tie, formal black pants, and black patent leather shoes. In his white-gloved hands, he held a black top hat lined with silk. The formal clothing suited him. He was more than good-looking, much more than could be conveyed by the word "handsome." Michele felt an unfamiliar ache as she watched him.

Her heart racing, she stared at him as he carelessly peeled off his gloves and dropped his hat, the three items falling together in a heap on the floor. He then reached for the hand of the girl in the mirror. And to Michele's astonishment, she felt his touch. She quickly looked down, but though her hand was empty, she could feel his fingers interlacing with hers, the sensation causing a flutter inside her.

What's happening to me? Michele thought frantically. But

suddenly she couldn't think anymore, for as she looked at the boy and girl embracing in the mirror, she felt strong arms encircling her own waist.

"I'm waiting for you," he murmured, smiling a slow, familiar grin that seemed to hint at a secret between them.

And for the first time, Michele and the mirror reflection were in sync as they both whispered, "Me too."

Michele Windsor awoke with a shock, gasping for breath. As she took in the sight of her darkened bedroom, her heartbeat slowed and she remembered—it was just The Dream. The same strange, intoxicating dream that had haunted her on and off for years. As always, waking up from it brought the pain of disappointment into the pit of Michele's stomach, as she found herself missing him—this person who didn't even exist.

She'd been just a little girl when she'd first begun dreaming of him, so young that she hadn't yet resembled the teenager in the mirror. The dreams were infrequent then; they came just once or twice a year. But as she grew up, looking like the twin of the girl in the mirror, the dreams began to flood her consciousness with a new urgency, as if they were trying to *tell* her something. Michele frowned as she slumped back against her pillows, wondering if she would ever understand. But then, Confusion and Mystery had been principal players in her life since the day she was born.

Michele rolled over onto her side, facing her bedroom window, and listening to the waves lapping the shore outside the Venice Beach bungalow. The sound usually lulled her to sleep quickly, but not that night. She couldn't seem to get those sapphire eyes out of her head. Eyes that she had practically memorized, without ever having seen them in her waking life.

"See that I'm everywhere, everywhere, shining down on you . . ."

The pulsing hip-hop beat of the Lupe Fiasco song "Shining Down" blared from Michele's iPod alarm the next morning. She unearthed her head from the covers and pressed the Snooze button. How could it already be morning? It felt like just moments earlier that she had managed to fall back to sleep.

"Michele!" a voice sang out from across the hall. "Are you up? I made pancakes, come eat them before they get cold."

Michele's eyes flickered open. Sleep or pancakes? That was a no-brainer. Her mouth was already beginning to water at the thought of her mom's specialty. She threw on a robe and fuzzy slippers and padded through the modest house until she reached the cozy kitchen. Marion Windsor was in her usual morning mode, sipping coffee while studying her newest clothing designs in her sketchbook. The crinkly sound of Marion's favorite old jazz record, by none other than her grandmother Lily Windsor, echoed from their vintage record player.

"Good morning, sweetie," Marion greeted her daughter, looking up from her sketchbook with a smile.

"Morning." Michele leaned over to give her mom a kiss and glanced at the sketch she'd been working on. A long, flowing dress with a bit of a Pocahontas-circa-2010 feel, it was right in keeping with the other bohemian-chic pieces in her mom's line, Marion Windsor Designs.

"I like it," Michele said approvingly. She settled into her seat in front of a plate of golden pancakes topped with strawberries. "And *this,* I definitely like."

"Bon appétit." Marion grinned. "Speaking of food, do you have lunch plans with the girls today?"

Michele shrugged as she inhaled her first forkful of delicious pancake. "Just the usual, nothing special."

"Well, I have a free afternoon, so I was thinking I could pick you up at lunch and we could go for burgers at Santa Monica Pier," Marion suggested. "What do you say?"

Michele gave her mom a sideways look. "You still feel sorry for me, don't you?"

"What? No!" Marion said innocently.

Michele raised an eyebrow at her.

"Okay, fine," Marion said, relenting. "I don't feel *sorry* for you, because I know you're so much better off without him. But I can't stand to see you hurt."

Michele nodded, looking away. It had been two weeks since her first real boyfriend, Jason, had broken up with her on the eve of the first day of school. His exact words had been "Babe, you know I think you're the best and all, but it's my senior year and I can't have the baggage of a relationship. I gotta live it up, play the field. You get it, right?" *Uh, not exactly.* So Michele had to begin her junior year with a broken heart, which grew all the more painful last week, when word spread that Jason was hooking up with a sophomore, Carly Marsh.

Marion reached across the table and squeezed Michele's hand. "Sweetie, I know how hard it is to see your first boyfriend with someone else. It's just going to take a little time to heal from this."

"But really, I *should* be over it," Michele vented. "I mean, all he ever talked about was water polo, and he was about as romantic as a toothpick. I just really miss—I don't know. . . ."

"That butterflies-in-your-stomach feeling of wanting to be with someone, and knowing they feel the same way about you?" Marion guessed.

"Yeah," Michele admitted sheepishly. "Exactly."

"Well, I can promise that you'll have that again, but with someone so much better," Marion said intently.

"How do you know that?" Michele asked doubtfully.

"Because we mothers have an intuition about these things. So when you see Jason with Carly, do your best to just shrug it off and think how lucky you are to be free for a guy who's actually worthy of you."

Michele shook her head wonderingly. It never ceased to amaze her that her mom had such an optimistic outlook on Michele's love life—or even still *believed* in love—after all Marion herself had been through in that department.

"I'm serious," Marion insisted. "And in the meantime, are you using all this as fodder for your writing?"

"Oh, you know it," Michele said wryly. "Lots of angsty song lyrics and poems."

"That's my girl," Marion encouraged. "You'd better let me read some of it soon."

"Once I edit everything down to perfection? Sure," Michele

said with a grin. "And I think I will take you up on burgers at the beach."

Even though she was more than a little skeptical of Marion's predictions about her love life, Michele always felt better after confiding in her. It had been the two of them against the world since Michele was born, and there was never a problem or a heartache that Marion couldn't fix with her stubborn resolve and humor.

"Honey, you're looking pretty pale," Marion noticed, eyeing her with concern. "Did you sleep well last night?"

"Not really. I woke up in the middle of the night after dreaming about Mystery Man, and then it took me forever to fall back to sleep."

"So you saw him again," Marion said, her eyes lighting up. "Do tell."

"Mom, I know you think the dreams are cool and all, but I can never meet this guy in real life," Michele reminded her. "So the whole thing is actually really irritating."

"Well, I think it's romantic. Maybe it's your subconscious telling you not to worry about Jason, that you *will* find someone special." Marion glanced at her watch. "Yikes, it's seven-thirty! You'd better go get ready."

"Okay, I'll be back in fifteen." Michele hurried to her room and changed into a fitted white tee, Abercrombie jeans with a skinny metallic belt, and a pair of black flats. She quickly ran a brush through her hair and dabbed on some concealer and lip gloss before tossing the three beauty essentials into her messenger bag.

Michele found Marion waiting in their Volvo outside the

bungalow. As they set off toward Santa Monica, Marion flicked on the CD player. "I want you to hear my latest discovery," she said. "Well, maybe that's not the most accurate description, since she's a Grammy-winning artist who's been around for decades. But I only recently heard about her, and she just might be my new favorite singer—after my grandmother, of course."

Michele curiously waited for the music to start. Her mom had such eclectic taste she never knew what to expect. This music surprised her. It managed to be heavy and light all at once, both breezy and aching. As soon as she heard the opening chords of the two Spanish guitars and the swaying Brazilian rhythm, Michele felt like she was transported to an exotic paradise. But when a woman with a deep, husky voice began to sing in Portuguese a melody rich with minor keys, Michele instantly knew that she was singing about pain. And yet the song wasn't sad, exactly.

"Nostalgia," Marion explained. "That word she keeps singing, *sodade*—it's the Portuguese word for a nostalgia so intense we don't have a direct translation for it in English."

"Wow." Michele picked up the CD case and looked at the cover photo of the singer, who appeared to be in her sixties or seventies. Her name was Cesaria Evora. Michele and her mom listened to the rest of the song in silence, and as the final chords played, Michele asked, "What does it make you think of?"

Marion paused. "Home," she said so quietly that Michele almost wondered if she had misheard.

She stared at her mom. "Really?"

But they had just pulled up in front of her school, Crossroads High. Marion didn't answer; she just smiled at Michele and smoothed back her daughter's hair. "See you at lunch, honey."

"Bye, Mom." Michele gave her a quick hug. "Love you."

"I love you too. Good luck with—you know." Marion gave her a meaningful smile before zooming off, her long auburn hair flying behind her.

Michele dashed to her locker and found her best friends waiting for her, Amanda typing away on her iPhone and Kristen inspecting herself with a compact mirror. Seconds later, the girls were heading down the hall to class, arms linked as they chattered. Michele was conscious of eyes on them as they passed, but the stares were mainly directed at her friends. Amanda was a leggy blonde budding model, while Kristen was the star of the soccer team. Michele had to admit that growing up with both the school beauty and the star athlete had made her conscious of how painfully ordinary she was in comparison. In her most private moments, she'd fantasized about returning to school after summer vacation as a new and improved Michele. She would transform herself from the girl-next-door type into a mysterious, stunning beauty, and she would finally gather the courage to take her mom's advice and submit her song lyrics to record labels and singers, becoming a wunderkind songwriter—

"Uh, earth to Michele!" Amanda waved a hand in front of Michele's face. "Did you hear what I just said?"

Michele gave her friend a sheepish smile. She really needed to quit daydreaming in public.

"No, sorry, what?"

"I asked if your mom has any ideas for our Halloween costume this year."

"Oh, right. She's taking me out for burgers this afternoon, so I'll ask her then. But we still have over a month left."

"I know, but since we're hosting a party this year, our costumes have to be *extra* fabulous," Amanda said importantly. "I mean, people have come to expect a lot from your mom's designs."

Michele chuckled. "Okay, well, don't worry. You know she can live up to the hype."

Every year since they were little, the three girls had coordinated their costumes, with Marion designing and sewing their ensembles. From trick-or-treating as kids to Halloween partying now that they were older, Michele loved the sense of belonging she felt as she and her best friends sauntered into the night, arm in arm, wearing their beautiful costumes.

The three girls hurried into their first-period junior-senior economics class just as the final bell rang. As Michele slid into her seat, she couldn't help glancing at Jason. She tried to ignore the familiar pang in her chest at the sight of his sandy dark-blond hair and brown eyes, which were focused away from her.

"Morning, class," the teacher, Mrs. Brewer, greeted them. "So, in keeping with our study of the history of commerce, today's lecture will cover one of the greatest commercial merchants in American history."

Michele froze. She was pretty sure she knew who Mrs. Brewer was referring to.

"August Charles—" Michele felt her whole body tense up, as it did whenever the name was mentioned.

"Windsor," Mrs. Brewer finished. "Of the famed Windsor family. He was America's first multimillionaire. August Charles was born to a poor Dutch family in the year 1760, but from childhood, he was known for his brilliant mind and fierce ambition. At the age of twenty-one, he began a career in fur trade, which was the start of his meteoric rise to fortune through trade and real estate. His descendents furthered the empire by gaining control of the burgeoning New York railroad . . ."

Mrs. Brewer's voice seemed to fade as Michele looked around at her classmates, some of whom were listening and taking notes, the rest clearly zoning out. But none of them would ever have believed that Crossroads High's own Michele Windsor had been born into this very family.

Marion had often said that hers was a cautionary tale for all Manhattan heiresses, that privilege came with a dark underbelly that few could see. Their neighbors in the laid-back Los Angeles town of Venice Beach all thought of Marion and Michele Windsor as the average single mom and daughter, with no connection whatsoever to that famous East Coast family of the same name. And that was just the way Marion liked them to be: anonymous. So while Michele's aunts, uncles, and grandparents lived in New York splendor, spending their summers in Europe and snagging invitations to White House dinners and Broadway premieres, Marion and Michele struggled to make ends meet on Marion's modest clothing-design income, with Michele's after-school waitressing job providing some pocket money.

It would have been easy to feel bitter about the injustice of it all during the painful times growing up when there wasn't enough money for Michele to go to sleepaway camp with her friends or buy the cool clothes and cutting-edge gadgets everyone else had. But Michele knew she had no right to complain, since she never would have been born if it hadn't been for Marion's exile.

When Michele was old enough to understand, Marion had told her the story, just once. It was a story that had left an indelible imprint on Michele's mind, one whose details she could call to memory at any instant, without ever having to pain her mom by bringing up the subject.

In 1991, the sixteen-year-old heiress Marion Windsor fell in love with Henry Irving, a nineteen-year-old from the Bronx. They met in a photography class at the Museum of Modern Art, and Marion was instantly fascinated with him. *"He was so . . . completely different from every other boy I knew. It was like he came from another world. Everything about him, even his name, seemed special and unique to me."* Michele remembered how her mom had stopped at this early point in the story, swallowing hard and taking a few deep breaths, as if gathering the courage to continue. *"He lived alone—his parents were far away—and that made him seem so much older and more mature than everyone else. I'd become so used to the grungy guys of the nineties, with their low-slung baggy pants that were practically on the ground, their slouching, and the careless way they would treat us girls. Well, that first day of class when I met Henry, he was standing tall and well dressed, and he actually took off his cap as he introduced himself to me, just like a gentleman. I was hooked right then."*

As the class progressed, Marion grew to love the look of fierce concentration on Henry's face as he studied a print, the way he could see the beauty and worthiness in objects and settings that no one else would bother to photograph. He had a different way of looking at the world, and it drew Marion to him like a magnet.

"I was desperate to get to know him, so one day I decided to just bite the bullet and sit next to him in class. And what do you know, that was the day the teacher had us work in pairs with the person sitting next to us," Marion had told Michele in a voice that sounded tremulous and different from her own. *"Halfway through class, I could somehow tell that he was just as taken with me. He asked for my phone number, and we went on our first date that Saturday night."*

The relationship soon grew serious, and Marion was unable to believe her good fortune as Henry fell in love with her. But her conservative, strict Windsor parents considered this boy from the opposite side of the tracks a nightmare of a choice for their only child. *"At first they thought it was just puppy love, a passing phase. So even though they disapproved, I wasn't forbidden to go out with him. We were together through all of my last two years of high school. But during my senior year, my parents started forcing me to go on dates with their friends' sons and attend these ridiculous debutante parties to meet boys they had preapproved. Henry and I both knew that I was getting closer and closer to being trapped by my last name and what it meant."*

When Marion was eighteen and approaching her high school graduation, Henry decided to solve the problem for them—by proposing. He was ready to start a life together. Marion had always known that he was the one for her, and she ecstatically accepted.

"I wasn't expecting my parents to be happy about it . . . but I never could have imagined their reaction when I told them the news," Marion had said, her eyes darkening at the memory. *"Mom cried all night, and Dad ranted and raved about how I was the last in the centuries-old family line and that marrying Henry would disgrace the Windsor name. With no brothers, I was expected to marry a businessman who could run the Windsor empire, someone from a solid old-money family who would also help the Windsors continue their reign over Manhattan society."* Needless to say, Henry was neither. But Marion loved him and refused to give him up.

"It will never work for you two to be together. New York won't accept it, and neither will we," Marion's mother had declared. So Marion and Henry decided they had no choice but to leave New York . . . and the Windsors. As Marion explained to Michele, at the age of eighteen, how could she even contemplate spending the rest of her life without the person she loved most in the world? Henry had some money saved up from his part-time job, and a friend from their photography class who had recently moved to Los Angeles offered to take them in until they found a place of their own. So Henry and Marion began planning for a new life on the West Coast.

On the evening of June 10, 1993, the day after Marion's high school graduation, she stuffed her most important belongings into a backpack subtle enough to go unnoticed by the household staff, and waited nervously for her parents to leave for a dinner party. Half an hour after they left, Henry arrived to pick her up. Marion took one last look at the beautiful bedroom she had spent eighteen years growing up in, then stole through the house. She left a note in her mother's parlor on the second floor, then hurried out the front doors and into Henry's arms.

Los Angeles was an adjustment at first, with Marion and Henry both feeling homesick and out of place in California. Despite her conflicts with her parents, Marion still missed them and struggled with guilt over hurting them. But not once did she or Henry express any second thoughts about their decision. *"We always knew it was the right thing. And once we moved into our own place, it was what I had always pictured domestic bliss to be,"* Marion remembered with a sad smile. *"He was so brilliant that I encouraged him to take an unpaid assistant position with a UCLA physics professor, in exchange for free college classes. He worked long hours while I waited tables at a diner, but we were young and in love, and planning to go to Vegas to be married as soon as we had enough money for the trip. There was this feeling that we could have, do, or be anything—so long as we were together."*

But a few short weeks later, the dream turned into a nightmare. Marion came home from a late shift at work to find that Henry wasn't there. When he finally got back he seemed distracted and dazed, like he was in another world. Sure, he hugged and kissed her like usual—but without really *seeing* her. When Marion asked him what was wrong, he gave her a tense smile and said that it was nothing, that he was just tired. *"It was like he had something huge on his mind, something he couldn't share with me."*

The following day, Marion again came home to an empty

apartment. She didn't think much of it at first, assuming he was working late again. But then he didn't come home at all.

Panicked, Marion called everyone she could think of—his boss, the friend they had stayed with when they'd first come to L.A., acquaintances they'd made during their brief time in California—but no one had heard from him all day. She called the police, all the local hospitals, but there was no trace of him.

As Marion struggled to keep from hysterics, the phone sounded its shrill ring. She leaped up to answer it, sure that it *must* be Henry. But her heart sank when she heard the voice of his boss instead, the eccentric physics professor Alfred Woolsey.

"No, he didn't come in to work today," Alfred had said slowly. *"But . . . I want you to know, Marion, I honestly think he's all right."*

"Where is he?" Marion demanded, her voice rising. *"How in the world could you know that he's all right?"*

"I don't know where he is," Alfred said regretfully. *"But . . . I think you should know that yesterday your parents called my office to speak to him. They spoke for nearly an hour, and when Henry got off the phone, he seemed . . . well, different."*

Marion could scarcely breathe. Her parents had called him? Her own parents might have had a hand in his disappearance? She hurried Alfred off the phone, barely registering his parting words about something Henry had left behind in the office.

"I called Mom and Dad right away . . . and they admitted to having offered Henry one million dollars to break off our engagement. But they actually said he refused *their offer, and they were almost relieved, because they were overcome with guilt over the whole idea."* Marion snorted angrily. *"I know a lie when I hear*

one. They were capable of making that disgusting offer, so they were capable of following through and lying about it to cover their tracks. I know that's why he left me. My parents might have thought paying him off would bring me back home, but it only cut me off from them for good."

Two weeks later, while Marion was still reeling from the betrayal of her fiancé and parents, she discovered that she was pregnant. Now Henry hadn't just abandoned her—he had left their child fatherless.

"I'll admit that when I found out, I was at my lowest low. But then it hit me that I had lost everything—my fiancé, my family, my home—and now God was giving me something to live for," Marion had said, taking Michele's hand. *"There was a reason for all this pain. Maybe I had to meet and fall for Henry Irving in order to bring you into the world. And when I met my daughter, it was love at first sight. I vowed to myself that I would be a real parent to you. I'd be everything that your father and grandparents couldn't be."*

And Marion did just that. She was more than a parent— she was a best friend to Michele. And whenever Michele had gone over to friends' houses and seen a traditional two-parent family, with grandparents on either side, the usually tension-fraught relationships between parent and child made it easy for Michele to feel that she'd gotten the better deal.

Though Marion had never seriously dated anyone after Henry, she had thrown herself into being a mother and a designer and seemed to find fulfillment in those roles. So one could say that things had turned out surprisingly all right. Still, it was painful for Michele to hear or read about the famed

Windsors. While other people saw them as the symbol of the American Dream, Michele saw them for who they really were: the cruel, dictatorial characters who had nearly ruined her mother.

After hearing the story, Michele had asked the question that had stood out in her mind above all the others. *"How . . . how did you ever get through it? Didn't everything just make you want to die?"*

At that, Marion had grabbed Michele's shoulders and looked her firmly in the eyes. *"Listen to me, Michele. There is nothing in this life that can ever destroy you but yourself. Bad things happen to everyone, but when they do, you can't just fall apart and die. You have to fight back. If you don't, you're the one who loses in the end. But if you do keep going and fight back, you win. Just like I won with you."*

Even though she had been just a child, Michele knew in that moment that her mom was stronger than the rest. That she was special.

"Michele? Michele!"

Michele's head snapped up. Her teacher was eyeing her sternly.

"Let's see if you were paying attention," Mrs. Brewer said. "What is the name of the family that became the Windsors' greatest rivals in both business and society, and why?"

"The Walker family," Michele answered automatically. "They had a majority ownership in some of the railroads the Windsors wanted to gain control of. And the women in the two families were always trying to upstage each other in society."

Mrs. Brewer raised her eyebrows, clearly surprised by Michele's knowledge. "That's right," she said slowly.

Kristen caught Michele's eye and the two of them shared a knowing look. Kristen was the one who had told Michele about the Walkers. She and Amanda were the only friends who knew Michele's secret and, curious about her famous family, had done their fair share of research. But they had guarded the secret well. No one else ever could have imagined that ordinary Michele Windsor had been born to blue blood.

When the bell rang for lunch a few hours later, Michele jumped out of her seat, relieved to have calculus class behind her. Math was definitely not one of her strong suits. She threw her textbook and binder into her bag and hurried out of the classroom, heading toward the school's front entrance. Marion hadn't arrived yet, so Michele hopped onto a bench to wait. Friends trickled by on their way to lunch, stopping to say hi and share choice bits of the day's gossip.

Ten minutes later there was still no sign of her mom. Michele pulled her cell phone out of her bag and dialed Marion's number, but the call went to voice mail. Just as she was about to leave a message, her attention was diverted by a police car pulling up to the school. Michele stared at the officer who got out of the car, his face drawn. With a flicker of curiosity, she wondered which one of her classmates might be in trouble.

The policeman's eyes met hers and then he did a double take, glancing down at something in his hands. With a stab of fear, she saw that he was now heading in her direction. *He's probably just going to ask if I have any information on someone or something,* she reassured herself, shifting nervously on her seat. Still, she couldn't keep her imagination at bay as he came closer. She tried to stay calm as visions of drugs being planted in her locker and similar offenses danced in her head.

"Hello. Are you Michele Windsor?" asked the officer, a ruddy-faced man of middle age.

Michele nodded shakily and got to her feet. She cringed as she realized that her mom was probably going to pull up to the school at any moment, only to find her being interrogated by the police.

The officer placed a gentle hand on her shoulder. "I'm afraid I have some bad news. You should probably sit down for this."

Michele's body turned cold. She stumbled back onto the bench and looked from the policeman to the school parking lot, torn between a desperate need to find out what was going on and an equally desperate urge to run away.

"I've just come from Santa Monica Hospital," he continued quietly. "I can't tell you how sorry I am to have to say this, but your mother got into a car accident at eight-fifteen this morning. Another driver was speeding and ran a red light, colliding with your mother's vehicle. And I'm afraid . . . she didn't make it."

"What?" Michele asked uncomprehendingly. She had heard wrong. There was no way—

"Your mother is"—the policeman looked down uncomfortably—"dead."

No. No no no no no no. Michele shook her head frantically and jumped off the bench. Her mother's words to her that morning echoed in her ears: *"See you at lunch, honey."*

"No!" Michele gasped. "That's impossible. You've got the wrong person! I just saw my mom this morning, she dropped me off and she'll be here any minute to take me to lunch—" She looked around wildly, willing the Volvo to pull up in front of the school. "You'll see, she'll be here any second!"

"Miss Windsor, it's understandable for this to be a terrible shock," the officer said, his voice grave. "She got into the accident just after dropping you off. I wish it wasn't true, but . . . We were called to the scene immediately, along with an ambulance. Everyone did all they could, but we were unable to revive either of the drivers. We found your mother's wallet in her purse, and that's how I located you." He handed her the object in his hands—Marion's faded brown leather wallet, with Michele's school picture peeking out from one of the flaps.

As she stared disbelievingly at her mother's wallet, Michele lost all sense of herself. Her head felt light, her vision nothing more than black-and-white dots swimming before her eyes, and the only audible sound was a vicious ringing in her ears.

"It isn't true." She gulped, fighting back the bile rising in her throat.

The officer tried to console her, but Michele pushed him away. If she could just get away from the school . . . if she could find her mom and make it okay . . . But as she tried to make her escape, she felt as if the ground was shaking underneath her. With a cry, she fell back onto the pavement. And everything turned black.

"Michele?" came a tentative voice.

Michele didn't answer, keeping her eyes shut as she lay in bed. It was the tenth day after Marion's funeral, and Michele was spending it the same way she had spent all her time since: holed up in the guest bedroom at Kristen's house. She couldn't set foot in her own home, couldn't bear to see it now that Marion was gone. Her friends had collected her things for her, and she had visitors at Kristen's every day, but nothing eased the unbearable pain. Michele had barely spoken or eaten since her mom's death. She had dropped nearly ten pounds, and she knew somewhere in the back of her mind that her behavior was scaring everyone. Kristen's parents had even pleaded with her to let them take her to Cedars-Sinai Medical Center, but Michele refused. She didn't *want* to get better. She only wanted her mom back.

"Michele?" Kristen's voice persisted.

Michele reluctantly opened her eyes and turned onto her side to look at Kristen. Amanda hovered beside her. The two of them had dark circles under their eyes from lack of sleep.

"I'm really sorry to do this, but Ms. Richards is here and she's forcing us to let her see you," Kristen said awkwardly. "She has news. . . . I have to let her in."

Michele buried her face in the pillow. Ms. Richards was

the social worker who was suddenly thrust into Michele's life after Marion died, supposedly to help the courts decide where Michele should live from now on. *Because I'm an orphan now.* Michele had thought those words countless times over the past two weeks, but they never ceased to feel unreal.

"I'm not going to live with you guys, am I?" Michele asked Kristen dully.

Kristen looked on the verge of tears. "You know we want you to! My parents are ready to become your guardians this minute."

"Mine too," Amanda added, sitting on the bed next to Michele. "But it's not up to us. . . . You know that."

Michele didn't answer, and after a few moments, Kristen got up to let the social worker in. A petite woman with curly brown hair and gentle eyes, Ms. Richards came into the room and pulled up a chair beside Michele. Amanda and Kristen sat at the foot of the bed, watching anxiously.

"How are you feeling, sweetie?" Ms. Richards asked. Michele didn't bother answering that question. Ms. Richards reached into her briefcase and pulled out Michele's file. "Well, I have some good news."

"I get to live with Kristen or Amanda?" Michele asked.

"Well . . . no. The good news is that the court lawyer and I made contact with the guardians your mother named for you in her will, and they want to take you in immediately. I have a letter here from them."

"What?" Michele sat upright. "What guardians? I didn't know my mom had named anyone for me, and if she did, I know it would be Amanda or Kristen's parents."

"The will was very clear, and there was no alternate guardian named. Just Marion's parents, Walter and Dorothy Windsor."

"What?" Michele, Amanda, and Kristen gasped in unison. Michele's mind raced, as she felt something besides grief for the first time in weeks.

"That has to be a mistake," Michele said shakily. "My mom has been cut off from her parents since before I was born. They drove my dad away. I've never even met them! There's no way she would give them guardianship—"

"I've seen cases like this before," Ms. Richards interrupted. "Often a mother or father does not have the best relationship with her or his own parents but still recognizes that they're the right people to take care of the child, should something happen."

"It can't be." Michele shook her head in disbelief. "I don't actually have to go, do I? You can't force me."

"Since you're a minor, you are under control of the family courts," Ms. Richards said carefully. "Contesting the will in this case requires you to first live with the Windsors for a minimum of three months. And even after that, I have to warn you that fighting this could be a lengthy process. Since you're nearly seventeen now, you're probably better off sticking it out with your grandparents until you turn eighteen."

"So wait . . . Michele has to move to New York?" Amanda asked, looking stunned.

"Yes." Ms. Richards handed Michele a FedEx envelope. "I can't explain it, but it's what Marion requested."

Michele stared at the thin package for a few moments before ripping it open. Inside was a cream envelope with her name written in fancy calligraphy. The return address was a stamp reading: *Windsor Mansion, 790 Fifth Avenue, New York, NY 10022.* Michele began to read.

September 30, 2010

Dear Michele,

It is very difficult to believe that this is only our first correspondence. I have thought of you and wondered about you every day. Despite the fact that we weren't in each other's lives, you and your mother were always in my heart, as well as your grandfather's. We so wish things had been different between all of us.

We are devastated by Marion's passing. We've been so worried about how you would get on without your mother, and thus were relieved to learn that Marion had named us your guardians in her will. To that end, we submitted an application on your behalf to Berkshire High School, one of the finest private schools in the nation. This was the alma mater of Marion and most of the other Windsor girls over the last century.

We would like to fly you to New York as soon as possible. In this painful time, getting to meet you and have you live with us will be the one bright spot for your grandfather and me.

Love,

Dorothy Windsor

Michele read the letter three times, waiting for the words to feel real. Did her grandmother mean what she had written? Moreover, *why* would her mom choose her parents to be Michele's guardians? She had to have known that Michele would try to fight it.

Ms. Richards broke the long silence. "I know this wasn't what you wanted, Michele. I know we're asking a lot of you, to leave your school and friends and home. But think about this: you'll be living in the same house your mom grew up in. Mr. and Mrs. Windsor told me that you'll have Marion's old bedroom and you'll be attending her school. Maybe your mom chose her parents as your guardians so you could stay connected to her in this way."

Michele was quiet as Ms. Richards's words sank in. What she wanted most in the world was to feel her mom with her again. What if this was the way?

Suddenly, Michele's mind flashed back to her last car ride with Marion, when they had listened to the song about nostalgia, *"Sodade."*

"What does it make you think of?"

"Home."

"Okay," Michele said after a pause. "I'll go."

"Flight attendants, be seated for landing," the pilot announced over the PA system.

Michele took a deep breath. She turned to look through the airplane window as New York, a mass of bright lights and buildings, became visible below the clouds. She nervously twirled a lock of hair around her finger. This was it. She was about to meet her new city—her new life.

She leaned back against the plush seat, which felt almost too comfortable. Her mom had never approved of wasting money on first-class tickets, but that was what Walter and Dorothy had arranged. For a moment, Michele felt guilty.

It seemed impossible that she had read her grandmother's letter only one week earlier. Everything had happened so fast after that. Amanda, Kristen, and their families had insisted on helping with her packing, and the Windsors had arranged for her boxes to be shipped to New York three days before the move. Ms. Richards had gathered all Michele's school and medical records, withdrawn her from Crossroads and enrolled her in Berkshire High to start on the eleventh of October. *Just three days from now,* Michele realized, her stomach lurching at the thought.

The previous night had been Michele's farewell sleepover with Amanda and Kristen. She'd expected to be inconsolable over saying goodbye to them, but the loss of her mom had made everything else pale in comparison. So while her friends tearfully spoke of how strange life would be without her and promised to call, text, and Facebook her every day, Michele simply sat there, numbly observing this latest step in the dismantling of her life.

Now she glanced back out the window and saw that the plane was lowering to the ground. She was almost in New York.

Michele made her way to baggage claim at John F. Kennedy International Airport, her heart hammering with nerves. It was hard to believe that she was just moments away from meeting her mom's parents for the very first time. But to her surprise, she instead spotted a man in a crisp business suit standing by the luggage carousel and holding up a sign bearing her name.

"Hi," Michele said as she approached him. "I'm Michele."

The man's face lit up and he gave her a goofy little bow. "Wonderful to meet you, Miss Windsor. I'm Fritz, the family chauffeur."

Chauffeur? Michele thought with a jolt. This was going to be different from California, all right.

"Um, you can call me Michele. And it's nice to meet you too," she replied. "So I take it my grandparents aren't here?"

"Oh no." Fritz looked at her as though that were a wild leap. "They're waiting for you at home, of course."

"Right." Michele nodded. But she couldn't help feeling hurt that her grandparents didn't want to be at the airport to welcome her.

A few minutes later, after retrieving her two suitcases, Michele was in the backseat of the sleek black Windsor SUV. As Fritz drove from Queens into Manhattan, Michele gazed out the window. She watched as they passed the suburban homes, shops, and restaurants of Queens and headed onto the highway. The blue-gray East River shimmered below while lit-up marquees advertising the latest Broadway hits dazzled overhead, like an opening act for the city that was about to make its entrance.

Mom must have seen dozens of Broadway shows while growing up here, Michele realized with a pang of grief.

As they exited the freeway, Michele sucked in her breath at her first glimpse of Manhattan, watching as snapshots of New York City came to life: the long avenues that seemed to stretch on endlessly, the soaring skyscrapers packed close together, and the bright lights casting a theatrical glow over all the sights. Before long, they arrived at Fifth Avenue, which was block upon block of five-star hotels, elegant restaurants, and high-end stores. Fashionably dressed locals zipped into and out of the shops, skillfully juggling their BlackBerries and iPhones with their shopping bags. As Michele watched the people go by, it seemed to her that all the passersby had someone—someone to hold their hand as they crossed the street, someone to hurry through the chill with. In this bustling new city, Michele felt even more alone.

Fritz continued up Fifth, driving past the majestic, Gothic St. Patrick's Cathedral and the Beaux Arts structure of the famed Plaza Hotel. And then he approached a four-story palace of shimmering white marble, which stood proudly behind towering wrought-iron gates carved with a *W.* Old-fashioned horse-drawn carriages and pedicabs transported giddy tourists past this mammoth estate into nearby Central Park.

"Here we are," Fritz announced. "Welcome home!"

Michele's mouth fell open in astonishment. "Are you kidding me?"

A portico of four hulking white Corinthian columns fronted the mansion's exterior. There were curved balconies and arched windows, and beyond the gates, Michele could see that the driveway and grounds were decorated with a rose garden and small sculptures. A group of tourists stood outside the gates, taking pictures of one of the last remaining relics of Gilded Age New York.

Fritz's eyes met Michele's in the rearview mirror and he chuckled. "I forgot, it's your first time seeing the home. Pretty incredible, huh? You know, it was modeled after the palazzi of the Italian Renaissance. Created by the foremost American architect of the late nineteenth century, Richard Morris Hunt."

Fritz used a remote control to open the gates and the tourists scampered out of the way, gawking at the SUV. As he drove around the circular gravel driveway that swept up to the imposing front doors, Michele had the strangest feeling that she had gazed upon this massive structure before. After climbing out of the backseat, she stopped for one more glance at the mansion's exterior before following Fritz up the white stone steps.

Fritz opened the doors of gilded bronze and glass. "Welcome to the Grand Hall," he said with a flourish of his hand.

Michele gasped. "Oh. My. God."

She had stepped into an enormous airy indoor atrium, built with domed arches, soaring marble columns, and frescoed ceilings. The upper-story galleries looked out on this indoor courtyard, giving the mansion an open-air feel. The east wall was made almost entirely of glass, offering a view of the mansion's back garden, with the hills of Central Park in the distance. Two Italian tapestries flanked the entrance, and the ceiling was painted to depict a summer sky, framed in ornamented gold. But the centerpiece of the room was the grand staircase of white marble with deep red carpeting, featuring ornate wrought-iron and bronze banisters. The staircase rose from the Grand Hall, breaking into two curving sections at the first landing. Opposite the staircase was a huge ornately carved fireplace, where a glowing fire was lit.

Our whole Venice Beach house could fit into this one room, Michele thought in amazement. Her eyes could hardly take in this overwhelming spectacle. Marion's brief description of the Windsor Mansion's grandeur had hardly prepared her for this.

At last she found her voice. "I can't believe Mom actually *grew up* here."

Fritz turned to look at her, his expression suddenly serious, but before he could say anything, a woman in a tweed suit entered the room. She had dark blond hair pulled back in a businesslike bun and kind blue eyes, and she looked like she was in her midfifties. Her face lit up with a smile at the sight of Michele.

"Michele! So wonderful to finally meet you," she greeted her. "I'm Annaleigh, the head housekeeper. I'm in charge of running Windsor Mansion, overseeing the staff, and keeping your grandparents—and now you!—happy."

"Nice to meet you," Michele replied. As she shook Annaleigh's hand, she thought for the second time that day that she *had* to have entered an alternate universe. Her mom had never hired any kind of domestic help before, so having this whole household staff sprung on her was more than a little overwhelming.

"Your grandparents are waiting for you in the drawing room. I'll show you the way." Annaleigh started toward the room, but for a moment, nerves rooted Michele to her spot.

Was she really ready to meet the grandparents who had ignored her for virtually her entire life? What was she going to say to them? Were they supposed to hug? Shake hands? She glanced down at her jeans and Converse sneakers, feeling that she didn't belong in this fancy world at all.

Annaleigh turned around, giving Michele a quizzical look. Michele took a deep breath and followed her out of the room. As Annaleigh led her through hallways decorated with French and Italian paintings, a prickly feeling rose on Michele's skin. She once again had the sensation that these hallways, this place, were strangely *familiar*.

They soon reached a large formal gold-paneled room, where crystal chandeliers hung from a coffered ceiling. And in the room stood a gray-haired couple. They were looking out the broad windows and murmuring to each other, their backs to the door, so Michele's first glimpse of her grandparents consisted of fancy-looking black fabric adorning two tall, reedlike bodies.

Annaleigh cleared her throat. "Mr. and Mrs. Windsor? Michele is here."

"Michele." Dorothy's soft voice spoke the name before she turned around, clutching her husband's weathered hand.

Michele's first reaction was that they looked nothing like what she thought of as grandparents. Amanda's grandparents lived with her family, and as a result Michele had grown close to them and considered them the gold standard. Amanda's Grammy and Papa were all round softness, a little like Mr. and Mrs. Claus, with Grammy usually knitting new sweaters for her beloved shih tzu while Papa belly-laughed over his favorite sitcoms. But Michele's grandparents looked more like an elderly king and queen, with erect posture, austere faces, and designer clothing. Dorothy looked like she had never knit in her life, and Michele couldn't imagine this regal man belly-laughing over anything. In fact, that was just it: both of them looked like they rarely, if ever, laughed.

Walter Windsor had a long, narrow face with sharp blue eyes, a salt-and-pepper beard and mustache, and ivory skin the same shade as Michele's. Dorothy's gray-blond hair was pulled back in a chignon, and her pale face was dotted with a few age spots, her cheekbones impossibly high. Michele was struck by her grandmother's hazel eyes. *They're just like Mom's . . . and mine.* Except that Dorothy's eyes had a hollowness to them that made Michele draw back in discomfort.

"Hello, Michele," Walter said, taking a few steps toward her. He and Dorothy looked just as unsure of what to do as Michele felt. They stood a few feet apart, looking at each other.

"H-hi," Michele stammered.

"You are beautiful, dear," Dorothy said quietly, studying her features. "Just as I expected."

Michele looked down, suddenly embarrassed. "Thanks," she mumbled.

"You don't know how long your grandfather and I have waited for this," Dorothy continued heavily. "We only wish we weren't meeting under such terrible circumstances."

Walter looked at her as though seeing a ghost. "You are so much like . . . her."

Michele couldn't reply. She just stared at these strangers, her mind buzzing with dozens of questions that she felt unable to ask out loud. After a few moments of silence, Dorothy placed a tentative hand on Michele's shoulder.

"Well then. You must be tired from the trip. Annaleigh will show you up to your room so you can get settled. We'll have dinner together later."

"Oh. Okay." Michele looked up and noticed that Annaleigh had been standing in the doorway all along. Evidently she had expected the big reunion to last only a few measly minutes. Michele followed Annaleigh out of the room, stung. Was *that* her grandparents' idea of a warm welcome?

Annaleigh turned to Michele with a friendly smile. "Would you like a tour of the house before I take you up to your room?"

"Sure. Thanks." Michele followed Annaleigh into the opposite hallway, which was decorated with tapestries illuminated by candelabra.

"I'm not sure if you noticed, but the furniture in the drawing room is entirely made up of reproductions of pieces from Versailles's Petit Trianon," Annaleigh announced proudly as she led the way. "Like some of the best Gilded Age homes, the Windsor Mansion followed the rule of being built like an Italian palazzo and decorated like a French Rococo chateau."

"Wow." Michele shook her head, having a hard time registering that this was all real.

The first door Annaleigh opened led into a room of pastel blue with gilt moldings. A mahogany dining suite stood at the center of the room. "Now, this is the morning room."

"Seriously? You have one room just for the morning?" Michele asked in disbelief.

Annaleigh chuckled. "Well, not exactly. Of course, the Windsors always have their breakfast in this room, but morning rooms are also traditionally used for lunch, tea, and any casual daytime gatherings."

There's nothing *casual about this place,* Michele thought as she followed Annaleigh into the next room, the walnut-paneled library. At the sight of this temple of books, Michele felt the flicker of a smile play on her face for the first time in weeks. She wandered through the room, scanning some of the titles of the leather-bound volumes lining the ceiling-high bookcases. A mural of angels was painted on the ceiling, and Baccarat chandeliers sparkled beneath it. The walls and desks were a deep mahogany, and plush dark leather armchairs and wing chairs scattered throughout the room all looked tailor-made for curling up with a novel.

"Come on, let me show you the ballroom. That's my favorite place in the whole house," Annaleigh said excitedly.

When they entered the ballroom, Michele's prickly sensation grew stronger, and she hugged her goose bump–covered arms to her chest. She moved away from Annaleigh, wandering slowly around the room. It was like something out of an Edith

Wharton novel, with its romantic white-on-ivory decor, gleaming dance floor, bronze and crystal chandeliers, and tall Roman columns. A Steinway grand piano stood at one end of the room, with a gilded balcony above.

"The most honored ball guests would sit up in the balcony and watch the dancers," Annaleigh said dreamily. "Isn't it incredible?" Michele didn't respond and Annaleigh seemed to notice her strange expression. "What is it, dear?"

"It's just"—Michele swallowed hard—"I keep feeling like I've *been* here before. But I know that's impossible."

"That is strange. Maybe you've seen ballrooms like this in a movie?" Annaleigh mused.

"Maybe." But Michele knew it wasn't that.

Annaleigh led Michele past the ballroom into a space she called the Moorish billiard room. It looked masculine and foreign, with walls covered in colorful Moroccan tiles and a glass dome ceiling.

"This is where the men would come smoke their cigars and play pool during parties," Annaleigh said, gesturing to the large billiard table in the center of the room.

"Are there a lot of parties here?" Michele asked.

"Well . . . no," Annaleigh admitted regretfully as she led her out of the room. "Not in the ten years that I've been here. But the Windsors were once famous for the society balls they hosted. I think once it was just your grandparents living here, they didn't have much use for parties." She broke off as they reached the covered patio, with a view of the back garden. "Now, this is where your grandmother plants her beautiful flowers and palms."

Michele shook her head in amazement. "This place . . . it's unreal," she blurted out. "It's like . . . it doesn't belong in the modern world. It almost seems . . . enchanted. You know what I mean?"

"I do know what you mean," Annaleigh agreed. "It's all the history here. You can almost *see* the spirits of Windsors past when you walk through the halls."

Michele stopped short, thinking of her mom. "Really?"

Annaleigh winced. "Oh, Michele, I'm sorry. That was tactless of me. I just meant . . . well, there's so much history here is what I meant."

Michele dropped her gaze. "It's okay. I know."

"Anyway," Annaleigh continued nervously, "I would show you the dining room, but since you'll be there in an hour for dinner, we can save that. I'm sure you must be curious to see your room."

Michele nodded and followed Annaleigh up the grand staircase. They stopped on the second landing (the mezzanine, Annaleigh called it) for Michele to look into Walter's study and Dorothy's parlor, which were on opposite ends. Michele shivered as she stepped into the parlor, realizing that this was the very room where Marion had left her fateful goodbye note.

Upstairs, the marble walls were light rose, matching the red-carpeted hallways. A railing bordering the third floor allowed one to lean over and gaze down at the mighty staircase and the Grand Hall below.

"Now, this is a *very* special room," Annaleigh said with girlish enthusiasm as she led Michele to the French double doors.

"Most of the Windsor daughters had this room when they were growing up, from the early 1900s to, most recently . . . Marion." Annaleigh opened the doors, and Michele drew in her breath.

The room was lilac, with white antique French furnishings that looked more appropriate for the court of Versailles than for a teenage girl. The sumptuous double bed was set on a raised platform, with an elaborate carved cream headboard and snowy white bed curtains. A floral Aubusson carpet added to the effect. There was even a large fireplace of gray and white with gold candelabra on either end. A gold mantel clock and a large mirror sat atop the fireplace.

"It's like going back in time," Michele murmured, fingering the lilac curtains on the tall windows. "To a time where no one wore denim."

She wandered around the room, taking in the delicate white mahogany vanity table and desk. She stopped short, a shiver running down her spine, at the sight of the accessories covering the vanity: china brushes, mirrors, and perfume bottles, all bearing the monogram MW.

"These . . . were my mom's?" Michele asked, her voice barely above a whisper.

Annaleigh nodded. "Your grandparents have always kept her room just as it looked when she was living here." She paused. "Is that all right?"

"Of course," Michele murmured, picking up her mother's hand mirror. There was something comforting about being surrounded by her mom's old things, as if Marion could walk in the door any minute to claim them. But it was also so hard to imagine her bohemian mother living in this formal princess bedroom, using a brush made of china. Michele felt that Marion Windsor the heiress was an entirely different person than Marion Windsor the mom.

"This is the only room in your suite that has almost all its original furnishings," Annaleigh continued. "Your grandparents asked me to add some modern touches to your adjoining rooms. I hope you'll approve!"

"My *rooms?*" Michele echoed, bewildered. That was when she noticed a single door on each side of the room. Annaleigh gestured for Michele to follow her.

The first door led to a huge dressing room—which Michele hardly had enough clothes to justify—and a marble bathroom. The opposite door led to a spacious sitting room, which featured an antique glass-enclosed bookcase (filled with recognizable books like the Harry Potter series and Jane Austen's tomes) as well as a flat-screen TV, a DVD player, and a state-of-the-art sound system. In the corner of the room was a round oak table with a place setting for one and a matching dining chair.

"Why do I have a dining set in my room?" Michele asked.

"For meals, of course. We'll have a dining cart sent up here for you at mealtimes, and every morning, you and I will go over your menu together. Look, the TV tilts at whatever angle you choose, so you can watch comfortably from your dinner table!" Annaleigh beamed, but her smile faded as she saw Michele's mystified expression.

"So you're saying my grandparents want me to eat all my dinners alone?" she asked incredulously. "After everything . . . ?"

"Oh, please don't misunderstand me," Annaleigh said anxiously. "It's just that your grandparents eat at such odd hours, often skipping dinner and just having a late lunch, so we thought this would be best, so you could be on a regular meal schedule."

"It's okay, I guess. Whatever," Michele murmured. *Sounds like it's going to be even lonelier than I thought in this gigantic old house.* She glanced at the portraits decorating the sitting room walls, which were of several different young women. Michele looked more closely at one of the portraits and felt a shock of recognition.

"Hey, that's my great-grandmother, the singer Lily Windsor!" Michele exclaimed. "But she looks so different with that hair."

"Well, yes, because she was just sixteen years old in this painting," Annaleigh explained. "It was 1925, the time of the flapper haircut."

Michele peered at the portrait. Her great-grandmother looked glamorous far beyond her sixteen years, with her sassy short hair, eyes rimmed in black, and a slinky sequined dress highlighting her figure. Michele's heart constricted as she thought of all the days her mom had played Lily's records in the house. Even though Marion had hardly been able to carry a tune, Michele always loved to hear her singing along to Lily's records. She had seemed happiest when music was on. And Lily was the only Windsor who Marion spoke of proudly. Lily had died in her eighties, when Marion was fifteen, but they'd been close throughout Marion's childhood.

Michele turned to the next painting, of a girl who could not have looked more different from Lily. While Lily wore full makeup and a confident, bold expression, this girl had a fresh-scrubbed face and a timid demeanor. She was dressed in an old-fashioned ball gown like those worn by Disney animated princesses, and her hair was a poufy red cloud atop her head, bedecked in jeweled hairpins.

"Who's that?" Michele asked.

"That's your great-great-aunt Clara. She was actually the only Windsor to be adopted into the family, and by Mr. George Windsor himself," Annaleigh said. "She had this very suite of rooms when she was growing up, and this portrait was painted on the occasion of her debut in society, in 1910. She would have been about your age then." Annaleigh's eyes glimmered. "Did you know that in those days, the wealthiest American girls were often married off to British royalty? So Clara's younger sister, Frances, became the Duchess of Westminster! In fact, you, my dear, are related to both a duchess and a countess."

Michele gaped at Annaleigh. "Jeez. This family sure doesn't hold back."

The next portrait was of a girl who looked a lot more accessible: a smiling dark-haired teenager wearing a pearl headband and a chic navy blue short-sleeved dress.

"How about her?" Michele wondered.

"That's your great-aunt, Stella, in 1942. Like the other portraits, it was painted for her society debut when she was still a teenager living in these rooms," Annaleigh said.

"Wait—so all these portraits are of the girls who had this room before me?" Michele clarified.

Annaleigh nodded.

"So then . . . where's my mom?" Michele was suddenly breathless.

Annaleigh silently gestured to a corner on the opposite wall, and Michele ran to it. There was her mom, alive in this painting

43

in a way that Michele had never seen her in a photograph. Her eyes were full of sparkle and mirth, and her mouth was stretched into a huge grin, as if she and the painter were sharing a great joke. Her normally straight hair was curled, and she wore a bright cocktail dress. Around her neck was a delicate jade and gold butterfly necklace. It was gorgeous, yet understated. *Just like Mom,* Michele thought.

"It's so hard to imagine Mom sitting for a portrait," Michele said, a lump in her throat. She was struck by the thought that Marion looked like the happiest of all the Windsor girls—but had been dealt such a tragic fate.

Tears welled up in Michele's eyes as she gazed at the portrait. She must have been staring at it for a long time, because when she finally tore herself away, she saw that Annaleigh had left her alone.

Just before seven-thirty, Annaleigh arrived at Michele's bedroom door to show her to the dining room. Michele's stomach felt queasy as she wondered what the conversation with her grandparents would be like.

She was nearly struck dumb by the sight of the Venetian-style dining room. Ten towering columns of rose alabaster flanked the room, and two Baccarat chandeliers sparkled above the carved oak dining table. The dining chairs were made of heavy bronze upholstered in red velvet, matching the crimson window draperies and the marble rose walls.

"Michele, welcome." Dorothy smiled. She and Walter were already seated, and Michele dropped into the chair facing them.

Almost immediately, a kitchen maid circled the table to serve the first course, a salad. Michele watched guiltily. She and Marion had always cooked and served their own meals at home.

"Can I help with anything?" Michele asked. The maid gave Michele a startled look, nearly spilling the salad she was heaping onto her plate, as Dorothy made a sound somewhere between a cough and a gasp. As soon as the maid had left for the kitchen, her cheeks blazing, Walter gently chided, "Michele dear, you shouldn't say things like that to the staff. It's not proper."

Michele stared at him, bewildered. "But . . . this is the twenty-first century!" she blurted out.

"Of course," Dorothy quickly interjected. "But since their job is to serve you, when you offer to help, it makes them feel embarrassed, as though they're not doing their job correctly."

Michele gave her grandparents a wary look. Something seemed very wrong with a world where offering to help "the staff" garnered a scolding.

"Now then," Walter said in a lighter tone, clearly eager to defuse any tension. "What do you think of your new home?"

"I—well, it's amazing, of course, like something out of a fairy tale. But I can't think of it as *home* when it's so different from everything I'm used to," Michele said honestly. "I mean, it's almost impossible to imagine Mom growing up here. She wasn't a fancy heiress, she was just . . . Mom. I would think that she didn't fit in here, but then, she looks so happy in that portrait in my room."

"She *was* very happy here," Dorothy said intently. "If it

45

hadn't been for—" She broke off at a look from Walter, and then she seemed to recover herself. "Anyway, dear, you're looking much too thin. Do try to eat something."

Michele frowned, taken aback by Dorothy's sudden change in tone. After a few moments of silence, while her grandparents ate and Michele looked at the floor, Walter cleared his throat. "Dorothy, are we meeting the Goulds before or after Carnegie Hall tomorrow?"

As the conversation steered away from Marion and turned to some concerto performance her grandparents were attending the following night, Michele felt herself begin to heat up with anger. Who *were* these people, with their strict snobbishness and total inability to communicate normally with her? Michele stirred the salad greens around her plate with her fork, fuming silently. She knew what her grandmother had been about to say—that her mom would have continued to be happy here if it hadn't been for Michele's father. It occurred to her that her grandparents, wishing her mom had never met Henry Irving, must wish that Michele had never been born.

Suddenly, she heard Walter speak her name. "Michele, you're not eating. What's wrong?"

Michele felt something inside her snap. She dropped her fork, which fell to her plate with a clatter.

"What's *wrong*? How can you *expect* me to eat? My mother is dead. But you don't really care about either of us, do you? You sent my dad away, even though you knew it would break my mom's heart. You didn't even bother coming to Mom's funeral! And since you hate my dad so much, I can't imagine why you would even want me living here." Michele paused mid-rant to take a breath, and she stopped short at her grandparents' expressions. They both looked like they had been slapped.

"You are completely mistaken," Walter said, his voice grave. "Yes, we made a lapse in judgment when we offered to pay Henry to leave, but you can never imagine the grief and panic we felt after finding out our only child had run away from home. Besides, we wouldn't have gone through with it, and we didn't. To this day, we still don't understand what happened to Henry. But let me say this: while your grandmother and I were made out to be the villains, there are things about Henry Irving that you don't know, that no one would have—"

"Walter!" Dorothy interrupted sharply.

Michele stared at the two of them. Walter's face had turned red, while Dorothy looked . . . fearful. What in the world was going on?

"What do you mean?" Michele felt her heartbeat quicken. "What do you know about my dad?"

Walter cleared his throat. "I only meant that he was never the person Marion thought him to be. Like we had expected, he was probably only in the relationship for the Windsor millions and took off when he realized he wouldn't be seeing any."

Michele flinched at his words. Dorothy opened her mouth as if to stop Walter, but he continued, his eyes clouding over.

"We made every effort to resume a relationship with Marion, and to be in your life. But she wouldn't take our calls, and all the letters and cards and checks that we sent to you both were returned, unopened. She broke our hearts a long time ago.

And of course we would have been at the funeral if we had been notified in time. We didn't hear about the accident or the funeral until the week after, when the news appeared in the *Times*." He reached for Dorothy's hand. Her face was as ashen as his.

Michele was at a loss for words. Could Walter be telling the truth? It was unimaginable that her mom could have been so wrong about her parents. She didn't know what to think, or what to believe.

"Why did Mom name you as my guardians, then?" she demanded. "It doesn't make any sense."

Dorothy smiled sadly. "We've been asking ourselves the very same question. It's the only bit of silver lining we've had in years. It shows that we must have done something right by our Marion, doesn't it?"

"I . . . I guess so," Michele said awkwardly.

"We know how painful a transition this must be," Walter said, his tone gentler. "But we hope you will manage to find happiness here in New York. Now, what do you say we try to forget this conversation and start over?"

Michele nodded uncomfortably. But as she looked at these strangers in front of her in this obscenely grand room, she felt a fresh wave of grief for her old home, for her mom.

"I don't feel well," she said suddenly. "Can I be excused?"

After a pause, Dorothy nodded silently.

"Thank you for dinner," Michele said quickly before hurrying out of the room.

On her first night in her new bedroom, Michele slept fitfully, her mind swimming with black-and-white images of the Windsor Mansion's former inhabitants. But then a smile lit her sleeping face as she succumbed to a new dream.

It was the most overwhelming feeling she had ever known. Like she was so happy she could burst, but at the same time, there was a constant, insatiable hunger inside her.

She was nestled in his arms under a dark night, at the foot of a tall elm tree. Miles of moonlit grass stretched out in front of them. He played with her hair as they laughed together, relishing a private joke.

"I can't believe this is real," Michele whispered as she stared into his sapphire blue eyes. "I don't want to be anywhere but here with you."

And suddenly Michele was awake, breathing heavily as she struggled to discern where she was. She almost expected her handsome stranger to still be beside her. But as her eyes registered the grand bedroom furniture through the darkness, Michele was reminded that she had just been dreaming. That happiness hadn't been real. None of it was real.

Why did I have a new *dream about him?* Michele wondered. She had grown so accustomed to the same vision of him as a reflection in the mirror that it was unbelievable to experience him as real and solid. *But he isn't real or solid,* she reminded herself. *He's just my imagination in overdrive.*

The next afternoon, the Windsor handyman, Nolan, brought up the boxes of Michele's belongings that had been shipped from California. She spent most of the day unpacking, trying to arrange her things so that this elaborate new bedroom would feel somewhat like hers. After organizing her clothes, she came across a box labeled with her mom's name. Michele hesitated.

Ms. Richards had brought her the box shortly before Michele left for New York, explaining that it contained jewelry and keepsakes Marion had kept in her safe at the bank. Michele had yet to open the box. The truth was that she was afraid to open it. For some reason, the idea of it made her mom's death feel that much more real. But after eyeing the box warily for a few moments, Michele took a deep breath and finally opened the lid.

Inside were three small jewelry boxes. The first two bore the logos of Van Cleef & Arpels and Tiffany & Co., while the third was unlabeled. Michele stared at the boxes in surprise. Her mom had never told her about these jewels. Michele figured they must be Windsor heirlooms, as Marion had never been able to shop at places like Tiffany's.

Michele opened the Van Cleef & Arpels box first. At the sight of the butterfly necklace from Marion's portrait, tears welled up in her eyes. She hugged the necklace close to her, as if Marion's presence could be found somewhere within it.

She opened the Tiffany box next and found a magnificent white gold necklace woven with diamonds. "Whoa," Michele murmured. She had never seen such fancy jewelry up close before.

Michele opened the unlabeled box last. And her heart nearly stopped at what she found inside.

Nestled in the box was a gold skeleton key that looked

centuries old. A key shaped like a cross with a circular bow at the top. And carved into the key's bow was the image of a sundial.

It was the key from her dream.

Michele felt her head spinning, felt chills running up and down her spine. "This can't be happening," she whispered to herself, her throat thick with shock. "It's not real."

She gingerly picked up the key—and felt it twitch, ever so slightly, in the palm of her hand. Michele yelped, dropping the key in horror. But once on the floor, the key was perfectly still.

How did Mom get this? Michele wondered desperately. *Why did it appear in my dreams?*

Michele noticed a folded piece of paper peeking out from the bottom of the box, and she quickly grabbed it and began to read.

September 1993

Dear Marion,

Enclosed is the key Henry left in my office. I know he wanted you to have it. Perhaps this will explain things. Don't hesitate to contact me if you need anything.

All my best,
Alfred Woolsey

Alfred Woolsey—my dad's old boss. The realization nearly knocked the wind out of Michele. This key had belonged to her *father?* This somehow seemed even more unbelievable than the very existence of the key from her dream. She had never in her life felt any sort of connection to her absentee dad, but now they shared something. She was suddenly reminded of the one time, when she was a young girl, that she had asked her mom if she was anything like her father. Marion had paused a long while before answering.

"Yes," she had finally said softly. "I can't put my finger on it, but there is something . . . something a little different about both of you."

Michele refocused on Alfred's note, wondering what on earth the eccentric old man had thought the key would explain. She hurried to her laptop to search for the professor on Google. Maybe she could find his phone number and ask him about it. But when the first link popped up on her computer screen, Michele's heart sank. It was to his obituary from a Los Angeles newspaper, dated eight years earlier. *So much for getting answers,* she thought glumly.

Michele remembered, with a pang of regret, that she had never even mentioned the key when telling her mom about her recurring dream; she had always just focused on the gorgeous stranger. *But if only I had given Mom all the details—then she would have told me she* had *the key,* Michele thought dizzyingly.

She nervously reached down to pick up the key, bracing herself for the creepy twitching. But the key remained still, and she placed it on her bureau. As she stared at it, she wondered if her mom had ever found out what it was—or if she had lived the rest of her life as perplexed by the key as Michele was now.

Later that day, Michele was brought back to reality by Amanda's voice echoing through her cell phone.

"Girl, how *are* you? We miss you so much already!" Amanda cried.

"I miss you guys too," Michele replied as she curled up on the couch in her sitting room. "What are you doing today?"

"Jen's having a party. It's probably going to be lame, but Kris and I promised we'd go."

"Oh." Michele swallowed hard as she thought of how Kristen and Amanda would be doing everything together from now on—without her.

"But anyway," Amanda said hurriedly, as if sensing Michele's discomfort. "What are your grandparents like?"

"I haven't seen too much of them, to be honest. We had a pretty awkward dinner last night and I've kept to myself since then. They're . . . I don't know. What you'd expect, I guess." Suddenly, an intercom in the room buzzed. "Hold on a sec."

Annaleigh's voice came through the tinny speaker. "Michele? Your grandmother is with one of your new classmates in her parlor. She wants to introduce the two of you."

Michele groaned inwardly. Why hadn't Dorothy told her ahead of time?

"Okay. I'll be right down," Michele answered. She turned to her cell. "Mandy, I have to call you back. Apparently I have a guest."

"Okay. Try to hang in there," Amanda said. "Love you."

"Love you too." Michele hung up reluctantly and glanced in the mirror. She had barely slept since Marion's death, and it was taking its toll on her appearance. She thought briefly of freshening up for her visitor as she surveyed her uncombed hair and bloodshot eyes, but she couldn't summon the energy. It felt like a long time since she'd cared about such things.

Downstairs in the parlor, Michele found Dorothy sitting in her regal armchair, facing a petite girl on the couch with long strawberry blond hair and green eyes. The girl was dressed in a buttoned-up black vintage tuxedo vest and skinny jeans tucked into black platform boots. An older blond woman stood behind Dorothy's chair, a pencil behind her ear, as she flipped through a notepad.

"Hi," Michele greeted them.

"Michele." Dorothy smiled. "This is my secretary, Inez Hart, and her daughter, Caissie."

Inez hurried forward and held out her hand. "It's so nice to meet you, Ms. Windsor. And please accept our family's condolences on your loss."

"Thank you. Please call me Michele."

Caissie gave her a smile. "Hey."

"Hi." Michele took a seat on the couch next to her.

"I asked Inez to bring Caissie with her to work today, since she's also a junior at Berkshire," Dorothy continued. "I thought it would be nice for you to have a friend when you start school on Monday."

At those words, Inez shot Caissie a stern look, as if to say, *Don't let me down here!* Caissie looked at the floor, clearly embarrassed.

"Thanks. That would be great," Michele said, trying to muster up some enthusiasm.

"Why don't you show Caissie your room?" Dorothy suggested.

"Okay," Michele agreed. Caissie followed her out of the parlor and they headed up the stairs silently, as Michele wondered why this felt so uncomfortable. When they reached the third floor, Michele led her into the sitting room. Caissie looked around.

"You don't have a bed?" she asked in surprise.

"Oh, that's in my other room," Michele replied. Caissie's eyebrows rose, and Michele flushed, aware of how ridiculously ostentatious this all must seem.

"Sit down," Michele offered. The two girls sat in armchairs opposite each other. "So, what part of the city do you live in?"

"I live with my dad right next door, in one of the apartments that used to be the old Walker Mansion. Probably the closest I'll ever come to living in a place like this," Caissie said with a laugh.

"The Walker Mansion? The same Walkers that were enemies of the Windsors?" Michele asked, casting around for some subject to talk about. "Pretty weird that they'd live next door to each other."

"Yeah." Caissie chuckled.

"So, what's our school like?"

"Honestly? It kind of sucks. Practically everyone there is an entitled preppy." Caissie made a face. "My best friend, Aaron, and I both got in on scholarship, and we'll definitely have an edge when applying to colleges—but public school would have been *way* preferable socially."

"Great," Michele said dryly. "Now I'm even more excited about starting there."

Caissie bit her lip, possibly regretting her bluntness. As Michele looked at the unfamiliar girl sitting in her room, she suddenly felt like she was watching the scene from outside her own body. None of this seemed real. The funeral, the mourning, and now this new life in New York all felt like scenes from a movie she was simply acting in. This couldn't actually be her life. Michele imagined that her real body, her real self, was far from this mansion, back in California with her mom and her best friends, and life was blessedly normal. There had never been a car accident, and the biggest problem on Michele's plate was still her breakup with Jason—which felt like a lifetime ago. Michele envisioned coming home that fateful day to find Marion waiting for her with an after-school snack, eager to hear about her day. Just like always . . .

Michele felt tears brimming in her eyes, and she stared at the carpet to hide them from Caissie. "Sorry to be a lame hostess. It's just that my grandmother didn't tell me you were coming over and I'm not feeling well today . . . I'm not really up for doing much."

"I get it," Caissie replied awkwardly. "I should get going anyway."

Michele got up to walk Caissie to the door. "Well, it was nice meeting you," she said, still looking away so Caissie wouldn't see her tears.

"You too. Bye." And with that, Caissie practically flew down the stairs.

Late that night, Michele was jolted awake by the sound of a terrible wail. She sat bolt upright just as a second sob sounded. Unable to sit there listening, Michele threw off the covers and jumped out of bed. She opened her bedroom door and stepped into the pitch-black hallway.

For a moment she shrank back. The darkness cast a frightening pall over the mansion, transforming it from the light palatial home of daytime into a creepy Hitchcockian setting. But as the wailing continued, Michele moved forward determinedly. She had to find out who was making this horrible noise.

Leaning against the walls and feeling her way across the

third floor, she crept closer to the sound. And suddenly she realized that the sobs were coming from the master bedroom. It was her grandmother.

Michele stopped short, taken aback. And then she heard Dorothy moan in a hoarse voice, "We should have told her. . . ." Or was it "*shouldn't* have told her"? Michele couldn't quite make out the exact words. And did the "her" refer to Michele or Marion? Michele's head spun with questions, but one fact was certain: the stoic, composed Dorothy she had met was a facade. It was clear that her grandmother wasn't well at all.

Walter murmured something in his low voice that Michele couldn't hear. She walked up to the master bedroom door, but when she reached it, she stood uncertainly in place. What could she do? Barge in and ask what was going on?

"No, Walter! It hurts when I look at her—it's like there's a ghost in the house," Dorothy burst out.

Michele gasped and started to back away from the door. But just then, the door flew open. Walter stood staring at her in shock.

"What are you doing eavesdropping?" he snapped.

"I'm sorry—I didn't mean to—I heard crying," Michele babbled.

"Your grandmother is not herself right now," Walter said in a softer tone. "She's grieving for Marion. As we all are."

Michele nodded, desperate to get away. "I'm going back to my room now—sorry."

Without looking back, Michele turned and took off for her room, tears springing to her eyes. She suddenly felt afraid of her grandparents, and despite what they said to the contrary, she had a strong sense that she wasn't really wanted here. One thing was for sure: Michele was determined to stay away from them as much as possible.

Michele lay on her stomach, her notebook propped up on her pillow, as she tried to write. She chewed anxiously on the end of her pencil, wondering if she had lost her talent along with her mom. She hadn't been able to write one decent line since Marion had died.

Heavy rain pounded outside, and the gray sky lent an eerie hue to her bedroom. Michele shivered, pulling her robe more tightly around her shoulders. A glance at the mantel clock atop her fireplace showed that it was just after six-thirty. The next day was Monday, October eleventh—her first day at Berkshire High School. With that miserable thought, Michele flung her notepad and pen across the room, where they just missed her desk.

She wondered, for what felt like the millionth time, how her mom could *ever* have imagined that Michele would fit in or be comfortable in this new world. *How could she not even* tell *me she was naming her parents as my guardians in her will?* Michele had never known Marion to keep secrets from her. Why now, when she had no way of uncovering the truth?

Michele lay on her bed, staring into space and trying to quiet her frantic mind. And that was when she saw it, something she hadn't noticed before: a lock on the bottom drawer of her antique desk.

Curious, Michele got up and rattled the knob of the locked

drawer. A thudding sounded inside, and Michele felt a flare of interest. Something heavy was locked in that drawer. What could it be?

Michele grabbed a couple of hairpins off her vanity table and stuck them inside the lock, wiggling them around, but to no avail. The lock stayed firm. *Oh well,* she thought with disappointment. Just as she was heading back to bed to continue her wallowing, she saw the key from her father twitch, ever so slightly, on her bureau—just as it had done the day before. But she had to be imagining it . . . right?

Michele sank back onto the bed, eyeing the key warily. Suddenly there it was again—the key twitching, *moving* from left to right. Michele yelped, scrambling back in terror. *Am I going crazy?* she thought fearfully. *Isn't this what happens when people lose their minds?*

The key continued its strange movements, as if it were anxious to get Michele's attention. Michele pinched herself as hard as she could and flinched from the pain. She definitely wasn't dreaming.

Her gaze fell on the locked drawer. As she glanced back at the animated key, an idea flickered in her mind. It was crazy . . . but then, she had to try something to stop the key's spasmodic movements.

Steeling herself, she walked over to the bureau. She squeezed her eyes shut as she reached for the key. It stopped moving and she picked it up. Barely able to exhale, Michele approached the desk. With a shaky hand, she tried to fit the key in the lock.

The key burst to life. Michele cried out in shock, stumbling backward, as the key didn't fit into the lock but instead *melded* to it like a magnet, sparking and moving as if it contained a hidden battery.

The desk drawer swung open, the key falling forward into it. At first Michele was too afraid to look inside. What other bit of crazy witchcraft or voodoo could be waiting there for her? But her curiosity got the best of her, and she gingerly took a peek.

Lying flat in the drawer was an ancient-looking leather-bound journal. The skeleton key was pressed to it like a paperweight. Michele's heart raced. Had this journal belonged to one of her parents? Were they trying to communicate with her somehow? She quickly stuck the key into her pocket and opened the worn and dusty diary. But to her disappointment, the name "Clara" was engraved in calligraphy on the inside cover. Beside that was written the year—*1910.* Michele flipped open the diary to the first yellowed page.

10/10/10
Today began just like any other day, but it quickly turned into much the opposite. . . .

As Michele stared at the date, her jaw dropped. Today was also 10/10/10—October 10, 2010!

Just then, the gold mantel clock sounded a chime. And suddenly Michele had the inexplicable feeling that her hands were stuck to the diary pages. She tried to pry them off, but she couldn't let go! *What is this?* she thought anxiously as she continued her attempts to yank her hands off the diary. *Did the pages turn to glue over the past century or what?*

In the most terrifying motion Michele had ever experienced, the diary seemed to *pull* her into its binding, and she found herself falling headfirst into an abyss of pages. She screamed at the top of her lungs, her stomach swooping sickeningly, as though she were on an upside-down roller coaster.

"Help!" she shrieked. "What's happening to me?"

She was swimming now, in a sea of papers and ink, as the diary had somehow enlarged to a monstrous size, able to swallow her whole. Then the diary pages vanished, and Michele screamed again as her body involuntarily spun and swirled around her bedroom—a bedroom that seemed to change with every glance, strange-looking figures entering and disappearing at the speed of light. The room seemed to turn older and older as she spun, and without warning, the spinning stopped and everything was once again clear and in focus.

Michele hit the floor with a thud. The scream she heard when she landed was not her own.

Standing right in front of Michele was a waif of a girl with pale skin, red hair tied back in a braid, and green eyes. She looked just like the painting of Clara Windsor hanging in Michele's room, but unlike the aristocrat in a sumptuous ball gown, this pale-faced girl wore a ratty, ill-fitting black dress and looked entirely out of place in the elegant bedroom. Michele scrambled to her feet in terror, but she fell to the carpeted floor again, dizzy and weak.

Clara stared down at Michele, her eyes wild.

"What—who—*who are you?*" she gasped. "Wherever did you come from?!"

"I—what are *you*—" Michele could barely speak as she

gaped at Clara. She looked frantically around the room. Every trace of modern life was gone. Michele's desk, laptop, and iPod were all missing, and her toiletries on the vanity table had been replaced with funny-looking powders and thick hairbrushes. Instead of cars whizzing by outside the window, Michele could have sworn she heard the clip-clop of *horses* trotting up Fifth Avenue. What *was* this?

Suddenly, a young woman burst into the room, her expression alarmed. She wore a maid's uniform of a plain black dress with a starched white apron.

"Miss Clara! What is it? What's the matter?"

Clara shakily pointed at Michele. "She—she appeared in my bedroom like an apparition! *How did she get in here?*"

The maid frowned. "I don't understand what you speak of, miss."

"Why her! The girl in the abominable clothing, right there!" Clara's voice was hysterical.

"Miss . . . nobody is there," the maid said after a pause. She eyed Clara with concern. "Now, you've had a very strange and exciting day, and it's to be expected that your imagination would run away with you after all that. It's late. You must lie down and get some sleep before you have a fainting spell."

"You don't . . . you don't see her?" Clara asked, her voice rising higher in panic.

"No, Miss Clara. There is nobody there," the maid answered patiently. "Would you like me to bring you up some tea or warm milk to help you calm yourself? Perhaps some smelling salts?"

"No . . . No, that's quite all right, thank you," Clara said, attempting to collect herself. "I'll just be off to bed, then. You're right. I must be feeling faint."

The maid gave her a reassuring smile. "Good night, miss. Ring the bell if you need anything. Rest well, and do feel better."

After the maid had shut the door behind her, Clara fixed her attention back on Michele, looking fearful. "Why could she not see you? Are you a ghost? Have I gone mad?"

Michele pinched herself again, and the pain followed on cue. As she stared at the crystal clear scene in front of her, she felt her stomach drop further in alarm. Was it possible that she *wasn't* hallucinating all this? But in what alternate universe *could* this be real?

"What year is it?" she asked, though she was afraid she already knew what Clara's answer would be.

"Why, 1910, of course," Clara replied, giving Michele an aggrieved look. "But please, *what are you?* What do you want with me?"

Michele stared back at Clara, her mind whirring. How could she possibly have traveled back in time *one hundred years?* Why in the world had she been sent here? And how was she going to answer her terrified great-great-aunt? She couldn't very well say, "Actually, I'm one of your relatives from the future. A hundred years in the future, to be exact." So Michele said the first thing that popped into her head: "Yeah, I am, um, a ghost. My name is Michele." *After all, I'm not technically alive yet,* she thought grimly.

Clara let out a frightened moan.

"No, I'm a good ghost. More like a spirit," Michele hurriedly added. "You know, like Casper."

Clara looked blankly at her, and Michele realized that Casper the Friendly Ghost probably hadn't been created yet.

"What I mean is . . . I'm here to help you." Michele thought this was possibly the dumbest thing she could have come up with, but to her surprise, the fear seemed to leave Clara's eyes at these words, and she looked at Michele eagerly.

"Did my mother send you?" Clara whispered, her face brimming with hope.

"What? I—I don't know," Michele stammered.

"I was just now praying for her to help me—or to send help for me," Clara said.

"Wait . . . so your mom died too?" Michele asked. This could not be eerier or more unbelievable. "What did you want help for?"

Clara took a deep breath and then told Michele her story. As Clara spoke, Michele could see the words in her mind, written in Clara's handwriting. She remembered that these were the words on the pages of the October 10, 1910, diary entry that she had been reading when she'd been sent back in time.

"Tonight you see me surrounded by gilt and glamour . . . but until now, all I've ever known is the grime and grit of the streets," Clara began. "While other girls my age were experiencing their first kisses and first automobile rides, I spent my days at the local orphanage—my home since my parents died when I was little. All I've ever had is cleverness. I tutored the other orphans to earn my room and board, and I taught myself through books at the library . . . my one safe haven.

"Today began just like any other day, but it quickly turned into much the opposite when the butler from the famous

Windsor family made a surprise appearance at the orphanage. It happened that the family patriarch, George Windsor, had somehow learned of my existence and insisted on taking me in, as a foster daughter. I cannot understand it, and from what I am told, it sounds as if I am being given a trial family. But who would take in a teenager, and a stranger at that? What do they want with *me*?

"I wasn't permitted to object or question it. I was simply ordered to pack my bags and leave the only home I've ever known. I arrived and my new family was waiting for me in the Grand Hall. Now I have a railroad-president father, a socialite mother, an eighteen-year-old brother, and two sisters: seventeen-year-old Violet and ten-year-old Frances. But none of these people besides Mr. Windsor seems to want me here. I do believe the others want me out. So then, what is going to happen to me? Why am I here?"

Clara clasped Michele's hand and looked at her pleadingly. "Will you help me? Help me learn the truth about why I was brought to live with the Windsors? That is why you came here, isn't it?"

Michele had no idea what she could do to help—but she was struck by the similarities between Clara's plight and her own. Both of them, though a hundred years removed, had been inexplicably sent to live in this new world with the Windsors, and both of them sought the answer why.

"I'll do whatever I can," Michele promised.

"Michele!"

She jerked her head up, and in one instant, the world returned to normal. She was back in her bedroom in 2010. Clara's belongings were gone, except for the diary in Michele's hands. And Annaleigh was calling Michele through the intercom, asking if she was ready for her dinner to be brought up.

For a moment, Michele was too stunned to reply to Annaleigh. She stared down at the diary, wondering if that exchange with Clara had actually happened . . . or had it all been in her head? Was she certifiably crazy? And how come the trip back in time had been such a nightmare, while returning to the present was instantaneous? One thing was for sure: Michele had no appetite that night. She slowly made her way to the intercom.

"Annaleigh? I'm actually not feeling well. I think I'll skip dinner."

"Are you sure? Should I have medicine sent up for you?" Annaleigh offered.

"No, that's okay," Michele replied. "I think I just need to rest. I'll see you in the morning."

Michele pulled the skeleton key out of her pocket and stared at it in wonder. Did this mean . . . that her father was a *time traveler*? Had Alfred Woolsey somehow guessed? Was that why he'd given Marion the key? If only there was someone to explain . . . But Michele was on her own.

5

The next morning Michele woke up at the crack of dawn, her stomach churning with nerves. She had been up nearly all night, unable to stop wondering about the key and her unbelievable trip back in time. Had it all actually happened? But now she had her first day of school to face.

She had never been the new girl in school before, and starting in the middle of the year made it extra brutal. With a sigh, she pulled her cell phone from her bedside table to check her messages. The first text was from Kristen's phone: *WE LOVE YOU, GIRL! Good luck tomorrow, we're thinking of you and hoping it goes okay. Call us after! Xoxoxoxoxo, K & A.* Michele read the text a second time, overcome with a fierce longing for her friends. It was going to be so weird being in school without them.

Unable to sleep any longer, Michele decided to use her extra time for getting ready. The strict Berkshire dress code meant that most of her own clothes were out, but her grandparents had instructed Annaleigh to buy her a first-day outfit: a white button-down shirt paired with a knee-length plaid skirt. Bare legs weren't allowed, so Michele found a pair of nude nylons to wear with her black ballet flats. She couldn't help cringing as she looked in the mirror. This überpreppy look was *not* her.

Michele blow-dried her hair, put on some light makeup, and then headed downstairs to the morning room. As usual, Annaleigh was at the table, sipping green tea while she looked over her to-do list. Classical music played lightly from the nearby radio. Annaleigh had offered to have breakfast brought up to Michele's room in the mornings, but it made Michele feel even lonelier to eat alone in her room, so she preferred to join Annaleigh.

"Good morning," Michele greeted her, plopping into an empty chair.

Annaleigh looked at her approvingly. "Good morning, dear. You look great. How are you feeling?"

"Pretty nervous," Michele admitted as the kitchen maid, Lucie, placed a glass of orange juice and a plate of sizzling bacon and eggs in front of her. She gave Lucie an awkward smile of thanks, still uncomfortable with the whole concept of being served like this.

"Don't worry. I can't imagine that you'll have any trouble making friends," Annaleigh assured her. "I bet everyone's excited to have a Windsor back at Berkshire. And besides, you already know Caissie."

Michele nodded politely, thinking that Annaleigh clearly underestimated the Exclusive-with-a-capital-*E* high school clique system, which rarely admitted intruders.

The two of them fell silent, and as the symphony playing on the radio faded out, a new one began—and Michele nearly spilled her juice in shock. She knew that music. It stirred something in her, an aching for something that she couldn't quite remember. She had heard this symphony before, somewhere important. She *knew* she had. But where?

Suddenly, those mesmerizing blue eyes filled her mind. This was the song that *he* was whistling in the hall of mirrors from her recurring dream—the handsome stranger.

"Michele, what in the world is the matter?" Annaleigh asked, clearly alarmed by Michele's sudden frozen state.

"This song—I've heard it before," she said shakily.

Annaleigh looked at Michele quizzically. "Well, yes, I would imagine that you have. It's one of Schubert's most notable compositions."

Michele nodded, but she knew that she had never heard it before, aside from in her dream. As the song ended, the deejay announced, "You're listening to 96.3 FM, New York's premier classical music station. You just heard Phoenix Warren and the New York Philharmonic with Schubert's *Serenade*."

"Phoenix Warren," Michele said with a small smile. "My mom named me after his composition *Michele*. That's why my name is spelled with only one *L*."

"Really? I love that piece. It's so beautiful." Annaleigh began humming it under her breath. Just then, her phone beeped with a text message. "Oh, Fritz just arrived. You'd better get going. You can't be late for the first day of school!"

Michele nodded nervously, pushing back her chair and heaving her bag over her shoulder.

"Good luck!" Annaleigh called.

"Thanks," she replied, forcing a smile. "I'll need it!"

Michele stared at the scene in front of her as she reached Berkshire High School. The white stone Upper East Side school looked a little like the Windsor Mansion, with its Roman-inspired facade, Corinthian columns flanking the front doors, and wrought-iron gates surrounding the building. The front entrance seemed to be a makeshift runway, as glamour girls strutted up the steps one at a time, each managing to turn the dress code into a fashion statement. A willowy blonde with voluminous hair wore a flouncy, pleated black and red plaid skirt with an embroidered short black blazer, platform pumps, and a black leather designer satchel moonlighting as a backpack. Next up was a gorgeous African American girl wearing a stylish red trench coat over her green plaid jumper, with a large Chanel quilted handbag slung over her shoulder. The guys looked equally polished, with their perfectly coiffed hair, dark blazers over white button-down shirts and colorful ties, and gray or khaki belted pants. Feeling infinitely less glamorous than her classmates, Michele followed them up the stairs, her eyes on the ground.

With the help of her school map, Michele eventually found

her first-period class, U.S. history. As the students filtered in, Michele approached the teacher.

"Mr. Lewis? I'm the new girl, Michele Windsor."

Mr. Lewis beamed and gave her a hearty handshake. "Welcome to Berkshire, Michele! We're so happy to have you here."

"Thanks. Where should I sit?"

"Oh, just wait here with me. I want to introduce you to the class!" he said, grinning at her as if Michele really ought to be excited about this. She stood awkwardly at the front of the classroom as the students looked at her curiously. Caissie Hart was among the last of the small group of students to arrive, and she gave Michele a tiny smile before getting into her seat.

As soon as the bell rang and everyone else was seated, Mr. Lewis announced, "Class, this is our new transfer student. Meet Michele Windsor, of the very Windsor family some of you studied in the New York history elective last year. She's the first Windsor we've had here at school in almost twenty years, so let's be sure to make her feel welcome!"

Michele smiled tentatively and quickly slid into the only empty seat. She could feel her classmates eyeing her up and down, surveying her appearance, and her face burned with embarrassment. She couldn't help wondering how she measured up to their expectations of the newest Windsor princess.

The boy sitting next to Michele turned to her and gave her a friendly smile. He had a very all-American, Abercrombie look: dark blond hair, brown eyes, and a boyish grin. Michele smiled back shyly.

As she was leaving at the end of class, Michele heard Caissie call her name. "Hey, wait up!"

Michele turned around, but she soon realized that Caissie wasn't talking to her. She watched as Caissie caught up with the other Michelle in class and the two of them sauntered out of the room together. With a sigh, Michele followed them out the door, hoping they hadn't noticed her stop. But a quiet chuckle over her shoulder told her that someone had witnessed her embarrassing move.

"Hey." It was the guy she'd sat next to. "I'm Ben, by the way. Ben Archer."

"Hi. I'm—" Michele stopped short, feeling her face flush. "Well, you obviously know who I am, after that whole introduction."

"Yeah." Ben laughed. "Actually, the teachers told us last week that you'd be coming here. There's been a lot of buzz going around about what you'd be like."

"Oh." To her mortification, Michele felt her face grow even redder. "I'm not really used to being the center of attention. Not at all, actually."

"Yeah. You're really normal for a Windsor," Ben commented. "In a good way." He grinned at her.

"Oh, well . . . thanks." Michele looked at him with faint curiosity, wondering if he was flirting with her. The thought would have thrilled her in the past, but now it barely registered.

"Well, I have to go to the science hall now, so . . ." Michele's voice trailed off and she glanced down at the school map in her hands.

"Oh, I'm going in the opposite direction. I'll see you around?" Ben said hopefully.

Michele nodded. "See you around."

A few hours later, Michele was suffering an acute case of New Girl Self-Consciousness Syndrome, compounded by the effort it took to keep up in her classes. Ms. Richards had clearly forgotten to give her the memo about how academically advanced New York private schools were, and Michele had a feeling she'd have to fight to hold on to her A average here.

She breathed a sigh of relief when the bell rang for lunch—but then had the painful realization that she had no one to lunch with. She lingered at her desk in the English classroom, wondering where she should go and what she should do, as everyone else took off for the school's dining room. Suddenly, a hand gripped her elbow. "Windsor, you're eating with us," someone said in a high-pitched voice.

Michele turned around to face a girl who looked like a designer version of a 1950s housewife. She wore a pale pink cashmere sweater with a tweed skirt and black Mary Janes. The outfit was topped off with a pink plaid headband and a string of pearls that looked suspiciously real.

"Hi. Sorry, I don't think I got your name," Michele said as the Prepster dragged her toward the door.

"Olivia Livingston. Of *the* Livingston family, of course," the girl answered with a proud smile.

Michele had never heard of the Livingstons, but she had the instinct not to admit it. "Well, thanks for the lunch invite," she said instead.

"Oh, it's not just an invite; it's a duty," Olivia said, giving

Michele a dead-serious look. "We old families have to stick together. It's up to us to lead the new generation of society."

"Um—what?"

But before Olivia could answer, they had arrived at her table in the posh Berkshire dining room, where three other girls, all of whom looked like they shared Olivia's sense of style, were seated.

"Here she is!" Olivia said triumphantly to the members of her tribe. "I told you we'd be able to add a Windsor to our club. Okay, Michele, this is Madeline Belmont, Renee Whitney, and Amy Van Alen. You'll of course recognize their last names."

None of the names rang a bell for Michele. She sat gingerly in her designated chair. "Hi. So . . . what is your club exactly?"

Madeline gave Olivia a quick glance, as if to get permission to speak, then explained, "We're the only students here from families of the New York Four Hundred. Our mission is to take over where Mrs. Astor left off and rule the next generation of society with elegance, and defend against the antics of the nouveau riche—who just make us look bad." With that, Madeline turned and sniffed in disgust at the sight of a miniskirt-clad girl giving her boyfriend a whole lot of PDA at the next table.

"Uh, I really don't know what you're talking about," Michele admitted. "The New York Four Hundred?"

Olivia stared at her, clearly astounded by her lack of knowledge on the subject. One of the other girls, Renee, hurriedly explained, "Caroline Astor ruled New York society from the late eighteen hundreds through the turn of the twentieth century, and she's, like, the *most* famous socialite in American history.

Anyway, she created a list of the four hundred most important people in New York to invite to her balls, because only four hundred people could fit in her ballroom. Genius, right?"

"Totally," Michele said dryly. No one seemed to notice her sarcasm. Across the dining room, she spotted Caissie sitting with a cute African American guy who Michele figured was the Aaron she had spoken of. For some reason, the two of them looked strangely annoyed by the sight of Michele sitting with this group.

"Anyway, to be a part of the Four Hundred was the most important honor of New York society," Renee continued. "You got written up in all the papers, and, well, you pretty much ruled. The Four Hundred was made up of the two hundred most prominent families in America, really. And *we* come from them!"

Amy looked darkly at the PDA-happy couple, who were surrounded by a throng of friends. "But nowadays, people don't recognize our importance and they're all over the latest trashy new It people."

"Well, that's probably because we really didn't do anything to deserve any attention; our great-great-great-grandparents did," Michele commented.

"What?" Renee and Olivia gasped in unison.

"Well, it's true," Michele said mildly. "And honestly, I have no desire to rule society or anyone. I just want to make it through the year."

"Just wait. Your pride will kick in soon," Amy insisted.

As Olivia started on a tangent about the legendary cachet of being one of the Four Hundred, Michele's mind drifted off. If these were her friend options at this school, then she'd have to settle for being a loner. Thoughts of her life with Marion and her friends in California haunted her, but she squeezed her eyes shut, trying to force them from her mind. That life was gone now.

Michele would have liked nothing more than to escape her current reality. And that was when Clara Windsor's diary flashed in her mind. True, the whole thing might have been one insane hallucination . . . but it could have been real. And if it had been real, maybe it wasn't as terrifying as she thought. Maybe it was her escape.

⚬⚬⚬

That night, Michele had a new dream of the handsome stranger with the striking blue eyes.

She was in his arms at a Windsor Mansion ball. An orchestra played Schubert's stirring Serenade *as the two of them danced, waltzing like they were floating on air. She beamed up at him, and he smiled down at her.*

Suddenly, Michele saw the scene from a different perspective. She was no longer in the boy's arms. He was dancing alone, but as though with an invisible dance partner. He smiled at no one, held an invisible waist. Party guests gawked and murmured uncomfortably. I don't exist, *Michele thought in horror.*

Michele woke with a start but didn't attempt to go back to sleep. Instead, she pulled on her robe and tiptoed down the two flights of stairs until she reached the ballroom. Taking a deep breath, she swung open the door and switched on the lights.

It was like the ghost of the ballroom in her dream—no

guests, orchestra, or glittering gowns and jewels, but undeniably the very same place. Michele suddenly had the eerie sensation that she was not alone. She could hear snatches of sound—a man's dignified chuckle, a woman's light giggle, the crinkling of fabric as skirts swished against each other on the dance floor. And then she heard the song that had been haunting her dreams.

In her nightgown and bare feet, Michele started to dance to the music with an invisible partner, the same way the boy in her dream had danced with her. She couldn't see her handsome stranger, but she felt him smiling down at her, moving with her. As she swayed to the music in her head, Michele once again wondered if she was going crazy . . . but this time she didn't care.

"Michele! What in the world are you doing here?"

Michele jerked awake to find that she was lying on the cold ballroom floor, morning light streaming in through the glass doors. Annaleigh stood frozen in the doorway.

"I—I must have been sleepwalking. I did that sometimes in California," Michele fibbed, stiffly pulling herself up off the floor.

"I got worried when you didn't come down to breakfast today and you weren't in your room," Annaleigh fretted, leading Michele out of the ballroom. "I'll have the cook put your breakfast in a lunch bag for you to eat on the way. You'd better hurry and get ready if you want to make it to school on time."

"Thanks, Annaleigh. Sorry to have worried you."

Annaleigh looked at her uneasily. "Sleepwalking in a big house like this seems pretty dangerous. Let me make an appointment for you with the Windsors' doctor—she could have some suggestions to help you sleep normally."

"No, I'm fine," Michele interrupted hurriedly. "It's nothing. It hardly ever happens, seriously."

"Okay," Annaleigh said, sounding unconvinced. "As long as it doesn't continue."

"It won't," Michele assured her. "I'll go get ready."

Upstairs in her room, Michele dressed at a breakneck speed, but her mind was in a dreamy fog the whole time. She could still see his eyes in her mind, could still feel the electrifying touch of his hand on hers—whoever he was. The music echoed in her head, and she hummed under her breath as she splashed some cold water on her face in the bathroom. As she looked up into the mirror, she could have sworn she saw a sparkle of blue . . . his eyes watching her.

As soon as she got home from school that afternoon, Michele raced up to her room and seized the diary. But before opening it to Clara's next entry, she glanced in the mirror at her school clothes. She didn't want to shock Clara again by wearing another "abominable" outfit. Maybe it would help put her at ease if Michele dressed a little more . . . vintage.

She quickly searched until she found what she had worn to a wedding the year before: an iridescent blue chiffon floor-length dress, with three-quarter lace sleeves. She styled her hair in a bun and couldn't help giggling at her reflection in the mirror. She looked like an old-fashioned ballerina. But she would probably fit into 1910 much better in this getup.

Michele scribbled a note to leave on her bed, in case she didn't return in time for dinner. *Going to study group and then dinner with some people from school. Not sure how late I'll be out. See you soon.* She crossed her fingers that her grandparents and Annaleigh wouldn't question her alibi. As she reached for the skeleton key on her bureau, her mind flashed back to her recurring dream. On impulse, she opened her jewelry box and rifled through it until she found a plain gold chain. She attached the key to the chain and clasped the new makeshift necklace around her neck. Michele turned to look in the mirror and shivered—it was just like gazing at the reflection from her dream. Her hand rested on the key, and she suddenly felt that she must never take it off.

Michele returned to the diary, her fingers trembling with anticipation as she flipped to the second entry, dated 10/25/10. She figured she would try to repeat the October 10 phenomenon by bringing the key to the old diary entry. *What if it doesn't work this time?* Michele worried. But no sooner had she thought that than the dizzying journey back in time had begun again, with the roller-coaster plunge downward and the room changing before her eyes at the speed of light—only the whole process was much quicker this time. And then Michele landed once again with a thud on the bedroom floor, arriving to the sight of a very pretty red-haired girl slipping on a pair of white suede gloves. The girl's face broke into a delighted smile at the sight of Michele.

"Clara?" Michele's jaw dropped. "You look so . . ."

"Different? I know." Clara laughed ruefully. "The day after I arrived, I was scrubbed to perfection, my hair dressed in a pompadour, and my face doused in powders. And now this." She smoothed the skirt of her bead-trimmed pale green silk princess-style dress, which matched her eyes. "Society ladies and debutantes have to wear dresses like this simply to go out shopping. I still can't fathom being one of them."

Clara suddenly took in Michele's appearance, and she said in a tone of utter surprise, "Why, you look quite pretty yourself! Though I cannot imagine why you don't wear gloves. Would you like to borrow some of mine?"

Michele laughed. "No thanks, I'm good. Besides, you seem to be the only person who can see me, remember?"

Clara nodded and then clasped Michele's hand excitedly. "I am so happy you're back—my very own friendly ghost! After you vanished like that, I was afraid I had imagined you. And you picked just the day to return—Mr. and Mrs. Windsor are hosting a Halloween masquerade ball! It's my debut in society, so I couldn't be more nervous."

Michele's chest suddenly tightened with grief as she remembered the Halloween costume party she and her friends had been planning and the costumes her mom would have designed, all that she would have had if only . . .

"Are you all right?" Clara asked, clearly noticing Michele's expression.

Michele refocused on Clara and slowly nodded. Remembering the date of the diary entry, she asked, "Is today October twenty-fifth?"

Clara nodded. "Henrietta Windsor is taking me to Lord & Taylor now, for the final fitting on my dress for tonight. Would you like to join us? Though I know no one else can see you . . ."

"I'd love to go," Michele said, feeling a flicker of excitement at the prospect of a 1910 sightseeing trip.

Clara put on an extravagant picture hat adorned with clusters of osprey feathers and set with a veil. Michele gave the hat an incredulous look, and Clara said, "What, have you never before seen a Le Monnier hat? It's my first. Mrs. Windsor gave me a good scolding yesterday for being seen in public without it."

Michele bit back a giggle as she imagined Kristen's and Amanda's reactions to Clara's Edwardian ensemble. She followed Clara down the stairs to the Grand Hall, and she was entranced by the sight of the Windsor Mansion in all its Gilded Age glory. While the house in 2010 had a bit of an old-relic feel, like something out of a museum, the 1910 version was like a freshly painted portrait. Everything from the walls to the floors sparkled with newness, and the home was abuzz with activity as some twenty servants scurried about, preparing for the ball. *This is no hallucination,* Michele realized with a firm knowledge that surprised her. *I've really done it; I've really gone back in time!*

As they descended the staircase, Michele spotted four women waiting for them in the Grand Hall. Her eyes were immediately drawn to the most beautiful of the group, one of the most striking girls she had ever seen. She looked around Michele's age, so Michele figured that this must be the new older sister Clara had spoken of—Violet Windsor.

Violet's black hair was piled atop her head in a waterfall of curls, and her eyes were the very color of her name. Her eyebrows were perfectly arched, her lashes seemed endless, and her lips formed a bee-stung pout. She wore a floor-length dress of ivory satin, festooned with ruffles and a long train. Even with all that clothing, Michele could see that she had an enviable figure—tall and slender, with curves in all the right places. *These people sure dress up to go shopping*, Michele thought, taking in Violet's doeskin gloves, strands of white pearls, and picture hat every bit as elaborate as Clara's.

An older woman stood beside Violet, and Michele guessed that she was Violet's mother, Henrietta Windsor. Though Michele figured she must be in her forties, since her youngest child was only ten, she looked significantly older than the women of her age from Michele's time. Henrietta's copper-colored hair was streaked with gray, and there was no makeup to diminish the lines and creases in her face, but she was attractive in a regal way. She looked powerful and proud in her black velvet dress and pearls. Her hat outdid both Clara's and Violet's, with not just plumes but fake *fruit* on it!

The remaining two ladies were both young maids, one of whom Michele recognized from her first meeting with Clara. They stood deferentially off to the side, in their matching plain long black skirts with tucked-in white blouses. Two footmen flanked the front doors of the mansion. Michele chuckled at the sight of them, thinking that they looked straight out of the movie *Cinderella*, with their striped vests, gray knee-length trousers over white stockings, and black patent leather Louis XVI–style shoes.

When Clara and Michele reached the foot of the stairs, Henrietta Windsor gave Clara a curt nod of hello. Clara quickly dropped into a slight curtsy, clearly eager to win over her foster mother. Violet didn't acknowledge Clara's presence with anything other than a narrowing of her eyes, and Michele could instantly tell that she was hardly thrilled about the new addition to her family.

"We are ready now," Henrietta announced to the servants. The footmen quickly swung open the front doors and led the two Windsors, Clara, and the ladies' maids to the horse-drawn carriage awaiting them at the entrance. The footmen helped the women into the carriage, beginning with Henrietta and ending with the maids. The invisible Michele climbed inside after them, squeezing between Clara and one of the maids.

"Wow," Michele whispered, enthralled by the elegant and cozy carriage interior, which was upholstered in maroon silk and lit by gilded lamps.

Once they emerged from the Windsor Mansion gates, Michele caught her first glimpse of turn-of-the-century New York. She let out a gasp of amazement. It was entirely different than she had imagined. The looming apartment and office buildings and upscale shops around Fifth Avenue were gone, replaced with grand marble and limestone homes. In fact, a dramatic redbrick and white stone mansion, with gables and balconies facing both Central Park and Fifth Avenue, now stood at the site of Caissie Hart's apartment building next door. *That must be the old Walker Mansion,* Michele thought. It reminded her of a French château.

Gone were the modern cars zooming through the labyrinth streets, but the cobblestone roads of 1910 were just as clogged with traffic. All kinds of carriages, a few old-fashioned buggies, and several boxy cars like Henry Ford's Model T filled the streets. Policemen, both standing and on horseback, were at the center of packed intersections, trying to manage the lines of vehicles as the extravagantly dressed pedestrians waited to catch a safe moment to cross. Above, a steam locomotive chugged on elevated train tracks. The rumble of early automobiles, the ringing of trolley bells, and the clip-clop of horses were like a strange symphony to Michele's ears.

The Windsor coachman persevered through the traffic, then stopped at Broadway and Fourteenth Street. Michele gave the street signs a double take, unable to believe that this was the area known as Union Square. The Union Square Michele knew from film and TV was an unexceptional, thoroughly modern part of the city, surrounded by trendy restaurants, the W Hotel, office towers, and New York University buildings. But *this* Union Square was something else entirely. Surrounding the expanse of the square were blocks and blocks of resplendent department and specialty stores, bringing to mind the famed shopping boulevards of Paris. Elegant carriages lined every curb, with liveried footmen standing on the sidewalk before them. Michele recognized a few of the names on the store awnings, like Lord & Taylor and Tiffany & Co., which looked even more lavish than its current incarnation on Fifth Avenue.

"Here we are, then, Ladies' Mile," the coachman announced, leaping out of the driver's seat to help the women out of the carriage.

Clara and the Windsors exited and Michele jumped down after them, then followed as they walked into Lord & Taylor. As soon as they entered the store, two young men in formal uniforms appeared at Henrietta's and Violet's elbows, showing off their latest wares and urging them to try on the newest gloves and jewels. Michele thought that this was pretty pushy

and annoying of them, but only Clara seemed overwhelmed. Violet and Henrietta were perfectly at ease with the badgering salesmen.

"Clara, please do not linger or we won't have much time to ready ourselves for the ball," Henrietta suddenly called sharply. Clara flushed and quickened her steps to meet their pace.

A liveried salesman handed an enormous garment bag to one of the Windsor ladies' maids, who led Clara into the dressing room. Several minutes later, Michele watched as Clara emerged in a shimmering beaded gown with a white satin overskirt and bodice over a white and cream brocade underskirt.

"Wow!" Michele mouthed to Clara, who smiled shyly. Out of the corner of her eye, Michele noticed Violet's expression sour at the sight of Clara in the stunning gown.

"That will do," Henrietta said disinterestedly. She turned to give instructions to her other maid, and when she was out of earshot, Violet commented, "Well, it is very nice—for Lord & Taylor. But you must know that all the *best* gowns come from Worth in Paris. That's where my gown for tonight is from, of course, as well as Mother's. I *wonder* why Father didn't order your gown from there as well."

"I am very grateful for all your father has done for me," Clara answered stiffly.

"As you should be," Violet replied. "I advise you to make the most of it, for we don't know how long this charitable whim of his will last. After all, you are not family."

Clara lowered her eyes, clearly hurt. Even though Michele knew that Violet couldn't see her, she couldn't resist throwing a dirty look her way.

"Clara, please change so we can leave," Henrietta called in her same chilly tone.

Clara headed back into the dressing room, one of the ladies' maids trailing her to help her change. When she returned to Henrietta and Violet in her afternoon dress, for a moment she hesitated, as though unsure of whether to follow them or run away.

It was eleven o'clock, and the Windsor Ball was in full swing. Michele sat unseen at the foot of the grand staircase, watching the dazzling ladies and distinguished gentlemen floating through the front doors and into and out of the ballroom. It seemed to Michele that all the guests were striving to outdo each other with their Halloween costumes, each one more spectacular than the last. She ached for her mom to be there alongside her to watch this procession of high society in costume as historical figures, goddesses, kings, queens, and gypsies. Yet no one managed to steal the spotlight from the Windsors.

George Windsor was dressed as Louis XVI, in an embroidered cream satin coat over an ornamented white shirt, with silver satin knee breeches and silk stockings. His costume was complete with a powdered wig under a feathered tricorn hat, and a diamond sword, which he carried proudly with him throughout the house. Michele giggled at how ridiculous her great-great-great-grandfather looked—but somehow, it worked in this setting. Standing proudly on his arm, Henrietta Windsor was costumed as Queen Elizabeth I, complete with a realistic red wig and extravagant neck and wrist ruffs. Her embroidered black velvet gown was set off by a long black velvet train falling from her waist, lined with red satin. She dripped with diamonds: a diamond crown atop her head, long strands of diamonds draped from her shoulders to her waist, a diamond-and-ruby pendant resting against her décolletage, and diamond-and-ruby brooches and bracelets. *This is unreal,* Michele thought as she watched Henrietta turn to greet a woman referred to as Mrs. Vanderbilt.

George and Henrietta's eldest son was away at university, and little Frances was too young to attend the ball, but Violet made for a spectacular representative of the Windsor offspring. While Clara's marchioness costume was a beauty, Violet was a smashing success as a Venetian princess. Her snowy white satin gown, embroidered with pearls, highlighted her striking black hair and violet eyes. A long train of royal blue velvet and satin draped from her shoulders. Ropes of pearls stretched from her neck to her waist, and it was clear from the longing gazes she garnered from the young men, and the envious stares coming from the girls, that Violet was the belle of the ball.

An orchestra in the ballroom played classical pieces, and American Beauty roses wreathed all the main rooms, their sweet smell perfuming the whole first floor of the mansion. Michele left her perch on the stairs to wander into the ballroom and watch the dancers. A colorful swirl of gowns swept across the floor, while debutantes whispered and tittered together in a corner and the elders watched carefully from the balcony above.

And then everything stopped.

A man entered the ballroom, arm in arm with Violet. He was dressed simply compared to the other costumed guests.

He wore white tie and tails and held up to his eyes a Venetian mask of black, white, and gold. There was something strangely *familiar* about him, from his tall, broad-shouldered body to his thick dark hair, to the slow curve of his smile as he looked down at the beauty on his arm. Where had Michele *seen* him before?

He turned toward her, and that was when Michele saw that behind the mask was a sparkling deep blue. Sapphire eyes. *His* eyes . . . the boy from her dream.

Michele felt the blood drain from her face, her heart racing unbearably fast. The music and the sounds of the party became inaudible and everything in her vision blurred—everything except him. Then his eyes flickered in her direction. For a moment he froze, and then he slowly lowered his mask.

"It's really him," Michele whispered in astonishment. Her eyes drank in every detail of the achingly handsome face of the boy who had haunted her dreams—now here, in the flesh.

Suddenly, his eyes locked with hers—and Michele could have sworn she saw a flash of recognition cross his face. Could he *see* her? But how? She felt nearly paralyzed with shock as she watched him. Who *was* he? How could a figment of her dreams just turn up in real life like this?

Michele watched as he murmured something in Violet's ear, then left her side and started to walk toward Michele. She felt spasms of terror inside her, alternating with thrills of excitement, with every stride he took. When he finally reached her, he stood in front of her, a few steps away, looking at Michele as though he had been waiting years for her. No one had ever looked at her that way before.

"I know you," he breathed. His voice was low and warm, just as Michele had expected.

Michele could barely speak, her mouth hanging open with shock. "You're real," she whispered. "You—you can *see* me. Then you had the—the dreams too?"

His eyes stayed locked on hers, though he looked puzzled by her words.

"Dreams?" he echoed dazedly. A few guests nearby turned to look at him strangely.

"Um, y-you should probably know that . . . well, no one else but you and Clara can see me—" Michele stammered. But he continued looking at her with intense concentration, as if he hadn't heard her.

"I must speak with you," he interrupted. "Come with me?"

Michele nodded. Though her legs felt like jelly, she managed to follow him as he strode out of the ballroom, leading her toward the back patio. As he made his way through the mansion, Michele could tell that he had been there many times before.

When at last they were alone among the ferns and wicker furniture, he stood gazing at her. "It was *you*—you were the girl I saw at my summer cottage three years ago," he said, his eyes bright with amazement. "My father and cousin didn't believe me about you, but I knew you were real. I never forgot your face." Michele felt a pang of disappointment as she realized he had mistaken her for someone else.

"No. No, that wasn't me. I've never met you until now. That is, I've had . . . dreams about you." Michele cringed with embarrassment. "I realize that sounds crazy, but, well, that's all I know you from."

He looked at her, shaking his head intently. "I know the face I saw. It was none but yours. I would stake anything on it."

Michele stared at him, wondering if he was right. She knew now that she was capable of time travel. Was it possible that she could go back further in time and meet him three years earlier? Or had his first meeting with her been a dream, just as she had dreamt of him all these years?

"Who—who *are* you?" Michele blurted out.

"Call me Philip," he answered. "And you?"

"Michele."

"Michele," he repeated, drawing out the syllables so that her name sounded like music. "You don't—you don't look or seem at all like the others." He glanced down at her ungloved hands.

Michele suddenly remembered how elaborately all the other girls were dressed, how stunning they all looked—especially Violet. Her own dress was like a peasant's in comparison. Michele felt a stab of envy. Though she knew in the logical part of her mind that it was ridiculous to be jealous of a girl from a hundred years earlier, a girl from another world, she couldn't help fervently hoping that Philip didn't think she looked shabby.

"You're right," she finally answered. "I am different. Very." *If you only knew!*

"I . . . rather like it," he said quietly. Michele blushed with surprise. Philip reached out as if to touch her hand, and then he seemed to regain a sense of propriety and drew his hand back.

"Where are you from?" he asked, studying her as though trying to solve a riddle.

"California," Michele answered, wishing he had gone through with taking her hand.

Philip stepped closer to her. "And you are a friend of the Windsors'?"

"Mmm . . . you could say that," Michele said. His closeness had caused her heart to start beating so loudly she was sure he could hear it.

The orchestra began playing a new piece—and Michele realized with a gasp that it was none other than Schubert's *Serenade*. Philip didn't seem to notice her reaction though his eyes sparkled as the song began. He offered his arm. "Might I have this dance, Michele?"

Michele linked her arm with his and her whole body seemed to awaken at his touch, even as something tugged at the back of her mind, telling her she shouldn't do this. She pushed the feeling away as he led her back into the ballroom, and they danced. Michele had never waltzed before, but somehow, in his arms she felt completely at ease. Her body seemed to melt into his as they moved together across the floor, just like in her dream. Each step and glance between them grew more and more heated, and as he danced her across the ballroom floor, she felt like she was floating—

"*Philip James Walker!*"

Philip stopped suddenly. Michele dropped his hand, her mouth falling open in shock. Philip was a *Walker*?

A ferocious-looking man in yet another Louis XVI costume grabbed Philip's arm and yanked him roughly away from Michele. "*What* do you think you are doing? Trying to make a scene?"

"Do relax, Uncle. I was only dancing," Philip argued, pulling his arm free.

"You may find it amusing to dance with yourself, but mind you, everyone here thinks my nephew has gone mad," Philip's uncle spat.

Oh, God. In the heat of the moment, Michele had forgotten how it would look to everyone else at the party—like Philip was dancing alone.

"Dancing with *myself*? Whatever do you mean? I was simply dancing with a friend of the Windsors', her name is Michele, she's right there—"

"Enough of this foolishness!" Mr. Walker hissed. "No other man of eighteen years and good breeding would dare act this way. You are far too old for imaginary friends."

Dumbfounded, Philip turned around to stare at Michele as it dawned on him that she was invisible to all but him. As Philip's uncle dragged him away from Michele, Clara raced over, casually lifting her fingers to her lips so nobody would see her speaking.

"What are you doing?" she whispered. "How can Philip see you?"

"I have no idea," Michele replied weakly.

"He's engaged to Violet," Clara said, glancing at her new older sister, who was now glowering at Philip.

Michele gaped at Clara, feeling as though she had just been punched in the gut. The boy from her dreams was *engaged*? And to the snotty, devastatingly gorgeous *Violet*? It couldn't be.

The rest of the ball was agony. Michele wished she could just get back to her own time, away from this confusing scene and all the feelings it was stirring up inside her. But although she clutched the skeleton key and whispered a pleading request to

Time to send her home, she remained at the ball. It hit her that she knew of no surefire way to get back to 2010, and the thought sent a streak of terror through her.

From the ballroom to the dining room, where a gluttonous buffet supper was served, Philip's uncle kept him planted firmly at his side. A woman costumed as a French courtesan stood with them, and though she didn't seem very maternal with her cold and detached expression, Michele could tell she was Philip's mother. Michele wondered where his dad was, why this uncle was acting so authoritative.

Philip seemed unable to take his eyes off Michele, his expression a mixture of distress and intrigue. As she gazed back at him, a part of her knew that she should stay away after what she had just discovered. Yet she still felt drawn to him.

After supper, Henrietta clapped her hands and happily announced that the quadrilles would commence in the ballroom. Michele noticed that the icy woman from that afternoon seemed to come to life in the party setting.

"What are quadrilles?" Michele asked Clara.

"Formal French square dances," Clara explained, again discreetly shielding her mouth with her hand. "They're performed at all the high-society balls. Mr. Windsor hired a private instructor to teach them to me, so I'll be dancing for my first time tonight. Oh, do wish me luck!"

"Good luck," Michele said with a grin, trying not to chuckle at Clara's earnestness over a square dance. While the guests returned to the ballroom, Michele noticed Violet and George Windsor hanging back from the crowd, looking like they were in the middle of a tense discussion. They made a funny pair,

Louis XVI and a Venetian princess, arguing under their breath. George abruptly stalked out of the dining room, away from the ballroom, with Violet on his heels. Curious, Michele followed them into the morning room, which was closed to the party. Being invisible to all but two people had its disadvantages . . . but it happened to be great for eavesdropping.

"Is now really the time for this, Violet?" George asked impatiently.

"It's just that I cannot *stand* pretending Clara is our ward, or foster daughter—however you choose to conceal it—when we know full well what she *really* is, Father," Violet said frostily.

"Violet," George warned, his face getting red.

Michele was suddenly alert. What was George hiding?

"In fact, I'm sure the sudden inclusion of Clara in our family has finally given Mother proof of your infidelities," Violet snapped. "Do you endeavor to cause the greatest scandal New York society has ever seen?"

Michele clapped her hand over her mouth. Did Violet mean what Michele thought she meant—that George Windsor had fathered Clara?

George's expression turned furious. "You have *no* right to talk to your father like that—"

Michele backed away but bumped into someone as she turned around. Clara. From the look on Clara's face, it was clear to Michele that she had heard everything.

Violet and George looked up, George's face turning pale when he saw that Clara had overheard them. Clara raced away from the morning room, Michele following closely. Suddenly, a family departing the ball got between the two girls, and Michele lost Clara in the crowd.

There was no sign of her among those dancing quadrilles in the ballroom, mingling in the Grand Hall, or downing iced lemonade and pastries in the drawing room. Figuring that Clara might have escaped to her bedroom, Michele hurried up to the third floor. And sure enough, as she neared the bedroom door, Michele heard quiet sobs coming from inside. She felt a pang of protective worry for Clara. She entered the room to find Clara kneeling on her bed, clutching a battered black-and-white photograph.

"Hi," Michele said tentatively. She sat beside Clara and glanced down at the photo. It was faded with age, but Michele could make out the form of a couple: a mustached man dressed in a suit and a bowler hat standing hand in hand with a young woman in a long dark coat over a plain floor-length skirt and blouse, her hair knotted atop her head. The photo was stamped with the date April 9, 1897.

"Are those your parents?"

Clara nodded. "They died when I was four. This picture was all I had of them to bring with me to the orphanage." She looked at Michele with wide, watery eyes. "Michele, do you think my mother was George Windsor's mistress? And that he . . . he's my *father*?"

Michele bit her lip uncomfortably. *How do I answer this one?*

"Yes. It seems like it," she finally admitted.

"I won't believe it," Clara said in a low voice. "These horrible rich men, they think just because they have money, they have the right to any woman, all women. I won't believe that my mother was someone who would have bedded another man. I *know* George Windsor forced himself on her. But how, *how* can I be the daughter of a sordid tryst like that?"

Michele didn't know what to say. So she wrapped her arm around Clara's shoulder and held her as she cried, just as Marion used to soothe Michele. There were two knocks at the door—one from Mr. Windsor and another from the housekeeper, both checking on her—but Clara refused to see them.

When her tears subsided, Clara asked Michele, "Will you stay with me until I fall asleep? I don't want to be alone with these thoughts."

"Of course," Michele agreed gently.

Once Clara had been asleep for a good fifteen minutes, Michele pulled the skeleton key out from under the neckline of her dress. She held it tightly, squeezing her eyes shut as she repeated a silent prayer: *Please send me back. Please send me to my own time.* But she opened her eyes to find herself still in 1910. She gulped nervously, her palms clammy. What if she couldn't get home this time? What if she was stuck in the past, forced to live this ghostlike existence forever?

Just then, the mantel clock struck four a.m. The house was eerily quiet now, the ball over and the Windsors and their staff all in bed. Michele felt desperate to get out. She hopped off Clara's bed and approached the bedroom door. So far, she'd followed Clara everywhere; she hadn't had to use her physical form at all. Taking a deep breath, she gently turned the door-knob and smiled when the door silently swung open. *I guess I can get around on my own,* Michele thought with relief.

She tiptoed out of the room and crept down the stairs, then reached the front door of the Windsor Mansion. She stood in the front garden for a moment and then pushed open the gate, stepping onto Fifth Avenue.

Michele found old New York to be dark, quiet, and deserted, a stark contrast to the action-packed and bright late nights of the city in her time. The only illumination came from the faint glow of streetlamps. Michele shivered, frightened by the thought that she was alone in the wee hours of one hundred years earlier.

Suddenly, she saw a figure approaching—coming from the Walker mansion. Michele froze. Was it Philip? He was walking with his head down and was still dressed in his tux from the ball. As he came closer and saw her, he stopped short. They stood a few yards apart, looking at each other. Michele felt her breath catch in her throat. Even the dark couldn't hide his extraordinary good looks.

"What are you doing out at this hour?" Philip asked after a long pause.

"I could ask you the same thing," Michele replied, trying her best to sound breezy.

He took a step closer, his face coming under the light of a streetlamp. Michele gasped at the sight of his left cheek—bruised and painfully red. "What happened to you?" she cried.

"Uncle got to me," Philip said stoically. "Our little dance cost me a good beating."

"Oh, God. I'm so sorry." Without thinking, Michele rushed toward him, closing the wide space between them. "How could he do that to you? Where were your parents?"

Philip let out a bitter laugh. "My father's brother is master of the house now. He's been free to do whatever he likes since Father died two years ago. And my mother wouldn't care. She can't be bothered with anything except her social engagements."

For a moment, Michele just looked at him. He was clearly unhappy, so unlike the carefree, smiling Philip from her dreams. "I'm sorry," she said quietly, gently reaching up to touch his wounded cheek. He winced but didn't move her hand.

"Who are you?" he asked in a low voice. "What have you done to me?"

Michele drew back. "What do you mean, what have I done to you?"

"Why am I *seeing* someone no one else sees—why am I feeling things I shouldn't feel?"

"What—what sort of things?" Michele couldn't help asking.

Philip looked away. "I . . . don't know."

After a pause, Michele said, "I don't think I can explain. I mean, I don't even understand it myself."

"Please try." Philip looked at her pleadingly. "Answer my questions, at least."

Michele swallowed hard. "Okay."

"Are you a human being, or—or a phantom?"

For a moment Michele wanted to laugh out loud. That was one question she had never expected to be asked in her lifetime. "Um, I'm a human."

"But then how can no one else see you?" Philip's forehead creased in frustration. "You are alive, are you not?"

"I am alive . . . but not in the same way you are," Michele confessed, surprising herself with her honesty. She hadn't planned on telling him the truth, but there was something about him. She couldn't lie to him.

"Michele." She looked up and his eyes were suddenly warm and soft. "You can tell me."

Michele nodded slowly as she thought of what it could be like to tell someone. Maybe they could figure this thing out together, and maybe they could discover how it was that they'd known each other before they had even met. "Okay," she agreed. "But let's walk."

They began slowly walking down Fifth. Her eyes on the ground, Michele blurted out, "The truth is I'm a Windsor. My mom died and I just moved to New York to live with my grandparents at the Windsor Mansion. The only thing is I'm . . . I'm from the future—2010."

Philip stopped in his tracks and stared at her. He let out an uneasy laugh. "You have quite the imagination."

"No, it's the truth." Michele looked at him seriously. "Philip, why do you think other people can't see me? It's because I don't exist in your time. Clara Windsor can see me, because I traveled here through her diary, and you . . . well, I don't know how you can see me, but—I can't help thinking it has to do with the fact that I've dreamt of you." Her voice lowered to a whisper. "All my life."

Philip's face was pale with dismay. "But—this *can't* be. I am going mad, aren't I?"

"No, I promise," Michele insisted, suddenly desperate for Philip to believe her. "I'm real, flesh and blood, and I'm really here. I'm just from a different time."

"Show me," Philip said hoarsely. "Show me that you're real, and not just my own madness."

Michele nodded and took a step closer to him. She gently took his hand, and the butterflies in her stomach fluttered. She slowly reached his hand up to her face, and let his fingers brush against her cheek.

"See? Solid and real," Michele said, with a shaky laugh. "Otherwise you wouldn't be able to—to feel me."

Philip gazed at her, his eyes deep with an emotion Michele couldn't place, one that brought a blush to her cheeks. Suddenly he reached for her again, and began to slowly, tentatively trace the outline of her face with his hands. Michele gasped involuntarily, as she felt electricity spark through her at his touch. She closed her eyes as his hands swept across her eyelids, as he ran his fingers through her hair, and then came to rest his fingertips on her lips. Michele leaned in to him, her heartbeat quickening with anticipation as their heads moved toward each other—

But he abruptly pulled away from her, his hands dropping awkwardly to his sides.

"I'm sorry," he said quietly. "I shouldn't have . . ." His voice trailed off.

"What?" Michele stared at Philip, her face burning with embarrassment. Had she done something wrong?

"Allow me to walk you home," he said uncomfortably.

"Wait—what just happened?" Michele asked, trying in vain to keep her voice steady.

Philip looked at her, his expression torn. "I'm engaged. And now you enter, a girl from another time, invisible to others, and I shouldn't feel . . . this."

Michele looked at the ground, feeling sucker-punched. For a moment, she had forgotten about Violet, forgotten that Philip wasn't hers. *Why* had she dreamt of him all her life, why did she now have this undeniable chemistry with him, when it turned out he was engaged to another girl?

She nodded stiffly. "Right. Okay."

They walked back to their street in silence, Michele feeling like a deflated balloon. It felt wrong, unnatural, to walk side by side without touching. She had met him only that night, so why couldn't her mind and body shake the feeling that she belonged with him? As Michele glanced up at him out of the corner of her eye, she caught him watching her. They both quickly looked away.

"Here you are, then," Philip said. Michele looked up and saw that they were in front of the Windsor Mansion gates.

"I, um—I don't have the key," Michele realized.

"Then what's this?" Philip gently reached for the skeleton key around Michele's neck, and his fingers brushed against her collarbone. Michele felt another shiver at his touch.

"Oh . . . well, that's not the house key but it's definitely done bigger things than unlock a gate," Michele said wryly. "I guess it's worth a shot."

"Whatever do you mean?" Philip wrinkled his brow in confusion.

"It's a long story." Michele grasped the key and pressed it to the lock on the gate. She felt a force pulling her into the gate with such speed she cried out in shock. She looked down and saw that the ground underneath her was shaking, moving, changing. Michele whipped her head around to face Philip, and saw him watching in astonishment as she floated away from him. For a moment their eyes met, and in his expression, Michele saw a flash of regret.

I'm back.

Michele looked around her in amazement. She was standing in the front garden, just behind the gate where she had left Philip. It was a starless, chilly night, and from the stillness around her, she knew that it was just as late as it had been in 1910. She instinctively turned to the site of the Walker Mansion, and when she saw the modern apartment complex in its place, she felt her heart clench. *He's gone now,* she thought. *He doesn't exist anymore.* But how could that be when her face still tingled from his touch, her stomach still felt queasy from his subsequent rejection?

The front doors flew open. Annaleigh rushed outside, her usually polished hair undone and her eyes frantic. "There you are!" she gasped. "Where have you *been?* We've all been terrified! Come inside."

Michele nervously followed Annaleigh into the house. "I— I'm sorry," she stammered, racking her brain for a good explanation . . . one that didn't involve time travel. "I left a note in my room. I was at a—a study group and we all hung out afterwards, and I guess I just lost track of the time. I had no idea how late it was."

"Well, you'd better get ready to explain everything to your grandparents," Annaleigh said grimly. "They've been sitting up all night waiting, and they instructed me to buzz them as soon as you got home."

"Oh no," Michele muttered. The last thing she felt like doing was being interrogated by Walter and Dorothy, especially after her last unsettling encounter with them.

"I'm going to go call their room. Stay right here," Annaleigh instructed.

Michele sank onto one of the settees in the Grand Hall. What in the world was she going to say to them? The memory of Walter's angry face from the other night flashed in her mind, and she shuddered. She leaned back, and as she closed her eyes wearily, the image in her mind changed to Philip's intense gaze. . . .

"Michele."

She winced at her grandfather's voice, tight with fury, and reluctantly opened her eyes to face him and Dorothy. They looked similar to the way they had the other night, both of them in their long cashmere robes, hair undone and faces aged considerably without the makeup and other solutions of daytime. Michele felt a twinge of guilt as she noticed Dorothy's red, swollen eyes.

"What do you have to say for yourself?" Walter demanded. "Where have you *been* until four-thirty in the morning?"

"I—I'm so . . . so sorry," Michele said anxiously, tripping over her words. "I didn't realize how late it was. I never meant to worry you."

"Where have you been?" Walter repeated. "Who were you *with*?"

At those words, Dorothy looked as though she was bracing for the worst. As Michele saw the fear in her grandparents' eyes, she had the feeling that her absence had triggered something in them, that there was more to their anxiety than worry about a wayward granddaughter staying out too late.

"I was just with . . . Caissie Hart. And her other friends," she blurted out, the lie coming faster than she could process it.

"Caissie?" Dorothy's eyebrows shot up. "That's impossible. Inez was here this afternoon and she would have told me."

"Well, Caissie lives with her dad, so she probably just didn't mention it to her mom. We were . . . at her friend Aaron's," Michele said, improvising. "We had a study group, and afterwards some of us stayed at Aaron's to order pizza and watch a movie. It got so late that I fell asleep during the movie. I'm really, really sorry."

Her grandparents studied her as though unsure whether to believe her story—but it was clear that they wanted to believe it.

"All right, then," Walter said quietly. "Here are the house rules from now on. Your curfew is ten-thirty p.m. on weeknights and midnight on weekends. If you plan to spend the night anywhere, it has to be girls only and you must call to let us know first. Break any of those rules and you'll be grounded. Do you understand?"

Michele gaped at them. "But—I've never in my life had a curfew or been grounded. Mom always trusted me."

"Your mother was still a child when she had you," Dorothy said dismissively. "She didn't know what was best—"

Michele leaped to her feet. "Don't *ever* talk about my mom

like that," she snapped. "She was ten times the mother you were."

Dorothy drew back as if she had been slapped.

"That's enough," Walter said tersely. "Those are the rules. End of discussion."

Without a word, Michele turned on her heel and left the room, thinking that these episodes with her grandparents were sure making her appreciate her freedom in 1910.

Michele walked into her first-period U.S. history class the next morning in a fog. The ride to school had felt surreal, the modern cars and skyscrapers all wrong, as she found herself yearning for the sound of horse hooves, the rumble of the elevated train, and mostly, the warm sound of Philip's voice. She tried to focus during class, but her mind was years away.

When the bell rang, Michele caught Caissie's eye and remembered that she had to ask Caissie to cover for her. Michele nervously approached her desk, wondering how on earth she would explain this one.

"Hey," she greeted Caissie, giving her a smile.

"Hi." Caissie smiled back, looking a little surprised.

"Listen, I have a huge favor to ask—and it's kind of weird," Michele began awkwardly.

Caissie raised an eyebrow. "Um, okay. Shoot."

"So, um . . . I sort of stayed out until after four in the morning and my grandparents flipped. I couldn't tell them where I really was and I was put on the spot, and I just—well, I blurted out that I was with you at your friend Aaron's. I don't know why

I did it and I feel really embarrassed telling you," Michele confessed. "I'm sorry to have to ask, but would you be willing to tell your mom that's what happened? Just 'cause I know my grandmother's going to check my story with her."

Caissie gave her a strange look but shrugged. "Okay. I mean, why not, I guess. Where were you that you can't tell them?"

Michele bit her lip. "I can't really say," she admitted.

"Oh. Okay," Caissie said stiffly.

"I wish I could," Michele said hurriedly. "It's just—"

"I get it," Caissie interrupted. "Consider the favor done."

"Thanks," Michele said gratefully.

Caissie swung her backpack over her shoulders. "Well, see you around."

"See you." Michele watched her leave, feeling unsettled. She could tell that she had offended Caissie by asking her to lie for her and then not trusting her with the truth. Still, how was she supposed to tell *anyone* what had really taken place the previous night? *I should have just made up some story to tell her,* Michele thought regretfully.

As she set off down the hall for her next class, Michele thought of what it would be like to have someone to confide in about this unbelievable turn of events. It would be a relief in a way. But there was no one to tell. Amanda and Kristen would never in a million years believe it. There was only one person who would take this seriously, and that person was gone.

After school, Michele arrived at the Windsor Mansion just as her grandparents were leaving.

"Hello, Michele," Dorothy greeted her quietly as they passed in the Grand Hall. Walter gave her a polite nod, but his face still looked tense.

"Hi," Michele replied. She watched them walk out the door, dressed in upscale finery. They were probably headed to yet another gala for one of the many boards they served on. It seemed to Michele that her grandparents did nothing meaningful, just constantly attended board dinners and events. *What kind of life is that?* she wondered as she headed up the stairs to her room. She heard her cell phone beep with a text message, and she pulled it out of her pocket. The message was from Kristen, asking where in the world Michele was. Michele guiltily remembered that she hadn't returned her friends' calls for the past few days, ever since her first trip to 1910. As much as she missed them, she didn't feel quite ready to call them back yet. They knew her well enough that they'd immediately sense she was different—and she had no idea how she would explain that.

Not in the mood to start on homework, Michele headed into her sitting room to find something to read. As she opened the glass-enclosed library cabinet, she saw a small burgundy porcelain music box that she hadn't noticed before. Michele opened the lid, and strains of Chopin's haunting Nocturne no. 19 in E Minor began to play. The music box was clearly ancient, and the song played in fits and starts, the sound low and tinny. Yet the melody was still so beautiful Michele wished she could hear it played properly.

Suddenly, a sound from downstairs caused her to jump, and she nearly dropped the porcelain box in her shock. Just as she had been wishing to hear the song in all its glory, there it was:

she could hear it now being played below by someone who sounded like a virtuoso.

Stunned, Michele turned to examine her room. Her TV and entertainment console were gone, replaced with a delicate white tea table, and gas lamps had taken the place of electric. *I'm back in 1910,* she realized with amazement. Somehow, Time had sent her back instantaneously. But all Michele could focus on was the music. *Who in the world could be playing like this?* she wondered. She had always thought Lily was the only Windsor with any musical talent, but she would have been just a baby in 1910.

She hurried downstairs, following the sound to the ballroom. Michele stood in the doorway and found the Windsor women seated admiringly around a young man playing the piano, whose back was to Michele. Henrietta sat with a little girl on her knee. Michele guessed that she was the youngest daughter, Frances. The two of them listened solemnly, while Violet perched beside them with a satisfied smile on her face. *Where's Clara?* Michele wondered.

Michele looked closer at the young man playing the piano—and she froze. There was no mistaking that thick dark hair, those hands, that proud posture. It was *Philip.*

She watched in awe as his fingers danced across the keys. Philip's eyes were closed in concentration, his body moving fluidly with the music, as he played with the passion of someone giving every bit of his soul over to the song. Michele felt a stab of longing as she watched him.

When he finished, the Windsor women politely applauded. Philip turned to face them and then stopped short, drawing a sharp intake of breath, at the sight of Michele. For a moment she worried that he was unhappy to see her, but then his face broke into a beautiful smile that sent a warm glow through her body.

"Philip? What in the dickens are you looking at?" Violet asked.

"N-nothing," he answered, collecting himself.

"What are you playing next?" Frances piped up.

Philip paused, and though he spoke to the others, the quick glance that he first gave Michele made her feel that he was addressing her. "This is actually something I composed myself," he said.

He turned back to the piano and began to play a song that couldn't have been more different from Chopin's Nocturne. This music had a syncopated, swinging rhythm, making Michele think of New Orleans jazz, only sped up. Philip's fingers flew across the keys, his hands looking like they were in competition with each other. The song was intoxicating and catchy, and Michele couldn't resist moving to the rhythm. Although Violet's presence was a painful reminder that Philip was taken, Michele felt even more under his spell now, after seeing his talent.

"Stop that at once!"

Michele jumped at Henrietta's icy command. Clearly bewildered, Philip abruptly stopped playing. Violet's face was red and she looked like she had just swallowed something sour.

"We do not allow that music in our house," Henrietta sternly admonished him.

"I beg your pardon?" Philip asked in disbelief.

"You were playing *race music*!" Violet hissed. "What would people *say* if they knew?"

Michele's mouth fell open in shock. Philip fixed Violet and her mother with a cold look. "It's called ragtime," he said evenly.

"The music of red-light districts," Henrietta said, shaking her head with disdain. "As my future son-in-law, I expect you never to expose my daughter to that music again."

"It's a shame you feel that way." Philip pulled out his pocket watch and gave it a perfunctory glance. "I'd best be taking my leave now, as Mother and Uncle will be expecting me."

"Philip!" Violet sputtered, no doubt guessing the reason he was cutting the visit short.

"I expect I'll be seeing you soon, Violet," Philip said cordially. "Goodbye, Mrs. Windsor, Frances." As he picked up his hat and headed toward the door, his eyes locked with Michele's.

"Don't listen to them," Michele, not even bothering with a hello, burst out the second Philip had left the room. "What they were saying was totally ignorant. Most of your generation may still think there's a racial pecking order, but history proves them wrong. African American music isn't race music; it's just *good* music. And it's great that you're so inspired by it, because your song is amazing, and as much as I dig Chopin, the ragtime is way cooler."

The corners of Philip's mouth twitched with amusement. "I confess I couldn't make out any of what you just said. But I do detect a compliment somewhere in there," he said, his voice low so as not to attract attention.

"Oh." *Got to remember not to use slang in 1910,* Michele

thought. "I was saying that they're completely wrong, and that you have to keep playing ragtime. I've never heard anyone play like that, and it was . . ." Michele searched for the right word. "Spectacular."

Philip stopped and looked at her, his eyes bright. Then he unexpectedly reached for her hand. Their fingers interlaced as if by habit and he led her out of the house, not saying a word until they were outside the Windsor Mansion gates.

"There's so much I've wanted to say to you, and ask you, since I saw you last," he said intently. "I know it's not quite proper, but the only place for us to talk without my being seen is in my home. Can I take you there?"

Michele nodded, feeling a thrill at his surprising change toward her. "Of course."

Philip led her through the arched French doors of the Walker chateau and into the lavish mansion. They passed through crimson-carpeted hallways on the first floor, decorated with eighteenth-century French tapestries and paintings, until Philip opened a door into a formal room and closed it behind them. The room had white and gold paneled walls, a gilded ceiling, and elegant curtains and furniture in different shades of burgundy. In the center of the room was an intricately painted grand piano, beside a five-foot gold harp.

"This is the music room—the one room in the house no one ever seems to enter but me," Philip said with a grin.

"It's beautiful." *Who would have ever thought I'd soon be so familiar with houses on this scale?* Michele thought in amazement.

Philip gestured for her to sit beside him, and suddenly Michele couldn't contain her curiosity any longer. "Philip, what happened?" she blurted out. "I thought you didn't want . . . I mean, I thought you wanted to stay away from me."

"I didn't want to. I thought I *had* to," Philip said. "That scene you just witnessed with the Windsors? That's the life I've been accustomed to—tightly controlled, with my uncle and this society holding the reins, pulling me back from any freedom or happiness. I've been numb for years, and I didn't realize it until after you appeared and—and made me *feel* something. Since then, these past two weeks I've been . . . awake. Alive. Restless for you to return—and afraid that you wouldn't."

Michele felt her face grow warm, and for a moment she couldn't speak. "I'm glad," she finally replied, shyly. She moved an inch closer to him, and the two of them sat smiling at one another. Philip's eyes seemed to drink in her appearance, and his face flushed as he regarded her knee-length plaid skirt and short-sleeved white blouse. "You're—you're quite underdressed," he commented.

"Not for 2010," Michele said with a chuckle. "These are my school clothes. This is actually considered conservative in my time."

"I haven't been able to stop wondering about the future since I saw you last," Philip said, his eyes filled with curiosity. "Will you tell me about it?"

Michele hesitated. "Are you sure you want to know?" She wondered if there were rules about this kind of thing, if it was bad for her to reveal what was ahead. But Philip nodded so eagerly that she couldn't stand to disappoint him.

"Well . . . the truth is, it couldn't be more different from now," she began. "In my time, we fly around the world in airplanes. There are rockets that send astronauts into outer space. People have walked on the moon—" She broke off at Philip's expression. He looked so incredulous she couldn't help giggling.

"We've been trying to get man to fly since '03, but no one has quite managed it," Philip said. "So it really works, then? And to go to outer space and the *moon!*"

"That's not all," Michele continued, warming to her subject. "We have computers, which are kind of like typewriters, but with all sorts of programs and applications. Practically *anything* you can imagine, you can do on a computer. We have small portable telephones that we carry with us everywhere, and there's this amazing invention called the Internet, where you can communicate with people from across the whole world in just seconds. We have access to anything we want— entertainment, communication, news—whenever we want it, just by logging on to the Internet on our computers and phones. There are video cameras in computers too, so I can be in New York and speak with someone in Africa as easily as if we were in the same room."

Philip sat on the edge of his seat, looking befuddled but listening in awe. Michele realized that what she took for granted as the simple necessities of life, he saw as a story beyond imagination.

"Do you have movies in your time?" she asked him.

"Yes, they're the newest fad. Though the picture is always flickering and the stories are too brief, not even five minutes long. I much prefer stage plays," Philip remarked.

"Well, in my time movies are as long as plays, and they look perfect, with full color. And they have sound and special effects," Michele said. "And then there's this thing called TV, which everyone has in their home. It's a big box with a screen that shows a bunch of different channels, and each channel has a different show at every hour. Wherever you turn in my time, there's constant entertainment and new technology."

"It sounds incredible," Philip marveled. "You must find our world so dull in comparison."

"No, actually. It's just different. I like what I'm seeing of old New York," Michele replied.

"What is it that you like?" Philip asked.

"I love the colors . . . the open spaces and unpolluted skies," Michele said thoughtfully. "I don't know. I guess I like that it seems more . . . innocent, somehow."

Philip smiled at her. "You see our old New York quite well."

"Tell me more about 1910. What's it like for you?" Michele asked.

Philip stretched his arms behind him, thinking. "It's like . . . living between the old and the new. The city has one foot in its Victorian past, and one foot in your future. New skyscrapers are being constructed every day, aiming to break height records, and in just the past years, we've been introduced to the telephone, the automobile, phonograph records, Kodak cameras, and so on. But at the same time, we continue to obey the rules and customs of the 1890s."

"Living between the old and the new," Michele echoed. "That's just what I'm doing now."

"I suppose we're not so different after all," Philip said with a grin.

"I don't feel like we are," Michele said, suddenly serious. "I mean, I know we're a hundred years apart, but . . . I don't know why, I just feel like I know you so well."

Philip nodded slowly. "I know just what you mean."

She gestured to the piano. "Will you play something for me?"

"Of course." Philip smiled and went to the piano. Michele knew instinctively what he was going to play before he began. Sure enough, the moment Philip's fingers touched the keys, Schubert's *Serenade* filled the room.

"Our song," he said to her with a wink as he played.

Michele closed her eyes, soaking in the beautiful music, as goose bumps rose on her arms. When he finished the song, she asked him to play another one of his ragtime compositions. As he played a soulful melody with a swinging rhythm, Michele had the incredible feeling that she was listening to a legend in the making.

"Writing music is what you were born to do," she said passionately when he'd finished playing. "I'm serious." Michele thought for a moment of her own songwriting aspirations as a lyricist, wondering if she would say the same about herself. *But my abilities are nothing next to his. Especially now that I haven't written a word in a month,* she thought wryly.

"I believe you are the one and only person who enjoys my compositions," Philip confided. "I do love classical, of course,

but my real passion is this new music coming from the South."
He set his jaw in determination. "No one believes I can do it,
but more than anything, I want to make a name for myself as a
composer, and I want our society to be rid of the hateful term
'race music.' I've always believed in music bringing people together, not setting us further apart."

"You're right," Michele agreed firmly, sitting next to him on
the piano bench. "You're just ahead of your time. You'll see. People will finally start to get it. And if anyone can make it in
music, it should be you. I haven't heard anyone in my time play
like that."

He gazed at her. "It's a wonderful feeling—you believing
in me."

The way he looked at her was so intimate it made Michele
feel exhilarated and shy all at once. She glanced down at the
piano keys, trying to calm her racing heart. And then she felt
Philip's hand gently lift her chin, and she looked, mesmerized,
into those sapphire eyes. Their faces slowly drew toward each
other, and he softly brushed his lips against hers. Michele felt
her knees weakening, her stomach swirling, all from the simple
touch of his lips to hers. Wrapping her arms around his neck,
she pulled him closer to her, and they began kissing passionately, the searing kiss of two people who had waited a lifetime
for each other. *Oh, my God*, Michele thought, as she felt his lips
against her neck and her hair. *So* this *is what everyone writes and
sings and dreams about—this feeling.*

When they finally managed to pull away, Michele leaned
against him and he nestled her in his arms, wrapping his black
coat around her shoulders to keep her warm. She closed her

eyes, and for the first time since losing her mother, she recognized the emotion inside her as happiness.

She wondered what this meant for them, what it meant for Philip's engagement to Violet. As much as she disliked Violet, she felt a sinking guilt in her stomach at the notion of breaking up an engagement, especially when she was just a traveler in Philip's time, not able to fully be with him. But she also felt that she and Philip belonged together, that her dreams all these years and the key from her father were like a road map, leading her to him.

After a while, Michele realized that she must have been with Philip for hours. "I should get back to my time," she said reluctantly. "If I miss my curfew, my grandparents might put me under house arrest."

"Wait—what if I come back to your time with you?" Philip's eyes lit up at the thought. "I would give anything to see it."

Bring Philip home with her? Michele smiled. It sounded too good to be true. Could she do it?

"Let's try," Michele agreed. She took Philip's hand, and with her other hand, she held her key tight, willing Time to send them to 2010—together.

"What the—"

At the horrified shriek, Michele looked up, disoriented. She was lying on a cold kitchen floor. The hum of a refrigerator and the laugh track from a nearby TV let her know that she must be back in her own time. But she was alone. *It didn't work,* Michele thought, a wave of grief overcoming her as she realized that

Philip wasn't there, that he didn't exist anymore in 2010. *When will I see him again?* she wondered anxiously.

Michele blinked and a face hovering over her came into focus. It belonged to Caissie Hart, who looked stunned and terrified. *Caissie? Where did she come from?* Michele thought, bewildered. That was when she remembered that Caissie's apartment building used to be the Walker Mansion. *This kitchen must be where the music room was one hundred years ago,* she thought.

"You'd better explain what's going on before I call the cops," Caissie warned. "Did you just *break in?*"

"No, please, let me explain," Michele pleaded, slowly getting up off the floor.

Just then, a man's voice called from across the hall, "Caissie? What in the world are you yelling about?"

Caissie's eyes darted from Michele to the door as she no doubt planned to turn Michele over to her dad.

"No, please don't!" Michele whispered frantically. "I have a seriously good explanation for this. It has to do with—with what I talked to you about at school today."

Luckily, Caissie's curiosity won out. "I just—I just saw a spider," she called back to her dad. "I killed it, so all's okay now."

Michele exhaled in relief. "Thanks. Can we talk somewhere in private?"

"Fine. Follow me." Caissie marched through the narrow corridors of the apartment unit until they reached her bedroom. It was a cozy room, cluttered with clothes and books. Radiohead and Coldplay posters covered the walls.

"All right. Explain," Caissie demanded, closing the door

behind her. "And while you're at it, why are you dressed in formal menswear?"

Michele glanced down and realized she was still wearing Philip's jacket. She stuck her hands in the pockets, and to her surprise, she felt a small card. She quickly pulled out the card and looked at it. Her heart constricted as she saw Philip's name written in bold calligraphy on the card, his address underneath.

The presence of his belongings made the whole thing seem a lot less crazy, and she felt a rush of courage to tell someone. And who else could she tell? Amanda and Kristen didn't believe in magic in the slightest, so if anything, Michele's story would further convince them that she belonged at Cedars-Sinai Medical Center. While Michele barely knew her, Caissie was the one person who had seen Michele appear out of thin air, so that made her the one person who might have reason to believe her. Plus Michele owed her an explanation now. She took a deep breath, gathering her nerve and steeling herself for Caissie's reaction, and handed her Philip's card.

"This jacket and this card belonged to Philip Walker in 1910," Michele said. "My dad—who I never knew—had this old key that I got from my mom's safe after she died. Long story short, the key led me to my ancestor Clara Windsor's diary from 1910, and the key and the diary together sent me back in time. And I know this sounds crazy, but I met them all, Caissie! I danced at the Windsors' Halloween ball, and I was just with Philip, in his music room, and I was trying to bring him back to our time with me. That's how I ended up in your kitchen. That must be where the music room used to be. And that's who I was with last night, when I needed you to be my alibi."

Caissie stared at her incredulously. "Either this is a ridiculously over-the-top prank, or you've completely lost your mind."

Michele bit her lip anxiously. This was the reaction she had been afraid of.

"Please try to believe me. This is real," she insisted. "How else do you explain how I got into your apartment? How else do you explain all this?" Michele pulled off Philip's coat to show to Caissie.

"This is just some vintage jacket you bought and that card could easily be a fake. They did *not* belong to some old Walker," Caissie argued. She was giving the coat to Michele when something caught her eye. She yanked the coat back and stared at the inside collar.

"What is it?" Michele asked.

Her face suddenly pale, Caissie approached the wall by her dresser, where the corner edge of the wallpaper was peeling. Caissie pulled back the piece of wallpaper, and underneath was the old wall panel—designed with the Walker family coat of arms. The very same coat of arms was sewn into the jacket collar.

"The outside of the mansion was demolished when they decided to turn the place into an apartment complex, but they saved parts of the interiors. So this is the original old wall paneling," Caissie said, her voice sounding odd as she looked up at the Walker coat of arms.

"Don't you see?" Michele breathed. "It's the same. I was really with him a hundred years ago!"

"You still could have found this at a vintage store," Caissie replied, but her hands shook as she passed the jacket back to Michele.

"You know I didn't." Michele gave Caissie a serious look. "Please, you're the only person here I can tell."

Caissie sank onto a chair. "Honestly, Michele? You've got to be the weirdest person I know. First you barely give me the time of day when I come to your house, you don't talk to me at school, and now all of a sudden you've gone off the deep end and *I'm* the one you want involved in your insanity? No thanks."

Michele's jaw dropped. She couldn't believe what she was hearing. "*I* didn't give you the time of day? I'm the one who's the new student at your school and I had thought maybe, just maybe, you'd talk to *me* or sit with me at lunch and make me feel welcome, but you're the one who acted like we'd never even met!"

"That's because you rushed me out of your house so fast that day, it was obvious you weren't interested in being friends with the secretary's daughter," Caissie retorted. "And then I saw you with the elitist Four Hundred club, and everyone knows how they look down their noses at scholarship kids like me and Aaron."

"I'm *so* not part of that club!" Michele argued. "I didn't know anything about them that first day. I was just grateful for someone to sit with at lunch. Did you not notice I haven't sat with them since? That I've actually been spending my lunches in the library? And that day when you came over, I was a total mess over my mom, and I'd gotten in an argument with my grandparents the night before. I was trying not to cry the whole time you were over—that's why I rushed you out."

Caissie was silent for a few moments. Then she gave Michele a sheepish look.

"I'm sorry," she said in a small voice. "I was being an idiot. I just—I hate how that crowd treats me and Aaron. We're the only students at Berkshire with after-school jobs, subway cards, and no allowance. I wouldn't even live in this building if it weren't rent-controlled. You should see the size of my mom's place; there's barely room for my own bedroom. But I would be more than cool with my situation if it weren't for the fact that it seems to give the school snobs the license to treat me like a second-class citizen. And you and your grandparents know my mom as the *help*. So that made me take everything personally, I guess."

Michele sighed. "It's okay," she said, relenting. "You know, this whole upper class thing is completely new to me. I'm used to living in a small bungalow with my mom and never having enough money. . . ." Michele's voice trailed off as the memories of her old life brought a lump to her throat.

Caissie bit her lip. "I'm really sorry I misjudged you. And I'm so sorry about your mom."

"Thanks. I guess I can understand why you would feel the way you did. I've only been at Berkshire a week, and I've already got a complex."

Caissie laughed, and Michele held out her hand. "Truce?"

"Truce," Caissie agreed, shaking her hand.

"And . . . now that you know I'm not who you thought I was, any chance you can believe me about the time traveling?" Michele asked hopefully. "I mean, how else do you explain how I got into your apartment and Philip's jacket and everything else?"

Caissie shook her head slowly. "Look, I study science. That's how I got into our school, and that's what I believe in—scientific facts, not magic and time travel." She gave Michele a sideways look. "But it's weird. At the same time, I *don't* think you're crazy anymore. So maybe I should just hold off on believing or not believing until you can get me more facts."

"Fair enough," Michele said. Her gaze fell on Caissie's alarm clock, which read 10:30 p.m. "Oh yikes, I've got to get home. I just missed my curfew. Cross your fingers my grandparents are still out!"

"Will do," Caissie said with a grin. She walked Michele to the door.

Before leaving, Michele asked, "Can we keep this whole thing just between us? You won't tell Aaron or anyone?"

"Girl, if I tell anyone, they'll think I'm as crazy as you," Caissie said matter-of-factly. "So you can bet I'll be keeping it a secret."

"Yeah, I guess you're right," Michele agreed. "Well, see you at school tomorrow."

"See you tomorrow." Caissie started inside but then stopped and turned back to Michele. "Hey, have lunch with me and Aaron tomorrow, 'K?"

Michele grinned. "That sounds great."

The next morning, Michele woke up early, unable to sleep with thoughts of Philip in her head. There was a part of her that still believed he was a dream, like he existed only in a fantasy parallel universe. But now that they had touched, held each other, kissed, he felt more tangible than anyone or anything else in her life, even though he was a hundred years away.

Suddenly, inspiration struck. Michele hurried to her desk and grabbed the first pen and notepad she saw. For a moment, she hesitated. She hadn't been able to write since her mom had died. . . . What made her think she could now? But a second later, she had her title: "Bring the Colors Back." And then she had the chorus.

> *Why, when you're gone*
> *The world's gray on my own*
> *You bring the colors back*
> *You bring the colors back.*
> *Why, I feel numb*
> *I'm a sky without a sun*
> *Just take away the lack*
> *And bring the colors back.*

The words flew onto the page as she came up with a verse.

> *Feels like so long been only seeing my life in blues*
> *There comes a time when even strong ones need*
>   *rescue*
> *Then I'm with you in a whole other place and time*
> *The world has light*
> *I come to life . . .*

Michele wrote and wrote, until Annaleigh interrupted to tell her to come down for breakfast. Before leaving the room, Michele read over her work and smiled. It didn't matter to her whether she'd written anything brilliant. It just felt good to be able to write again.

Later that day, in English lit class, the teacher divided the students into two groups to fill out study questions about the book they were reading, *The Great Gatsby.* Michele, Caissie, and Ben Archer were placed in the same group, along with two guys from the school's tennis team and an overly tanned bodacious bombshell who looked like she'd be more at home on an MTV reality show.

"Fakin' Jamaicans," Caissie whispered to Michele, nodding at the two jocks as they approached their group.

"Huh?" Michele gave her a quizzical look.

"You'll see," Caissie said with a laugh.

Once their study group was situated around a table, Michele had to bite her lip to keep from snickering. The tennis players sat on either side of Bodacious Bombshell, their eyes not-so-subtly drifting to her chest while she giggled and made a big show of pretending not to notice. Meanwhile, Caissie kept gazing longingly at the door, clearly fantasizing about escape. The only person acting normal was Ben—although for some reason, Michele kept feeling his eyes on her.

"So, uh . . ." Ben looked around. "Should we do this thing?"

"Yeah, mon," Jock Number One said, then began reading the first of the study questions in a full Rastafarian accent. "How do Gatsby represent da American Dream? What be da condition of American Dream in da 1920s?"

Michele stared at him. *Is this guy for real?* But Caissie seemed to be the only one in their group who found anything bizarre about their blond, blue-eyed classmate talking Rasta. Her shoulders shook with silent laughter as she watched Michele's bewildered expression.

No one was making a move to answer the question, so Ben spoke up again. "Um, I think Gatsby represents the dark side of it. Like, how money and power was made to be so important that people would ruin their lives to attain it."

"Yeah, I agree," Michele said. Caissie nodded.

"I don't know," the bombshell interjected. "Gatsby only wanted money and power to get Daisy. And I think that's *so* romantic. It's not like *we* would complain if a guy ruined his life to win us over. Am I right, ladies?" She gave Michele and Caissie a conspiratorial smile.

"Uh, no—"

"Gatsby be a bad bwai," Jock Number Two said admiringly, in the same Rasta accent as his comrade.

"All right, then. Since we all seem to have different points of view here, maybe we should just fill this out on our own," Caissie hastily suggested.

"Irie," the Fakin' Jamaicans replied in unison.

"Boys," Caissie sighed in Michele's ear, rolling her eyes.

Michele thought of Philip—how opposite he was from this crew, and how different he was from her lame ex-boyfriend, Jason, back in L.A. Even a nice enough guy like Ben seemed miles away from Philip. Was it *possible* for someone like Philip Walker to exist in her generation?

During the car ride home from school, Michele was lost in thought. She needed to know, before she fell any further for him, if Philip was destined to marry Violet after all. And as much as Michele was trying to stay away from her grandparents those days, she knew that they were the ones to ask.

Once she arrived at the mansion, Michele headed to the library, where her grandparents could usually be found playing cards at that hour.

"Hi," she greeted them, standing awkwardly in the doorway.

Walter and Dorothy looked up in surprise.

"Hi, dear," Dorothy greeted her.

"How was school?" Walter asked. Michele could tell from

their expressions that they were pleased she had come to see them.

"Oh, it was fine. Actually, that's what I wanted to talk to you about. I'm doing a . . . a history project on the Windsor family," Michele fibbed.

Walter brightened. "That's wonderful! There are many incredible stories and people from our family, so you'll have a lot to write about."

Michele sat down in one of the leather armchairs. "Well, I actually wanted to ask you about something in particular. I heard a rumor that a Windsor and a Walker were married— Violet Windsor and Philip Walker, in the 1910s. Is that true?" Michele held her breath, waiting for the answer.

Walter and Dorothy looked at each other, clearly bewildered.

"I've never heard anything of that sort in my life," Walter answered. "Violet married a French lord and moved to Europe. She most certainly didn't marry a Walker."

As the words registered, Michele felt faint. *He didn't marry her! . . . Was it because of me?* She felt her legs trembling.

"I've never even heard of a Philip Walker," Dorothy commented. "Have you, Walter?"

Walter shook his head. "No. I don't think there ever *was* a Philip Walker."

Michele shrank back at those words.

"What's wrong, dear?" Dorothy asked, looking at her worriedly.

Michele swallowed hard. "I'm fine. I just . . . thought I saw something. It's nothing." *They're wrong,* Michele assured herself. *Philip is every bit as real as I am.*

"Since you're studying Windsor history, you should do some research up in the attic," Dorothy suggested. "All the old family photos and documents are up there in boxes labeled by year."

Michele felt her spirits rise. That sounded promising. Maybe she would find something there . . . some answers about Philip.

"That sounds perfect," Michele said. "I'm going to go up there right now."

The Windsor attic was organized and tidily lined with boxes—hardly the spooky, dank place Michele had imagined. The first row of boxes were labeled with names of unfamiliar Windsors, but lying on top of those boxes, oddly out of place, was a music composition book. Michele picked it up curiously. The front cover read *Songs by Lily Windsor, 1925.* Michele grinned. Lily must have been Michele's age when she'd written these songs; how incredible it was to find handwritten lyrics from when she'd been an aspiring songwriter like Michele! She held on to the composition book while she continued to look around.

As she made her way to the back of the attic, she saw a name that she recognized on one of the boxes: George Windsor, 1859–1922. Was that Clara's dad? Michele felt a stab of guilt as she remembered her promise to help Clara. She had all but forgotten her in the whirlwind of Philip.

Michele quickly opened the box. She found a number of

odds and ends inside: business documents, letters, and photos. Then one of the faded old black-and-white photos caught her eye. It was a photo of the woman in the picture Clara had shown her—Clara's mother! The photo was crumbling with age at the edges, but the words scribbled at the bottom of the picture were unmistakable: *I love you always. Alanna.*

As Michele studied the photo, the attic suddenly began to spin and shake. She fell to the ground, covering her head with her hands in terror. *Is this an earthquake?* But then, her hands gripping the wooden floor, her eyes squeezed shut, she felt the familiar downward plunge and knew she was being sent back in time.

When the spinning and shaking finally ceased, Michele gingerly opened her eyes to a blanket of darkness. There were no lightbulbs here anymore, and now the place was half empty, holding an assortment of cast-aside furniture and half a dozen brown boxes.

Suddenly, she heard the sound of footsteps coming up the stairs, and she quickly scrambled behind a broken dresser. The door opened, and a young couple walked in, hand in hand, the man holding up a small candelabra. Michele peered around the dresser and recognized the dark-haired man as George Windsor—but almost twenty years younger, with a carefree expression that she hadn't seen before on his face. He wore a crisp white shirt, a white tie, and a black vest with pin-striped trousers. The young woman was a beauty, with wavy red hair up in a pompadour, and she wore a simple white blouse with a long navy blue cotton skirt. It was clear from her plain, unembellished clothing and her lack of hat or jewelry that she wasn't part of the Windsors' upper class, but from the adoring way George looked at her, Michele could see that he didn't care in the least.

The young couple leaned side by side against the attic wall, grinning at each other, clearly relishing being in their own private world. The woman, who Michele recognized now as Clara's mother, Alanna, wrapped her arms around George and pulled him close. The two of them kissed tenderly.

She really loved him, Michele realized with surprise.

George pulled away and reached into his coat pocket. "A gift for you," he said, handing it to her in a shy, almost boyish way.

"George!" Alanna beamed at him before delicately opening the box. George stood behind her, his hands resting on her shoulders.

"A locket!" Alanna cried with delight. "It is so beautiful. George, you needn't have."

"I wanted to," George said, pulling her in for another kiss. "I only wish . . ."

"Yes, darling?" Alanna asked. "What is it you wish?"

George was silent for a moment, and when he spoke, his voice was hoarse. "I wish you could put our picture in the locket without fear of being found out."

Michele watched as Alanna nodded, leaning into George and whispering something Michele couldn't hear. Alanna pulled a pocket watch from her skirt pocket and sighed heavily. "It's nearly five. Henrietta will be home any moment. We must leave here." She looked up at him, her face filled with despair. "Why didn't Time let us meet sooner?"

George took her hand and held it up to his cheek. "It's not too late for us yet," he said urgently. "We can find a way to be together."

Alanna shook her head, and Michele saw her wipe her eyes. "You know you can't leave her. You might never see your children again. No, we must somehow bear it."

"How can I ever let you go?" he asked, his voice breaking.

Alanna shook her head, and began to sob on George's shoulder. And suddenly Michele wanted nothing more than to get away from this painful scene. She closed her eyes, clutched the key necklace, and willed Time to send her back.

Michele opened her eyes to find that she was back in the attic in her own time. Taking the photo and Lily's composition book, she ran downstairs to her room. She had to get back to Clara.

She tossed Lily's composition book into her desk, grabbed Clara's diary, and flipped it open to the third entry: November 1, 1910. Without even glancing at the first sentence, Michele held on tight to the diary, the photo, and the key. After a few seconds the spinning and swirling began again, sending her back to the November first of one hundred years earlier. She arrived to find Clara curled up on her bed, her head buried in a book.

"Michele!" Clara cried when she appeared, and jumped off the bed to give her a hug. "I'm so glad you're back."

"Me too. What have I missed?" Michele asked.

"Very little," Clara replied. "I've been spending nearly all my time in this room, avoiding the family—especially Mr. Windsor."

"That's why I'm here," Michele said, handing her the photo. "I found this in the attic with George Windsor's things." As Clara's eyes took in the image, her face turned white as a ghost.

"You have to talk to your dad," Michele urged. "She *gave* this to him. She must have had real feelings for him. You need to know what really happened between your parents."

Clara nodded slowly. "Will you come with me?"

"Of course I will."

Clara nervously gripped Michele's hand as they made their way down the stairs to George Windsor's study. Clara knocked on the door.

"Come in," George called.

Clara stepped into the room, and George's face paled when he saw who was there. He looked at her silently for a long moment. "Please tell me what happened . . . with you and Mother," Clara said, breaking the silence.

George hesitated. "I don't know what you speak of," he said, not meeting her eyes.

Clara slapped the photo onto his desk. "Why have you been lying to me?" she asked sharply.

George stared at the photo in shock. He looked up at Clara, opening and closing his mouth as if unsure what to say. When he finally spoke, his voice sounded ragged, years older. "I'm so sorry . . . my child," he said, his breath coming out in shallow gasps. "I never wanted to deceive you. I simply couldn't bear the idea of you thinking less of your mother."

Clara slowly sank into a chair across from her father. "I want the truth," she said quietly. "All of it."

George nodded. After a deep breath, he began. As he spoke, Michele sensed that he had never told this story before.

"I met your mother at the home of the Astors. I was fortuitously early that day, the first to arrive for a card game with the gentlemen. When I went into the library to wait, I bumped into Mrs. Astor's new social secretary—Alanna. The moment I laid eyes on her, I felt . . . well, it was the most curious thing. I felt as though I had rediscovered someone precious to me, someone who had been missing all that time."

Michele felt a jolt in her stomach. *That's just how I feel about Philip.*

"She was like a dream come to life," George continued, a faraway look in his eyes. "I had never forgotten my favorite journey as a boy, when I accompanied my father to County Kerry, Ireland. Since then, I had been entranced by the Irish culture, and so Alanna was simply fascinating to me, with her shining red hair and light Irish brogue, and the mesmerizing stories she wove about her homeland. As we grew to know and understand each other, it felt like we were kindred spirits." George closed his eyes for a moment. "I was married when we met. Henrietta and I already had a son, with Violet on the way. I've always been fond of my wife, of course. But what I felt for Alanna . . . well, it was simply the only time I've ever known real love or true happiness. You can imagine my joy when she told me she shared my feelings."

Michele and Clara both watched George intently as he spoke, riveted by the story.

"I desperately wished to marry Alanna, but please understand, as rare as divorces are now, they were even more impossible to obtain in the 1890s. The courts were extremely reluctant to grant them, and Alanna and I both knew that leaving Henrietta meant leaving my children. I couldn't do that to them. And then Alanna discovered that she was pregnant—and she panicked." George's eyes filled with tears. "She was terrified to be pregnant out of wedlock, and she couldn't bear for our child to be raised as an illegitimate."

Michele looked at Clara. She was sitting motionless, her face frozen, but her eyes too brimmed with tears.

"Alanna had a lifelong friend from Ireland—they had both immigrated to the States at the same time, and took care of each other here. His name was Edmond, and he had always loved her." George's face contorted with pain. "When Alanna confided in him her secret, he offered to marry her and raise the child as his own. Alanna thought this was the answer to her prayers for our unborn child. They were married immediately at city hall. And then, on the most terrible day of my life, she came and told me everything, the wedding band on her finger. She said that I'd always be the love of her life, but for your sake, she had to pretend you were Edmond's and move back to Ireland with him, where they would have the help of their families in raising you.

"I always wanted to be your father. I hated that Edmond was the one who got to hold you and soothe your cries and watch you grow. That should have been me." George's voice broke with anguish. "But Alanna wouldn't separate from you. She said we had to end our affair immediately, before anyone had a chance to speculate that you might be mine, and she insisted on taking you to Ireland as soon as you were strong enough for the journey. It was the most heartbreaking time of my life." George took a shaky breath. "I tried to find you and Alanna for years. I hired a detective, and it took a decade to uncover the truth, for my detective focused his search in Ireland. But you three had never made it there. Alanna and Edmond tragically died of the Spanish influenza when you were four years old, just before you three were set to depart for Belfast. You cannot imagine my shock and devastation when I learned that my Alanna was gone and our daughter had been living in an orphanage this entire time, right here in my city.

"I love you, Clara, and all I've wanted all of these years was to be your father," George declared, his tears now falling freely. "Might I have a second chance at that?"

Clara's hands trembled.

"I—I can't believe it," she whispered. "It's so much to believe. Everything I thought I knew about my mother and father . . . was wrong."

George shook his head. "Not everything. You thought you had a mother and father who loved you, and each other, very much. And that is true. I miss and love your mother every day—and I've loved you all this time, even before knowing you."

Clara stared at her father, and as the truth sank in, tears began to fall down her cheeks. She got up and took a tentative step toward him, and the two of them hugged, crying as they shared their first father-daughter embrace.

As Michele watched them, she was taken aback by her own mix of emotions. She was thrilled for Clara, but a painful ache had settled into the pit of her stomach as she'd heard George's story and watched him embrace his daughter. She thought of her broken family: her mother, who was gone; her grandparents, who were in their own distant world; and her father, who she would never know. She had never before felt the loss of him, but now, watching the emotional reunion of Clara and George, Michele felt as if her heart were being twisted by an invisible fist. She lifted the skeleton key necklace and stared at it. If only Henry Irving could somehow find her and give her the answers she needed . . . If only she could wake up the next morning and find herself no longer an orphan . . .

Michele quietly left the study and drifted off to Clara's room to wait. When Clara returned a while later, her eyes were watery but bright. She threw her arms around Michele.

"I cannot thank you enough for uncovering the truth and bringing me and my father back together," she said, clasping Michele's hands gratefully.

"I'm glad I could," Michele said. "You're so lucky to have this chance at being part of a real family."

"I'm so accustomed to loneliness," Clara remarked. "It's difficult to believe I might actually be loved."

"Well, it's clear your dad really loves you," Michele said, giving her a tremulous smile. "And you also had a mom and a surrogate father who would have done anything for you. I think what Edmond did for you and your mom was pretty amazing."

"Yes, it was," Clara agreed. "I feel grateful and saddened by it, all at once."

"When is George going to tell the rest of the family about you?" Michele asked.

"He wanted to tell them straightaway, but I asked him not to," Clara replied, sitting down at her vanity.

"What? Why did you do that?" Michele looked at Clara in confusion.

"Well, Father is going to adopt me. So I am officially going to be Miss Clara Windsor." Clara's cheeks flushed with happiness. "And Violet has guessed the truth. But I don't want to cause Henrietta and little Frances pain, and I know it would hurt them if Father confirmed that I'm his daughter. It's enough for me that he and I know. And I know that I was conceived in love, but . . . well, you know how it would look to society. It would ruin the family reputation. I could never let Father do that for me."

"Wow," Michele marveled. "That's really generous of you to keep that a secret your entire life!" *So I'm the only person alive in my time who knows the truth,* she thought with amazement.

"Father doesn't like it, but I know in time he will see that it is the best thing for all of us," Clara said.

"But how will he explain why he's adopting you?" Michele asked.

"We're going to say that my father was a childhood friend of his, and he couldn't bear knowing that his close friend's daughter was a penniless orphan," Clara explained.

"Hmm. That's a good one."

"I admit I am nervous about how Violet and Henrietta and the others will react to Father adopting me," Clara said, biting her lip. "But he says there is nothing they can do to object. He says Henrietta wouldn't dare leave him over it, for fear of what society would say. And even if she and Violet do shun me, as long as I have Father, it'll be all right."

"I bet they'll get over it and grow to love you," Michele said encouragingly. "You'll be a good influence on those snobs!"

Clara covered her mouth, giggling. Just then, one of the maids knocked on the door.

"Dinner is about to be served, Miss Clara. Will you be requesting a tray again this evening?"

"No, thank you. I'll join the family downstairs." Clara grinned at Michele.

Before heading to dinner, she gave Michele another hug. "Thank you so much. You are the kindest ghost I could ever hope to meet."

"Thanks." Michele laughed. "Good luck, Clara."

Michele lingered in the room after she left. *Clara's so lucky she has a real family to have dinner with every night,* Michele thought wistfully. As she pictured the solitary dinner in her room that awaited her back in 2010, the loveless atmosphere in the Windor Mansion of her time, she felt a fresh surge of pain. She had to get out of the house. She had to try to escape the dull ache inside her.

"Michele!"

Her heart leaped as she looked up. She had just passed through the Windsor Mansion gates and was heading toward the Walker Mansion—and there was Philip, grinning ecstatically at her. Michele raced toward him, overcome with emotion. But before they could embrace, he grabbed her hand and led her to the back of the Walker Mansion, where no one would see him. Once they were alone, he pulled her into his arms, kissing her lips and hair and eyelids.

"You're back!" He broke off, looking at her with concern. "What's the matter? Have you been crying?"

Michele looked away self-consciously. Philip tilted her chin toward him.

"Tell me. What's wrong?" he asked soothingly.

"I'm just—" Michele swallowed hard.

Philip stroked her hair. "It's all right. Go on."

"I'm so alone," Michele whispered. "Except when I'm with you."

Philip held her closer. "What do you mean?"

"I mean I don't have—I don't have any parents." Suddenly, Michele's tears broke forth with sobs. "And I might as well not even have grandparents. I just—I feel like I don't have any family in the world, like I've just been thrown out there to fend for myself."

Philip stroked her trembling back, kissing the top of her head. "I'm sorry . . . so sorry," he murmured. "I know what you mean. I feel just the same."

Michele wiped her eyes. "Aren't we a pair?"

Philip leaned his forehead against hers. "Someone once told me that friends are the family you choose. So here's an idea—I'll be your family, and you can be mine."

Michele felt a warm glow inside her. She gave him a watery smile. "Okay . . . That sounds nice."

"Now, it's time we cheer you up," Philip declared, the sparkle returning to his eyes. "I'm taking you on a proper date."

"Um, where can we go?" Michele replied with a giggle. "No one else can see me. They'll think you're pretty crazy if you try to get a table for two at a restaurant."

"I have an idea," he said with a wink. He took her hand and

led her into the Walker Mansion, down the stairs and into the servants' quarters. Philip swung open the door to the kitchen.

"Mr. Walker!" "Oh, my goodness!" "What are you doing here?" The cries rang out among the cook and the scullery maids, all of whom looked stunned at the sight of Philip in their kitchen. Michele gave Philip a bewildered look. What was the big deal?

"Oh, do relax. Surely there is nothing wrong with me visiting the kitchen now and again," Philip said cheerfully.

"But the masters and mistresses of the house never come down to the kitchen!" the cook exclaimed. "It's not proper for you to see us. You know that, Master Philip."

"Well, it's about time we disrupted that silly tradition, don't you think?" Philip smiled. "Now, I was wondering if you might prepare me a picnic basket. Maybe enough food for two, as I am extra hungry tonight."

Michele grinned. A turn-of-the-century picnic! What a perfect idea.

"Isn't it rather late for a picnic?" the cook asked. "I'm not sure your uncle would—"

"Oh, I just need some fresh air and time alone to think," Philip said, improvising. "And please, there is really no need to tell my uncle."

"Well, all right," the cook agreed. She quickly put together a basket as Philip called out suggestions: "The best cheeses, salami, and fresh bread—oh, and chocolate truffles too!"

After the picnic basket was fully stocked, Michele and Philip ran up the stairs to the main quarters of the mansion. Staying close together, they walked into the still, starry night toward Central Park. Michele was nearly dizzy from all the stimulation to her senses. She was mesmerized by the passing sights of old New York at nightfall while her heart raced from Philip's scent and the feel of him next to her. They walked past the twenty-story emerald-topped Plaza Hotel and into the park through Scholars' Gate at Fifth Avenue. As they entered the park, Michele's heart rate picked up even more. She wondered what this famous landmark would be like one hundred years earlier.

The pastoral, picturesque landscape was just as Michele knew it, its wide, rolling meadows contrasting with a woodsy, untamed hiking area known as the Ramble and the more formal walking grounds, called the Mall. There was the park's most famed monument, Belvedere Castle, with its Victorian structure towering atop giant rocks. Surrounding Michele and Philip was the comfortingly familiar meandering lake. But the silence and emptiness of the park made it feel like an altogether different place. Even in all the movies she had seen that featured Central Park, Michele had never seen it empty but for two people. Yet tonight it looked like they were the only ones there.

"It's like our own private sanctuary," Michele said, marveling, to Philip.

As they walked through the park, Michele didn't see any playgrounds or boathouses, and the Great Lawn was missing too. *They haven't been built yet,* she realized. Philip led the way to the grassy Cherry Hill, which overlooked the eastern edge of the lake and the romantic cast-iron Bow Bridge, the star of many Manhattan-set movies. As Philip spread a blanket over a patch of grass for them, Michele stopped to admire the fountain at the center of the hill, a granite pool with a black and gilt cast-iron structure in the center, topped with a golden spire and round lamps.

"What are you concentrating so hard on?" Philip chuckled, gesturing for her to sit beside him.

"I just . . . I can't *believe* I'm here with you. I want to remember every detail of tonight. So I can relive it whenever I want," Michele answered shyly.

Philip smiled at her. "Why not write it down, then?"

Michele's cheeks turned pink. "It's funny you say that."

"Why?" Philip asked.

"Because . . . I actually do write. I've been writing poems and making up lyrics to songs since I was a little girl. My secret dream is to be a professional lyricist for singers and Broadway shows," Michele confided, smiling. "But I mean, I have no idea if I'm any good at it. The only person I've ever let read my work is my mom, and she loved it. But then, she was my mom, so how could she not?"

"I can't imagine you being anything but wonderful at it," Philip said encouragingly. "You have a poet's soul, the way you see and understand things, even things one hundred years in the past! How could your writing *not* be great?"

Michele felt her heart lift at his words.

"You know, I had stopped writing after my mom died," she said suddenly. "My writing was something I'd only ever shared with her. It was . . . our thing. When she died, I felt like I lost my writing too, like I was permanently blocked. But then, after meeting you, it . . . well, it all came back."

"Really?" Philip's eyes warmed. He touched her cheek. "What did you write?"

"Lyrics to a new song," Michele said shyly.

"Oh?" Philip looked even more interested. "What is the song called?"

"Um . . . 'Bring the Colors Back,'" she answered with an embarrassed giggle.

Philip grinned and kissed her.

"I like that title. You a lyricist, me a composer—you and I make a complete song." Philip sat up straighter, looking excited. "That's it! We have to write a song together. Perhaps I can try to find a melody for 'Bring the Colors Back.'"

"That—that would be amazing," Michele said slowly. "But . . ." She was too embarrassed to finish the sentence, but the idea made her nervous. What if Philip thought her writing *sucked*? Clearly sensing her hesitation, he smiled at her.

"I'm sure I'll love it," he said reassuringly. "You've told me a secret, so I will tell you mine. I haven't repeated this yet, since I know my mother and uncle won't approve—but after I graduate this June, I'm going to pursue a full career as a composer and pianist. In fact, I'm expected to attend Harvard next year, but . . . well, I've been accepted to the Institute of Musical Art here in New York, which is the nation's best music college. And that's where I intend to go."

"Wow!" Michele exclaimed, beaming at him. *That's Juilliard!* she thought, remembering from her own college research that Juilliard had originally been called the Institute of Musical Art.

"I want my life to have a purpose. Do you know what I mean?" Philip looked intently at her. "Something more meaningful than simply accumulating more wealth through the family holdings. I know Mother expects me to graduate Harvard and then help Uncle run the business, but she will be in for a bit of a shock when I enroll in music conservatory instead. I only hope that between that and . . . well . . . breaking off my engagement to Violet, she can forgive me at some point."

"Breaking off your engagement?" Michele repeated. "You—you've decided on that, then?"

Philip nodded seriously.

"Philip, are you . . . sure? About Violet, I mean." She bit her lip anxiously. "I feel like I'm disrupting your whole life."

"But in the best way," Philip countered. "Don't you see that my life needed to be disrupted?" When Michele didn't answer, he continued, "I was never in love with Violet. We were simply friends who had grown up together, whose parents intended on creating even more wealth by marrying us. That's how all New York society marriages work—but it's not for me. I need my music, and I need—well, after finding you . . ." Philip flushed, suddenly looking awkward. "Well, how can I be expected to marry someone else now?"

"I know," Michele said tremulously, taking his hand. "That's how I feel too."

After they'd finished their picnic, Philip and Michele crossed Bow Bridge into the sumptuously designed split-level Bethesda Terrace, with its ornate stair rails and sculpted carvings. They climbed the stone staircase leading from the upper level to the Bethesda Fountain plaza. Sitting beneath the fountain and its statue, Angel of Waters, Philip took Michele into his arms and kissed her for what could have been minutes or hours—Michele had lost all sense of time.

"What do you think it all means?" she asked suddenly. "You know—the fact that we both recognized each other before we met, and you can see me when no one else can besides Clara?"

"That we belong with each other?" Philip suggested, pulling her close again.

"But . . . how can we? How can we really be together when I don't truly exist in your time, and you can't even get to my time?" Michele swallowed hard. "Sometimes it seems like a cruel joke."

Philip was silent for a moment and then he turned to her, his eyes intense. "We met for a reason, so I know that whatever . . . whatever force brought us together can keep us together somehow. And until we have a permanent solution, we have these moments. So many people never get to experience this—it's rare in my time. It may not seem like it, but we are lucky."

Michele smiled as his words sank in. "You're so right."

Hand in hand, they walked out of Bethesda Terrace on the majestic tree-lined path of the grand promenade. As they proceeded under the canopy of overhanging American elm trees, Philip suddenly leaned in to give her a kiss, and Michele found that she couldn't stop smiling, couldn't control the fluttering, thrilling sensation inside her.

❧ ❧

When they returned to the Walker Mansion, Philip led her into the music room. He lit a few candles and then gestured for Michele to sit beside him at the piano bench. "Can I hear your lyrics now?"

Michele let out a nervous laugh. "I don't know. I've never shown my writing to anyone but my mom . . ."

"Please? I want to hear your words." Philip took her hand and laced his fingers between hers.

"Oh . . . all right." Staring at the floor, her cheeks flushing red, Michele recited her lyrics for him. *He's going to think I'm totally obsessed with him,* she thought in embarrassment. When she had finished, she kept her eyes focused on the ground, until he lifted her chin with his hand, forcing her to meet his eyes.

"That's just how I feel too," he whispered. "But you're the only one with the talent to put it into words."

As he kissed her, Michele thought she might burst from the thrill she felt. When they finally managed to break away from the kiss, both smiling and flushed, Michele said, "So do you think you can put music to it?"

He grinned at her as he placed his hands artfully on the keys. "Let's see, shall we?" And he began to play, experimenting with different melodies until he found one that seemed to perfectly fit "Bring the Colors Back": a bluesy, soulful midtempo tune in a minor key. The melody and feel of Philip's composition reminded Michele almost of Ray Charles, and though he played it from a 1910 point of view, she could easily imagine hearing it in her own time as a contemporary song. Michele listened dreamily, humming along.

Suddenly, without warning, the music became faint. Michele looked up sharply to see Philip and the music room fading from view. Philip's mouth opened in a silent cry. His hand was outstretched toward her, and Michele tried desperately to meet his grasp. But then he was gone and there was nothing left but the modern, bright kitchen she was standing in.

I'm back in Caissie's apartment, she thought dully. *Why did Time have to take me away from that perfect night?* Her eyes quickly scanned the room, but fortunately she was alone. She spotted a window big enough for her to squeeze through and close enough to the ground for a non-treacherous drop. Before opening the window, Michele glanced at the digital clock on the oven. She gasped. It was just before ten-thirty—her curfew.

She held up the skeleton key necklace, looking at it searchingly. *Is someone—or something—controlling my time traveling?* she suddenly wondered. After all, it seemed that she nearly always returned to 2010 against her will. And she had yet to figure out a surefire way to get back to her time on her own.

As she walked back to the Windsor Mansion, she couldn't stop playing the question over in her mind: *What, or who, is causing all this?* She was desperate for the answer. She had to be sure that she would always be able to get to Philip.

During her U.S. history class the next morning, Michele rested her head on her desk, struggling to stay awake through Mr. Lewis's lecture. She hadn't slept a wink the night before, replaying the incredible evening with Philip over and over in her mind. But then Mr. Lewis said something that got her attention.

"As you all know, our field trip to Newport, Rhode Island, is just two weeks away. We'll be touring the historical mansions that belonged to New York's finest families, and getting a firsthand peek at the way of life back then." His voice was full of enthusiasm. "Per the annual tradition, we'll be staying at Hotel Viking for the weekend. I'm going to pass out permission slips for you to have your parents fill out today, as well as a form on which you can request the classmate you'd like to share a hotel room with. I'll do my best to meet everyone's requests, but I'm afraid some of you will have to make do with your assignments."

A weekend away with this *group?* Michele thought desolately. How had she missed the memo about this trip? And she hated to have a whole weekend away from Philip. Without thinking, Michele thrust her hand into the air.

"Yes, Michele?" Mr. Lewis called.

"Um . . . well, I was just wondering—is the field trip mandatory?" she asked.

The other students gawked at her in surprise, but Caissie grinned at Michele. Clearly she felt the same way about this trip.

Mr. Lewis frowned. "Of course it is. If you remember, it was part of the curriculum I gave you on your first day. Did you have somewhere else you have to be that weekend?"

"No. I was just . . . wondering."

When she was handed her roommate-request form, Michele wrote Caissie's name, crossing her fingers that Caissie would do the same.

At lunch, the topic everyone was buzzing about was not Newport, but the annual Autumn Ball, which had just been announced for the third Saturday in November at the Waldorf-Astoria Hotel.

"At least *that's* not mandatory," Michele remarked to Caissie and Aaron as they attacked their burgers.

"Yeah, no kidding," Caissie agreed. "The last thing I'm in the mood for is watching our classmates compete over who can spend the most money on a dress they'll wear once and forget about the next day."

"I say we go to the dance and shock them all by wearing thrift-store clothes and Chuck Taylors," Aaron suggested, a gleam in his eye. He nudged Caissie. "You down?"

Caissie blushed slightly. "Sure. Why not?"

Michele couldn't hold back her smile as she watched the two of them. It was obvious they liked each other. She didn't know why they bothered with the whole Just Friends routine.

"Hey, why does that Ben Archer dude keep looking over here?" Aaron asked.

Caissie grinned. "He *so* wants Michele. He's always looking at her."

"*Not* always," Michele said, rolling her eyes.

"Will you go with him if he asks you to the dance?" Caissie asked curiously.

Michele was momentarily thrown by the question. Since Philip, she hadn't even contemplated the idea of other guys asking her out. It would feel wrong, almost unbearable, to go out with someone else now. "I'd say no," she replied.

Aaron raised his eyebrows. "Seems like most girls here would be pretty psyched to go out with that dude. He doesn't do it for you?"

"It's not that. He's really cute and nice enough," Michele said honestly. "It's just—well, I'm sort of taken."

Caissie gave her a suspicious look, no doubt remembering the whole Philip Walker time travel conversation. "Oh yeah? By who?"

Michele looked down. "He . . . lives far away. It's a long-distance thing."

"Well, long distance almost never works at our age," Caissie said, giving Michele a knowing look. "So if Ben or any other cute guys here ask you out, I think you should go for it."

"Okay, well, let me remind you that no one *has* asked me out here," Michele said with a laugh. "So how about we change the subject?"

❧ ⸱ ❧

After school, Michele reluctantly brought the Newport permission slip to the drawing room for her grandparents to sign. They were seated beside each other drinking tea, Walter studying the newspaper while Dorothy looked over some correspondence.

"Hi," Michele said, standing in the doorway.

"Hello, dear." Dorothy looked up to give her a quick smile before turning back to her letters.

"Come in," Walter said.

"Um, I have a permission slip that I need you guys to sign. It's for a weekend field trip in two weeks to Newport, Rhode Island." Michele handed them the paper.

"Newport . . ." Dorothy's voice warmed. "We loved it there."

"Really? Do you have a house there?" Michele asked, suddenly a little more interested.

"We did," she answered. "It was one of the most treasured properties the Windsors had. It was built in 1898, but it burned down in the 1970s."

"I'm sorry. I would have liked to see it," Michele said sincerely.

"It's a beautiful town. You'll like it," Walter said, giving her one of his rare smiles.

Something occurred to Michele. "Do—do the Walkers have a house there?"

"Yes. *Theirs* didn't burn down," he replied, a trace of bitterness in his voice.

Michele's heart leaped. Maybe, just maybe, she would get to see Philip that weekend after all!

The next afternoon, Michele found herself staring contempla-
tively at Clara's diary. She wondered how things had turned out
between Clara and her new family, if Henrietta and Violet had
managed to accept the adoption, or if they had continued their
quest to make her miserable. It was strange, but she felt protective of this girl who was really her elder by a hundred years.
Would it hurt just to check on her? *Probably not,* Michele
thought. *And then I can go see Philip afterward.*

Michele carefully opened the diary to the fourth entry,
November 12, 1910, and braced herself for the roller-coaster
ride back in time. When she landed on the floor of the bedroom one hundred years earlier, she was surprised to find it

empty. She was used to Clara's being there to greet her. But then she heard the sound of high-pitched yelling coming from downstairs, and she hurried out of the room to see what was going on.

She stopped dead in her tracks at what she saw two floors below in the Grand Hall. Violet, her face red with fury, was pushing Philip toward the front door as Clara and several members of the household staff looked on in shock. Neither Philip nor Clara looked up to see Michele watching from the third-floor railing.

"You are a despicable, disgusting excuse for a man!" Violet shrieked. "Get out, get out of this house!"

"Violet, please don't. Don't make a scene," Clara begged, clutching her sister's arm. Violet threw her off.

"You would be *dead* if my father was home," Violet said menacingly, stalking toward Philip. "But you wait. We will ruin you."

"Violet, please try to understand—I never intended to hurt you," Philip pleaded. "I care about you—I have all my life—but we aren't right for each other in that way. I'm not the one who can make you happy. I'm only trying to save us both from an unhappy marriage—"

"Get out!" Violet cried. "I never want to see you again."

"I hope you can forgive me one day." Philip looked at her sadly. "Goodbye, Violet."

Violet stared after him, breathing heavily. Once the front door had closed behind him, she let out a terrible sob, crumpling to her knees. Clara wrapped a protective arm around her. "Please, leave us," she told the staff.

Michele felt guilt striking at her insides as Violet sobbed on

Clara's shoulder. She wondered what Clara would think of her if she ever found out that Michele had caused all this.

"Come, you need fresh air," Clara said gently. "Let's go outside." As she led Violet toward the back patio, Michele sensed that Clara was glad to be able to take care of her new sister.

Once the girls were gone, Michele tiptoed down the stairs and hurried out of the mansion. She had to see Philip. She raced through the Windsor Mansion front yard, out the gates, and through the Walkers' front door, which, fortunately, was unlocked. Once inside, she heard angry voices coming from down the hall. Her heart sinking, Michele followed the voices until she was outside a closed door.

"How *dare* you do something so unforgivable, and without even consulting us!" came an enraged voice that Michele recognized as Philip's uncle's.

"With all due respect, sir, you are not my father," Philip retorted.

"You may think nothing of my wishes, but to completely disobey your own mother? What kind of a son are you?"

Michele angrily balled her hands into fists as she listened outside the door. If only Philip's uncle could see her . . . She would have loved nothing more than to barge in there and tell him off.

"Mother, I do apologize if this causes you any pain. But marrying Violet would have been a lie," Philip entreated. "I can't stand up in a church and lie, and I cannot commit myself to a fraudulent life. Can you really not understand that?"

"I understand that you do not know your duty to this family," a woman's chilly voice spoke up. *Philip's mom,* Michele

161

realized. "You know that this scandal could be damaging for the family business, yet you acted of your own accord anyhow."

"Mother, you really think my breaking off with Violet affects the real estate market?" Philip replied, with an incredulous laugh.

"Ah, but your boy has no regard for the family business. In fact, today's *Town Topics* hinted that he plans to attend music school next fall," Philip's uncle spat. "*Music* school, not Harvard. Is that true, Philip?"

There was a shocked silence. Michele squeezed her eyes shut, in agony for Philip.

"Yes. It is true," Philip admitted. "Mother, I'm sorry if I am not what you expected of your son. But the Institute of Musical Art is the finest conservatory in the country, the hardest to get accepted into, and after hearing me play, they offered me a spot. I have to follow this opportunity. I *am* gifted, Mother, and music is what I am born to do. Please, let me have your blessing on this."

"You are not my son." Mrs. Walker said the words so sharply, Michele drew back as if she had been slapped. "*My* son made a promise to marry Violet Windsor. My son is due to start work at the Walker Company this summer. If you want to be my son, this is what you must do."

There was another long silence, and Michele held her breath. When Philip finally spoke, his voice sounded heavy, but brave. "Very well. If your regard for me is so conditional that it rests solely on whom I marry and what I do for a living, then you clearly don't love me. And I don't wish to have a mother who can't love her own son. I'll settle my affairs and be out of this house by graduation. You won't have to see me again after that."

With that, Philip swung open the door—nearly colliding with Michele. He looked weary and beaten, but his eyes still warmed at the sight of her. She took his hand and followed as he led her upstairs to his room. It was a spacious bedroom in the Empire style, with wood trim and mahogany furniture. Dark maroon curtains hung above his bed, and opposite was a striking desk in the Louis XIV style, made of gilded mahogany. Her first time in Philip's bedroom should have given her a thrill, but Michele was too sickened by all she had just seen and heard.

Once the door was closed behind them, Philip sank dazedly onto his bed. Michele sat beside him.

"Did you hear everything?" he asked dully.

Michele nodded. "And I also . . . I saw what happened with Violet. I was on the third floor. I got there in the—the middle of it."

Philip winced. "I'm sorry you had to see that."

"Philip, I can't stand this," Michele burst out. "I can't stand watching your life go up in flames because of me when I don't— I don't have anything to offer you instead."

Philip looked at her, clearly astounded. "What do you mean, you don't have anything to offer me? Since my father died, you're the only person in this whole world who has brought any happiness to my life."

"But I'm not *real* in your world. Violet is real. She can give you an actual family and a home—" Michele broke off, suddenly in tears. "You have to marry her."

Philip pulled her face toward his. "Look at me. You are real

163

for me, and that's what matters," he said intently. "Do you think I could ever be happy married to Violet, knowing you're out there, somewhere in time? And besides, I know I'm not the one she really wants. She wants a businessman, like my father, like her father. She's embarrassed by my music. She doesn't really want *me.*"

Michele looked up at him tearfully. She wanted so badly to believe him, to believe that her involvement in the past wasn't wrecking everything.

"I really ought to thank you," he said quietly. "If it weren't for you, perhaps I wouldn't have had the courage to go after what I really want in life. I know I can make my mark on this world, and not because of my last name—but because of my own talent."

Michele smiled through her tears. "I know you will. And, Philip?" Her smile faded as she took his hand. "I'm so sorry . . . about your mom and uncle."

Philip looked straight ahead, his expression dark. "I hate them."

"You don't—you don't really mean that," Michele said awkwardly.

"Of course I do," he said harshly. When he looked back at Michele, his eyes were pained. "I've always despised my uncle. He's a vile opportunist who made no secret of his delight at being head of the house when Father died. But I tried to love my mother. I *wanted* to love her. How could I, though, when I saw the way she hurt my father?"

"What?" Michele stared at Philip. "What are you talking about?"

"I watched her as she made Father miserable during those last years of their marriage—and I was powerless to stop it," Philip burst out, his voice breaking. "He was always infatuated with her, but it was clear she didn't feel the same way, that she had married him out of duty rather than love. Her flirtations with other men broke his heart. And even when he had the stroke, she couldn't show the love that a wife should. Maybe if she had, Father would have rallied. I'll never forgive her for it."

"Philip . . . I'm so sorry," Michele whispered. She wrapped her arm around him.

"They want to control and ruin my life the way they did his, but they won't," Philip said determinedly. "I'll be stronger and I'll fight back, starting by leaving here."

Michele nodded. "I know. You're doing the right thing."

"I'll never forget the day when Irving Henry—Father's lawyer—came to read the will," Philip began, but Michele's shocked expression caused him to break off midsentence. "What is it?"

"Irving Henry," Michele repeated, feeling a chill run up her spine. "That's my father's name, only backwards."

"That is an odd coincidence," Philip agreed.

Michele nodded, trying to take in this new information. "But go on. What were you saying?"

"When Mr. Henry came to read the will, he and I both knew then that Uncle had won," Philip continued. "You see, when my grandfather died, his will stipulated that his eldest son, my father, should inherit the majority of the wealth—but if Father died before my thirtieth birthday, then Uncle would have it all. My inheritance is in a trust, which I'm to receive in two parts, when I turn twenty-one and then when I turn thirty. Meanwhile, Father left this house to Mother and she knows Uncle controls the finances now, so she invited him to live here and sucks up to him like a leech, hoping he'll continue providing for her in the same manner Father did. I'm just a pawn in their game—marry Violet Windsor and add to the family fortune through her dowry and marriage settlement." Philip shook his head in disgust. "I won't play their game anymore, and I'm sickened that I did for so long. I'd gladly forfeit my inheritance now, just to know I'm not like them."

Michele touched Philip's cheek. "Listen to me. You are nothing like them. *Nothing*. You couldn't be. I told you—you're ahead of your time."

Philip managed a laugh. "And you're behind your time, here in the past. No wonder we're a . . . a perfect fit." He leaned in to kiss her. Michele closed her eyes, as the feel of his lips against hers never failed to send sparks throughout her whole body. She loved the way his kisses were both tender and urgent, the way he traced every inch of her mouth with his lips as he cradled her in his arms. She felt safe and protected in his arms, yet she had the same excitement and butterflies that came with taking a great leap.

When they had broken apart, Philip said quietly, "Father was proud of my music. I know he would have supported my decision. He was the only true family I ever had. I miss him every day."

Michele nodded sadly. "I know. I miss my mom constantly too. It's like there's always this hole in me—but remember what you said? You're my family now, and I'm yours."

Philip looked at her for a long moment. "I love you, Michele Windsor."

Michele sucked in her breath. "You do?"

Philip nodded, smiling at her. "You know I do."

"I love you back," she whispered. And suddenly his arms were holding her tight and they were kissing passionately. Barely able to control her thoughts, Michele fell back onto the bed, pulling him down on top of her. She wanted to feel his weight on her, to run her hands through his hair and down his back. He was all she had in the world, and it felt like she couldn't get close enough to him. And then he was kissing her neck, his hands exploring her, as she started to unbutton his shirt—

Philip suddenly rolled off her and sat up abruptly. "I'm sorry," he said, flushing as he tried to catch his breath. "I shouldn't have—"

"What do you mean?" Michele asked, hurt. "You don't . . . want to?"

"Of course I do," he said, laughing in surprise at her question. "But we're not married."

That was when Michele remembered: in 1910 anything beyond a kiss before marriage was considered scandalous.

"But we're together, aren't we? That's all that matters to me," Michele said softly.

Philip tucked a strand of her hair behind her ear. "Michele, I want you more than you can imagine. But to . . . *have* you . . . before we're married is disrespectful and dishonorable. I can't do that to you."

Michele tried to imagine a teenage guy in 2010 saying those

words to her, and she couldn't help chuckling. Time had definitely changed things a lot in this department.

"Okay. If that's what you want. But how could we ever get married when I don't exist in your time? I hate that there are all these normal things we can't do or have together." She bit her lip anxiously. "And . . . I'm scared, Philip. I still don't have total control over my time traveling. What if I . . . What if I can't always get to you? Especially with you leaving home, how will I find you?"

"I promise you that I'll never go so far where you can't find me," Philip said seriously. "I'll still be here in New York, attending music conservatory. And even though Time may have made a mistake by placing us in different centuries, we still found each other—we're together now. So I have to trust in Time. Don't you agree?"

Michele gazed at him. "When you talk about it, I feel . . . like it makes some sort of sense."

Philip grinned and wrapped his arm around her. "Good. Now let's try not to worry anymore today, not about anything. Let's just be here, together."

Michele smiled and snuggled into him. "Sounds like a plan."

That Saturday, Michele woke up to a text message from Caissie. *Are you free today? Need to talk to you. Want to meet at Burger Heaven for lunch?*

Michele raised her eyebrows, wondering what this could be about. *Sure, see you there,* she typed back. *Let's say noon.*

As she walked the several blocks to the diner, breathing in

the cool autumn breeze, she marveled over how much her life had changed since she'd arrived in New York a month earlier. She had been sure that her life was ending then—but now, with Philip, Michele realized that it had actually been the beginning of a destiny she was meant to fulfill. *If only Mom were still with me,* Michele thought wistfully. She ached to talk to her, to tell her all about Philip, to hear her reaction, see her smile.

Michele arrived to find Caissie already seated at a booth in the back of the diner, her head buried in a scientific-looking book with a picture of Albert Einstein on the cover.

"Hey, girl," Michele greeted her. "Did I miss the memo that we're studying for something today?"

"Hey." Caissie grinned. "You'll see in a sec why I brought this. But let's order first. I don't know about you, but I'm starved."

Once they had ordered, Caissie placed her Einstein book between them on the table so that they were both staring at his black-and-white wrinkled face.

"Okay, please explain why you brought Albert to lunch," Michele said as the waiter brought their drinks to the table. "Science is totally not my subject, FYI."

"Well, lucky for you, it's mine." Caissie took a sip of her soda and then continued. "Okay, so I have to admit that even though you did have a little evidence of your time traveling that night, and even though I got caught up in your story, after you left, I told myself that there was no way you had actually gone back to 1910. You *had* to be delusional."

Michele's face fell. "That's what I was afraid of. But—"

"Wait," Caissie interrupted. "I knew *you* believed it, I knew it wasn't a joke you were playing on me or anything, so I was tempted to talk to you about . . . you know, talking to a professional, getting help, that sort of thing. But I never did, because there was something in the back of my mind that I just barely remembered that made me wonder if you were right. You know how you can have a name on the tip of your tongue and not be able to remember it? Well, that's what this was, and I only remembered it last night. That's where our boy Albert comes in."

Caissie looked intently at Michele. "Albert Einstein believed in time travel. And what's more, he proved that it's theoretically possible."

"What?" Michele gaped at Caissie.

"I did some studying up on his theories last night and I brought the book for you to have. Check out his Special Theory of Relativity, which was published in 1905. His experiments basically *reversed* the belief that time is linear and the same for everyone. They showed that one person's past could hypothetically be another person's future!" Caissie opened the book to a dog-eared page. "Listen. Einstein says, 'The distinction between past, present, and future is only a stubbornly persistent illusion.' Just like your situation!"

Michele's head was spinning. "Wow. I can't believe this. I always thought it was just . . . magic."

"Well, I mean, there is something inherently magical about it," Caissie said. "But the point is, we now know that science backs it up."

"So how did Einstein think time travel worked?" Michele asked eagerly.

"It's all in the book." Caissie handed it to her. "But basically, Einstein proved that if an object is moving fast enough through space, it can change its passage through time. So time slows down as an object approaches the speed of light, meaning that traveling faster than the speed of light could send you *back* in time."

"But how could *I* be traveling faster than the speed of light?" Michele wondered. "I mean, from what you're saying, it sounds like that would take, like, a spaceship or something."

"Yeah, that confused me too. But didn't you tell me yourself that when you go back and forth through time, it feels like the speed of light?"

"Well—yeah," Michele admitted. "But I only meant it as an expression. I still don't see how . . ."

Caissie pointed to the key hanging around Michele's neck. "You said the key is what sends you back, right? Tell me more about how it works."

"Well, it sounds crazy, but . . . there's just *something* in this key. I don't know what it is—but whatever scientist or magician created it put something inside that causes it to open locked drawers and doors, to move and become animated. I can't even imagine where or how my dad got it," Michele said, marveling. "And when the key touches an object from the past . . . that's when I go back in time. But while that much is clear, I still don't fully understand how I'm returned to the present. That part is so often out of my control."

"Wow . . ." Caissie stared at the key. "My God, can you imagine the sensation this news would cause? We could get the top minds in the world to study the key—"

"Caissie, no!" Michele grabbed her wrist across the table.

"You promised, you can't say anything. Please. This is private. I don't want to become a freak show here. And besides, I could never hand over the key to someone else."

"All right, all right. I won't say anything," Caissie said, relenting. "But you're depriving the world of an amazing development in science!"

"How do you know it would be so amazing?" Michele countered. "I mean, I'm just one person going back in time. Imagine if everyone was doing it. The whole world as we know it could be over, or at least majorly thrown out of whack."

"I guess you have a point," Caissie conceded reluctantly.

"But . . . since you seem so interested, and you're my only confidante here, I'll tell you whatever you want to know about it," Michele offered. "And maybe at some point I'll let *you* study the key—but no one else."

Caissie's eyes lit up. "That would be awesome!"

"It's just so crazy that this is happening to *me*," Michele said. "I was always the ordinary one compared to my friends."

"Not anymore you're not." Caissie laughed. "Far from it."

"Okay, can I confess something else?" Michele felt a giddy smile stretching across her face as she began to confide in an amazed Caissie all about her relationship with Philip.

12

That night, Michele dreamt that Philip was calling out to her. "I have something for you, Michele," he said, his blue eyes intent. "Please, come to me."

When she woke up, it was three a.m., but there was no way Michele could fall back to sleep. She knew it, she felt it, that somewhere in 1910 Philip was trying to reach her. And she would have to go to him.

She got up and dressed nervously, her eyes continually darting to her mantel clock. *Please, please, don't let my grandparents or Annaleigh or anyone discover that I'm gone,* she silently prayed. She pulled on Philip's jacket, which he had let her keep, and wore her softest flat shoes, so she wouldn't make any noise going downstairs. Once she reached the Grand Hall, she held her breath as she opened the huge front door, willing it to close as quietly as possible. Outside, she ran through the gates to the apartment building next door. Standing in front of the building, she wrapped Philip's jacket tightly around her with one hand and clutched her key with the other. "Send me to him," she whispered.

And then, right before her eyes, the apartment building crumbled to the ground. Michele opened her mouth to scream, horrified by what she had done—just as the glorious Walker Mansion burst to life in its place, like an Etch A Sketch drawing appearing in a matter of seconds out of nothingness. Michele rushed up to the Walker Manison. She held her breath again, and sure enough, as she placed the key against the lock of the front door, it melded against it, and the door swung open.

Stepping into the chateau, she heard it right away—Philip's piano playing. With a smile, she hurried into the music room.

She stood in the doorway, watching him, as his fingers flew over the keys, playing one of his jazzy ragtime compositions. When he looked up and spotted Michele, his eyes lit in such a way that Michele felt her face instantly growing warm, her heart racing almost as fast as the syncopated rhythm Philip had been playing. He leaped off the piano bench and pulled her into his arms.

"You're here!" he cried, kissing her over and over. "You heard me! I can't believe it worked."

"So—you were really calling me?" Michele said breathily. "I didn't just dream it?"

"I really was," Philip said. "But I've tried it before and it never worked. You always seemed to come to me at different times. I wonder how it worked now."

"I don't know, but this is unbelievable!" Michele marveled. She pulled him to her for one more kiss. "What were you playing just now? I love it. It's so catchy."

"That's what I wanted to show you," he said eagerly. "I was thinking of you, and then the song just came to me—the same way you did. And I want you to write lyrics to it. That's why I called you here."

Michele smiled, her face flushing. "Wow. I'm flattered. But I don't know if I can do it on the spot like that."

"Of course you can," he said confidently. "It needs your words."

"Okay . . . I'll try. Will you keep playing the song while I come up with the lyrics? And do you have a pen and paper?"

"Right here." Philip stood up and lifted the top of the piano bench, where music books, blank sheet music, and a notebook were stashed. As Philip played the song over and over again, Michele sat beside him. Two words kept echoing in her mind as she watched him and lost herself in the melody: "chasing time." After a while of Philip playing and Michele frantically jotting down, crossing out, and rewriting lines, she finally had something. She took a deep breath, then sang along to Philip's melody in her soft voice.

> *"Catch my eye, tell me what you see*
> *Wonder if they could guess it about me*
> *Here I'm standing in a double life*
> *One with love, one with strife*

Try to act normal and play it cool
So afraid of breaking a rule
But now I'm falling too hard to stop
Can't help but take the next drop."

And then she sang the chorus.

"I can't live in the normal world,
I'm just chasing time
I belong in that endless whirl
The place where you're mine
So take me there, where I long to be
Inside time's mystery
Upside down and it feels so right
Take my hand, we'll take flight."

"How's that for a start?" Michele asked shyly.

"I love it!" Philip jumped off the piano bench in his excitement and spun her around. "It's perfect."

"Really?" Michele beamed. "Okay, let's keep working on it, then."

And that was how they spent the late hours: writing and playing, singing and laughing. Michele realized that she had never enjoyed herself so much in her entire life.

Philip copied "Chasing Time" and their first song together, "Bring the Colors Back," onto sheet music, and as Michele watched him move expertly from playing the songs to notating them, her admiration for him grew even more. "You're such a hot genius," she blurted out, grinning.

Philip smiled, but he seemed only to half hear her, his expression preoccupied. "Michele? Will you do something for me?" he asked abruptly.

"Anything."

"Will you find a way to get this song out in the world—and 'Bring the Colors Back' too—in your own time?"

"Me?" Michele let out a surprised laugh. "But I'm no singer, and I know nothing about the music industry."

"You could find a singer to perform the songs, just as you would find another pianist, since I won't be there. I know you can think of a way. And it could be the start of your career as a lyricist," Philip said.

"But that wouldn't be fair," Michele said uncomfortably. "Even if I was by some chance able to get the songs released, why should I get the credit as a songwriter when you're not there to get any recognition? I don't like it. If anything, you should publish the sheet music now, in your time. Then maybe your mom and uncle would understand about your music—"

"No," Philip said firmly. "I want these songs to live on in the future—when I can't. I want to know that I'm somehow . . . with you there."

For a moment Michele was too overcome with emotion to speak. "Okay," she whispered.

Philip reached over to ruffle her hair. "I love you, you know."

"I love you too." Michele leaned her head on his shoulder as he returned to playing the songs and transcribing them on sheet music. His face was filled with focus, as though he was convinced that the key to their staying together through time could be found in their songs.

As the first break of daylight streamed through the windows, Michele said reluctantly, "I should probably get back."

"Oh, God, I completely lost track of the time," Philip said guiltily.

"It's okay. I loved every minute." Michele smiled.

"Let me walk you home." Philip stood up, offering his arm.

"To 2010?" Michele laughed.

"I wish. But at least as far as the Windsor Mansion." Philip handed her their sheet music. "You'll be back soon?"

"Of course I will," Michele promised.

It was the night before the class trip to Newport, and as Michele packed her weekender, her cell phone rang. She glanced at the screen, which flashed with a picture of Kristen. Michele bit her lip guiltily as she realized how many days it had been since she'd spoken to her best friends. She quickly picked up the phone.

"Hey, girl!" she answered. "I'm so sorry it's taken me so long—"

"Michele! Where have you *been,* girl? Amanda's here too."

"Omigod, I can't believe we actually got you live!" Amanda piped up. "What is going *on* over there? Are you okay?"

"Yeah, I am. Actually, I'm doing . . . pretty well, believe it or not. But I really miss you guys. I'm so sorry I've been MIA," Michele said. "There's just been so much going on here—"

"You met a guy," Kristen declared.

Michele's mouth fell open and she couldn't help laughing.

How was it that obvious? "Why would you say that?" Michele asked, trying to sound innocent.

"Don't try to hide it. We know you practically as well as we know ourselves," Kristen warned.

"Plus it's kind of blatant. You disappear for days and now you're sounding all spacey and abnormally happy," Amanda pointed out. "What I just don't understand is why you wouldn't tell us! Helloooo, that's what best friends are for."

"I know," Michele conceded. "I'm sorry. I guess it's just that it's all a little . . . uncertain and I didn't want to jinx anything."

"You're super into him, aren't you?" Amanda guessed gleefully. "I mean, you sure didn't waste any time telling us when you started crushing on Jason. This guy must be special."

"He is," Michele admitted, smiling. If only she could tell them *how* special.

"Okay, details, please. Can we check him out on Facebook?" Kristen asked eagerly.

"Uh, no." Michele laughed. "He's not into that stuff. He's not on Twitter either."

"Wow," Kristen said, marveling. "Very mysterious and old-fashioned of him."

"Well, anyway, I'll tell you guys more later if—if anything happens," Michele said hurriedly, anxious to change the subject before she revealed too much. "What's the latest with you two? I want to hear everything."

Twenty minutes later, after she'd finished catching up with the girls, it occurred to Michele that her grandparents probably expected her to say goodbye to them that night, since she'd be leaving for the trip early in the morning. She hadn't heard them come upstairs yet, so she headed downstairs to find them. She spotted Annaleigh on the mezzanine.

"Hey, do you know where my grandparents are?" she asked.

"Yes, they had tea sent to them in the library fifteen minutes ago, so they're probably still there," Annaleigh replied.

"Thanks." Michele headed down the stairs and into the library. She found the room empty, but two half-full teacups rested on one of the reading tables, beside an open book. Michele figured her grandparents had probably just stepped out for a second, and she sat at the table to wait for them. She glanced at the book and saw that it was an old photo album. She peered at the photo the album was opened to—and her jaw dropped in shock.

The faded black-and-white photo showed an attractive man in a stiff Victorian suit, his wavy hair parted in the middle, his dark eyes looking away from the camera. He seemed somehow known to her, like an old acquaintance she hadn't seen in ages. But it was his name that surprised her. The photo caption read *IRVING HENRY, Attorney at Law. 1900.*

"Irving Henry," she whispered. The attorney who had worked for Philip's father . . . Her own father's name backward. What was this photo doing in a Windsor album?

"Michele!"

She looked up at Dorothy's sharply calling her name. Her grandparents had just returned, and they looked strangely discomfited by the sight of her. Michele was too preoccupied with the photo to bother being polite, and she blurted out, "Who is this? He looks familiar, and his name . . ."

"He's nobody important," Walter said, a little too quickly. "Just an attorney who worked for my family in the previous century."

Michele stared at them. "There's something you're not telling me," she said slowly. "He's not nobody, or you wouldn't be looking at his picture."

"Dear, your grandfather was simply showing me one of the old family photo albums," Dorothy said with a stilted laugh. "Mr. Henry was a loyal family employee. That's the only reason he's in the album. This is the only picture of him in the whole book. There's nothing to know about him."

Michele stood up, unable to contain her frustration. "Why are you two so secretive all the time? I know you're hiding something from me. I can tell, I'm not stupid."

"That's enough, Michele. You're being impertinent," Walter said sternly. "We aren't hiding anything. I'm sorry if it's disappointing for you to hear, but there's nothing more to the story."

Michele sighed. She could tell she wasn't getting anywhere with them—and she had to admit she was beginning to wonder if her time traveling was hurting her ability to discern the difference between reality and fantasy.

"Okay. Sorry," she said grudgingly. "Anyway, I just came to say bye. The Newport trip is tomorrow."

Walter gave her a nod of acknowledgment. "Have a good time."

"Good night, dear. Be safe," Dorothy added.

"Thanks. Good night." Before leaving the room, Michele was compelled to turn around for one more glance at the photo of Irving Henry. And as she did so, she could have sworn she felt the skeleton key pulse against her neck.

Michele settled into a window seat on the train in the row behind Caissie and Aaron. She was just about to slip on her headphones when she heard a voice beside her. "Is this seat taken?"

Michele looked up. It was Ben Archer, flashing her his dimpled grin. She'd been looking forward to some time alone to think, but she knew she couldn't say no. "Go ahead," she replied, giving him a friendly smile.

As Ben settled into the seat next to her, Michele could hear Caissie start whispering to Aaron in the row ahead. She had obviously noticed the Ben development, and Michele seriously hoped she wouldn't make too big a deal out of it. A moment later the train left Penn Station, heading for Rhode Island.

"Ever been to Newport?" Ben asked conversationally.

"Nope. You?"

"Yeah. A family wedding was there a few years back," he answered.

Michele nodded. "Cool."

There was a moment of awkward silence and then Ben said, "So how's New York treating you so far? It must be pretty sweet living in the Windsor Mansion. I remember passing by that place so many times as a kid, thinking how awesome it must be."

"It is pretty amazing," Michele agreed. "But what I love about it isn't so much the fancy stuff; it's all the history."

"Yeah? Then you're going to love Newport," Ben told her. He glanced at the iPod and headphones in her lap. "What are you listening to these days?"

"Honestly, a bit of everything. I'm obsessed with almost all genres of music." Michele grinned. "Right now I'm alternating between Thom Yorke's solo record and some vintage Nina Simone."

"Nice. Let me hear some of that Thom Yorke." Ben playfully took her headphones from her.

"Sure. Let me just cue up a track."

While he listened to the song on her iPod, Michele leaned back in her seat, glancing out the window. As the suburban towns whizzed by, she felt her eyelids growing heavy. She leaned her head against the window, closing her eyes for a moment and letting herself daydream about Philip. . . .

She felt a hand gently shake her arm. *Philip,* Michele thought happily, lifting her arms toward him. But as she opened her eyes, to her mortification she saw that it was Ben. She quickly pretended to be stretching her arms, her face burning. "Did I fall asleep?" she asked groggily.

"Yeah," Ben said. "We're actually here, in Rhode Island."

"Are you serious? I slept the whole way?"

"Guess you really needed the rest," Ben said with a chuckle.

"Sorry I wasn't much company," Michele replied sheepishly.

"It's okay. You looked . . . cute. Sleeping," Ben said, looking a little shy.

"Oh. Thanks." Michele glanced down, her face turning redder. She had a feeling she needed to discourage Ben—but how?

"Kingston, Rhode Island!" the conductor called out.

"That's us, everyone," Mr. Lewis called, standing up to address his class.

Michele, Ben, and the other students stood and gathered their luggage, preparing to disembark. Mr. Lewis had explained that there was no direct train to Newport, so a shuttle bus was picking them up from the train station and taking them to the island.

Michele discreetly moved away from Ben at the train station and caught up with Caissie and Aaron, sharing a row on the bus with them. As they drove into Newport at sundown, she smiled at Rhode Island's foliage, unlike anything she had seen in New York or back home in L.A. They drove under canopies of trees, with lush meadows on either side of the road. When they hit the coast, with its spectacular ocean views, Michele squeezed Cassie's arm, enthralled. Plunging cliffs set the stage for a dramatic expanse of shimmery blue water, dotted with boats and lighthouses.

Downtown Newport was like a historical timepiece, with nearly every building dating back to the eighteenth century. Mr. Lewis pointed out the sights to the class as they passed: "There's Trinity Church on the right, where George Washington and Queen Elizabeth worshipped. . . . And look, over here is the first incorporated library in the U.S., Redwood Library, from 1747! . . . White Horse Tavern is on your left, the oldest tavern in the nation, dating all the way back to the 1600s."

Then they turned onto Bellevue Avenue, and the sights changed dramatically. Colonial structures gave way to block upon block of massive palatial villas and mansions, just like the

Windsor Mansion and the other old Fifth Avenue mansions Michele had seen.

"Here are the famous Newport cottages, which we'll be visiting tomorrow and Sunday," Mr. Lewis announced. "Starting in the late 1800s, Newport became *the* summer destination for high society, and all the top families owned homes here to vacation and entertain."

"Wait—*cottages?*" Aaron blurted out in disbelief.

"Yes, that has always been the term for summer homes in Newport," Mr. Lewis said with a smile. "Even the Vanderbilts' house, The Breakers, is called a cottage—and it's four stories high, with more than seventy rooms. Most of the famous families that had homes here, like the Astors and Vanderbilts, are no longer with us, so the Preservation Society of Newport County has preserved their homes and turned them into museums. That's how schools like ours can experience what life was like in those days."

Caissie and Michele exchanged grins. Little did Mr. Lewis know, Michele didn't need a museum tour to experience life in the past.

"Are we going to see the Walker family's cottage?" Michele asked.

"As a matter of fact, yes," Mr. Lewis answered. "Tomorrow morning."

Michele bit back a smile, not wanting to draw attention to herself—but she felt her spirits lift. She might not be able to see Philip that weekend, but she knew she would feel close to him as she wandered through his summer home.

Soon they reached the Hotel Viking, a stately brick

boutique hotel at the top of what Mr. Lewis called Historic Hill. A plaque by the front doors read A HISTORIC HOTEL OF AMERICA. ESTABLISHED 1926.

The class followed Mr. Lewis into the hotel lobby and waited while he signed in and collected everyone's room keys. When he returned to the class and handed out room assignments, Michele breathed a sigh of relief at being paired with Caissie and not one of the Four Hundred snobs.

After dropping off their bags and settling into their rooms, the class gathered at the hotel restaurant, One Bellevue, for dinner. As Michele, Caissie, and Aaron gathered around a table for three, they couldn't help noticing Olivia Livingston giving Michele a disappointed look.

"Well, looks like someone still doesn't approve of a Windsor choosing her friends outside of the *Social Register*," Caissie said dryly.

"That girl has serious issues," Michele said, rolling her eyes. "Aaron, who's your hotel roomie?"

"I'm in with one of the Fakin' Jamaicans," he replied. "So far I've already been treated to some dancehall reggae, and I have a feeling I'm in for a whole lot more."

"Promise me you'll get through the weekend without developing a Rasta accent?" Caissie said.

"I think I can manage that." Aaron playfully tweaked Caissie's nose, and she blushed and quickly buried her head in her menu. Michele stifled a giggle. Those two so wanted each other.

13

The next morning, a tourist trolley transported the class to their first tour of the day at the Walker's Newport mansion. Michele felt light-headed from the dizzying combination of nerves and excitement as the trolley drew closer and closer, finally slowing in front of an entrance gate from which a flag waved and a large sign read PALAIS DE LA MER, BUILT FOR THE WALKER FAMILY OF NEW YORK, 1901. DAILY TOURS 9 A.M.–6 P.M. Behind the gate loomed a sprawling white stone structure. Caissie squeezed Michele's hand as the trolley pulled through the gate and into the driveway.

Mr. Lewis led the class through the arched French doors into the house, where they were instructed to wait in the entrance vestibule for the next tour, which was starting in five minutes. Michele was oblivious to the light chatter of her classmates as she eagerly looked around, imagining Philip bursting in through the front doors on a summer day or climbing the winding staircase up to his room.

The guide soon arrived, a Newport native in her sixties named Judy. As she led them through the social rooms on the main floor, she explained the Walker family history.

"This home originally belonged to Mr. Warren H. Walker of New York, who shared it with his wife, Paulette, and their son, Philip," she began.

At the mention of Philip's name, Michele stopped in her tracks, her heart about to burst. She realized that it was the first time anyone in her modern life had ever acknowledged Philip's existence, and it gave her an incredible feeling. Even when she had his jacket around her shoulders and his music in her head, it was sometimes hard to fully believe that he was real when she was firmly entrenched in 2010 soil. And now here was a tour guide telling them the story of the boy she loved and his family. Smiling to herself, Michele caught up to Caissie as they followed Judy and the class into the next room.

"Warren Walker's grandfather had established the family as a real estate giant back in the seventeen hundreds. After Warren's father died, he inherited the business and it grew even more successful under his leadership. Meanwhile, Paulette was an aristocrat of French origin, and since American high society worshipped the traditions, styles, and manners of the French, Paulette was one of the most popular hostesses of her day. And of course the son, Philip, attracted considerable attention, with his fine pedigree and even finer looks."

Caissie raised an eyebrow at Michele, who couldn't help grinning proudly.

Judy led the group upstairs to view the family and guest bedrooms on the second floor. Olivia and her friends oohed and aahed loudly over the period decor in Philip's parents' room, with the delicate antique furniture from the era of Louis XV and framed black-and-white family photographs above a striking gilded fireplace.

"Sadly, Warren Walker died of a stroke in 1908, at the early age of forty-seven. Upon his death, his younger brother, Harold, was appointed head of the Walker family and business, and he soon moved in with Paulette and Philip," Judy said. Michele thought of Philip's brutish uncle and shuddered.

At last, they arrived at Philip's bedroom door. Michele's heart lifted when she saw the engraved P.J.W. on his door. It was the strangest feeling to be this close to his life and yet a hundred years removed.

Philip's room at Palais de la Mer, decorated in the Empire style, had a similar feel to his New York bedroom. The room was painted a deep blue, with dark wood furniture and a frescoed ceiling. The sight of black-and-white photographs of him with friends and family, framed throughout the room, brought a lump to Michele's throat. If only he was really here with her in 2010, rather than a figure of the past.

"The Walker family had more than its share of losses," Judy said somberly, "and the greatest tragedy in the family centered on the occupant of this room, Philip Walker."

Michele's head snapped up in shock. Caissie looked at her anxiously as Judy continued.

"In the year 1927, at the age of thirty-five, Philip Walker was declared dead."

Michele choked back a scream. The room swayed around her, and she felt like she was going to be sick. Caissie grabbed her hand to steady her.

"His body was never found, and the location of his remains is still a mystery to this day," Judy said. "However, a cryptic journal entry written the night before his disappearance caused the police to rule his death a suicide."

Michele slowly backed away toward the wall and leaned against the cold wood as she tried to fight the nausea enveloping her. This couldn't be happening. It was just a nightmare she was going to wake up from. Her vibrant, beautiful, determined, and brilliant Philip could never have killed himself. Never.

"What did the journal entry say?" Amy Van Alen called out curiously.

"It was widely copied in newspapers at the time, and I actually have a section of it here to read to you." Judy looked down at her clipboard and began to read. " 'Sixteen long years of unbearable waiting. I can't do it anymore. She was supposed to return—she always did—and now I see the cruelty in this helpless waiting, living at the mercy of Time. Dragging through the days, I ask myself why I bother when I know that the one place I can find her isn't here on earth. That's it—that's enough of this—I'm done.' "

For a moment a hush came over the class. Michele felt herself sliding against the wall, her vision momentarily failing her, as she grappled with the sickening discovery. *Something happened and I couldn't get back to him, I couldn't get back for sixteen whole years! He thought I abandoned him and he died because of me—it's all my fault. He was supposed to be a great musician, live a long life. What happened, what have I done?*

"Philip's adult life was a sad one," Judy remarked. "Society columns from the Gilded Age described him as the popular life of the party in his youth, with everything going for him. But as he grew up, he became more and more withdrawn, and despite the countless eligible women vying for his attentions, he always said he was already spoken for. But no one ever saw the girl, and whoever she was—if she was even real—it seems she led to the end of his life. Now then, on to happier topics . . ."

As Judy led the class out of Philip's room, Michele and Caissie hung back, looking at each other in horror.

"I killed him . . . didn't I?" Michele whispered to Caissie. "How could a love so perfect, so right, turn out like this?"

Caissie just stared at her. "I . . . I don't know."

"I don't understand what happened. Why couldn't I get back to him?" Michele covered her face with her hands, her throat thick with sobs. "He was supposed to do so much. He was going to change the world with his music."

"You really love him, don't you, Michele?" Caissie asked.

"Of course I do!" Michele cried.

"Then . . . you know what you have to do."

Michele nodded, but she couldn't speak.

"You have to let him go," Caissie said quietly. "That's the only way. You have to . . . to somehow explain all this and end it with him, early enough so he still has a chance to move on. If you do that . . . well, maybe then you can change the past, maybe you can save him."

"Do you mind leaving me here for a little bit?" Michele asked numbly. "I just need to be alone."

"Okay." Caissie gave Michele a hug before leaving the room.

Michele felt herself sink to the floor. She knew that Caissie was right, but the reality of it was cripplingly painful. How could she give up the only person in her life that she truly cared about, the one person alive who really loved her? Now there would be no more happy distractions, no one to make things better when her grief for her mom became too much to bear. *If I do this, I'll be more alone than ever,* Michele thought. And how could she ever stand to break his heart, to leave him when she knew how much he loved her?

"I can't do it," Michele whispered. She wanted to get up, to leave this room, but something kept her stuck in place. She kept turning over and around in her mind what Judy had revealed— the terrible fate that had befallen Philip, all because of Michele.

I can't let that happen to him, Michele thought urgently. *Love means putting the other person first, and that's what I have to do. I can't let him torture himself waiting for me for years on end. I can't let him give up his dreams and his life. I have to get him to move on. I have to save him. No matter how much I'll miss him, as long as I know he survived, then I'll be okay.*

She clutched her key necklace and closed her eyes. "Please take me back to Philip. I need to say goodbye."

"Phil! The boat arrived!" a young, exuberant voice called out.

Michele's eyes snapped open, and she sprang up. A little boy of about ten, dressed in a sailor suit, dashed into the room and frowned in disappointment when he saw that Philip wasn't there. And of course, he didn't see Michele steadying herself and catching her breath.

Michele followed the boy out of Philip's room and was once again transplanted into a tableau of Gilded Age life. The Walkers' Newport home was glitteringly new, with costumed footmen marching importantly throughout, following their master's orders and seeing to the perfection of the house.

A man in his forties reached the top of the staircase, his arm around a teenage boy with thick dark hair and the most beautiful blue eyes—

Oh, God. It was Philip. Only—had she come to the right time? This Philip definitely looked younger. . . .

"Phil, the new boat is here, it's here!" the little boy cried, jumping up and down.

The man with Philip ruffled the little boy's hair and chuckled. "See that, Philip? Your cousin just might be more anxious than I am to show you the new Walker vessel. Didn't I tell you it was the finest?"

Philip grinned. "You sure did, Father."

Father? Michele was stunned. What year had she gone to? She raced back into Philip's room and rifled through the contents on his desk until she found a calendar, which was opened to the month of July . . . 1907.

Michele stared at the calendar in shock. How could she have ended up in 1907, a time when Philip's father was still alive and Philip didn't even know her? He *couldn't* know her. It would alter their whole relationship if he saw her now, too soon. What if it ruined everything? She had to get out of there and get back to her own time.

As Michele was hurrying out the door, she smacked right into someone. "Ouch!" she yelped, rubbing her bruised forehead.

She heard a sharp intake of breath, and she looked up. That was when she saw that she was in Philip's arms. He was holding her upright, staring at her in astonishment.

"*Who are you?*" he breathed. "Where did you come from?"

"I—I can't tell you now," Michele stammered. "I have to go."

"Please, don't go," Philip protested. "Just tell me your name."

But Michele turned around and broke into a run down the stairs. They weren't supposed to meet for another three years!

She heard footsteps behind her as she ran, and a hand closed on her wrist—but then it suddenly lost its grasp on her, and Michele let out a startled cry as she saw that she was literally running through time. The stairs above her and the landing were those of 1907, with fifteen-year-old Philip looking desperately at her, while the stairs below her and the ground floor were from 2010. Caissie was waiting at the bottom of the staircase, watching her worriedly.

"What happened?" she asked, when Michele reached the last step.

"I'll tell you later. I need to get out of here," Michele replied breathlessly. "Can you tell Mr. Lewis I got sick and needed to go back to the hotel?"

Caissie nodded anxiously. "Are you sure you're going to be okay alone?"

"Yeah, I just need to get out of here."

Michele ran out of the Walker house as the memory of her first meeting with Philip flooded back to her: *"It was you—you were the girl I saw at my summer cottage three years ago. . . ."*

So Philip had been right. He really *had* seen her years before the ball.

On the way back to New York the following night, Michele sat rigidly in her seat, her body cold. It was unthinkable how much circumstances had changed since her last train trip two days earlier. Then she had been consumed with the excitement of being in love; now she was practically numb with pain over the task that she knew awaited her back in New York.

She had done everything she could to put the impending breakup with Philip out of her mind during the rest of the school trip, knowing that the only way she could get through the weekend was to give herself a major dose of denial. But now that they were heading home, Caissie asleep in the seat next to her, Michele allowed herself to drop the act. She thought of Clara's mother, Alanna. Was this how Alanna had felt when she'd had to leave George Windsor? Michele felt a fresh wave of longing for her mom. How could she not *be* there when Michele needed her most?

When they reached Penn Station, Caissie and Michele

caught a cab home together. Michele followed Caissie into her apartment building, her face white as a ghost. Once the girls were in Caissie's room, Caissie knowingly offered to give Michele some time alone. "I'm going to go . . . catch up with my dad, fill him in on the trip. I'll let your grandmother know that you're spending the night. You know, in case you need to be . . . there awhile."

"Thanks." Michele swallowed hard.

Caissie gave her a warm hug. "Good luck. You're doing the right thing."

The second she was alone, Michele pulled Philip's card out of her bag. She kept it with her all the time. Closing her eyes and holding on tight to her key necklace, she willed Time to return her to him.

In mere moments, Caissie's room transformed before Michele's eyes, taking on dozens of different incarnations, until she found herself in Philip's bedroom. He was sitting at his desk, and he jumped out of his seat when he saw her appear.

"Michele!" He whirled her around and kissed her tenderly. "I've missed you."

Michele kissed him back, and it felt so good that the thought of never kissing him again, never being with him again, brought tears to her eyes. She broke away from him.

"Michele, what's wrong? Why are you crying?" Philip grasped her hands, looking at her worriedly.

"Philip, I have to tell you something and it's really . . . really hard for me."

Philip let go of her and sank into the nearest chair, possibly fearing the words to come.

"I have to say goodbye," Michele said, her stomach churning. "I love you, but . . . I have to stay in my own time, and you in yours."

The color drained from Philip's face. "No. You don't mean that, we can't do that. We belong together."

"But we can never actually *be* together," Michele said, her voice tight with agony. "I can't fully exist in your time, and you can't get to mine. And in the end, that will only ruin us."

Philip just stared at her, shaking his head.

Michele's tears were now falling freely. "I love you, but I can't be with you anymore. Please try to understand what I'm about to say. I've discovered that . . . that something is going to happen. I don't know what or why, but I won't be able to travel to you anymore, at least not for . . . for many years. And you're too good, you have too much life in you to throw it away on waiting for me." She realized she was babbling through her tears now, but she couldn't stop. She had to make him understand. "I can't live with myself knowing that your life ends because of me. I live in the future, so I've *seen* how this will go wrong if it continues. I need you to move on. Please . . . do it for me."

"But . . . how will I ever bear it?" Philip asked, his voice breaking.

"How will I?" Michele cried. "All I know is that . . . even when we're not together, I'll still love you and think of you every day. And the one thing that will get me through is knowing that you lived a long and happy life, that you were able to achieve your dreams and touch people with your music. I can't let our relationship stop you from having the life you were meant to have. Please promise me that you'll move on, pursue your music, and not let anything bring you down."

Philip was silent a long moment, blinking back tears. "I promise," he finally said, his voice barely above a whisper. "For you."

As Michele gazed at him, she realized that she was shaking. He wrapped his arms around her, and she threw her arms around his neck and kissed him. He kissed her back with a new urgency, and as their kisses grew more and more heated, he pulled her onto the bed with him. And for a while, in each other's arms, they managed to forget about goodbyes.

⤜⁂⤛

She was asleep in his arms, her head nestled on his shoulder. Even with the terrible knowledge that this was their last night together, she managed to find comfort and peace in being this close to him. And then, without any warning, she wasn't anymore.

"Michele?"

At Caissie's voice, Michele blinked and looked up—as 1910 vanished. She was lying on Caissie's bedroom floor, with no arms holding her. When Michele saw that Philip was really gone, a wave of fresh tears came over her. Caissie helped her up off the floor and comforted Michele as she cried.

"Is there anything I can do to make you feel better?" she offered anxiously. "We can rent a really distracting movie, or . . . ?"

"Thanks," Michele replied, wiping her eyes. "But I feel so sick—I think I should just go home and go to bed."

"Okay. You're going to be all right. I know it." Caissie gave her a tight hug. "Call me if you need anything."

On the short walk from Caissie's apartment to the Windsor Mansion, Michele was unable to stop her tears. She knew she had done the right thing for Philip, but how was she ever going to get through the days, months, and years ahead without him? Their love had saved her after her mom died. What was going to save her now? And now that she had found the kind of real, true love that everyone dreamed about but hardly dared to hope for, how could she ever even contemplate being with someone else? *I can't*, Michele thought. *There's no one else I can marry, or even date. Philip was the one. And now I'm condemned to a lifetime of missing him. God, if only Mom were here.*

And suddenly, Michele realized something: these were the exact feelings her mom must have suffered when Henry had disappeared. This was what Marion had lived with every day for nearly seventeen years. The one and only person who could ever understand what Michele was going through was gone too. And now Michele cried for all of them, her parents and Philip. By the time she walked into the mansion, she was a wreck.

Dorothy was in the Grand Hall talking to Annaleigh when Michele walked in, but they both stopped short when they saw her.

"Michele, what happened?" Annaleigh cried.

In an uncharacteristic move, Dorothy ran to Michele and wrapped a protective arm around her. "Annaleigh, I should talk to my granddaughter in private."

"Of course." Annaleigh nodded and left the room. When they were alone, Dorothy asked Michele, "What happened, dear? I thought you were spending the night at Caissie's. Did you two get in a fight?"

"No," Michele managed to choke out.

Dorothy was silent a moment and then she said, "Are you missing your mother?"

At this point Michele was crying so hard she couldn't even speak. Dorothy pulled her into a hug, their first embrace since Michele had arrived. Michele leaned her head on her grandmother's shoulder as Dorothy stroked her hair, murmuring soothingly.

"Why don't you change into your most comfortable pajamas and get cozy in bed? I'll bring you up some chamomile tea," she said kindly.

Michele nodded and went dazedly up to her room, changed into pajamas, and crawled into bed. Dorothy came in a few moments later with a mug of warm tea for Michele. For a moment Michele was surprised she had shown up. Dorothy had never visited Michele in her room before, and it was out of character for her to be taking care of Michele like this. But now her grandmother was here, tucking her in and stroking her hair until she finally fell asleep.

The next morning, Michele woke up feeling like she had been run over by a truck. Her whole body ached, there was a painful lump in her throat, her eyes were swollen, and her stomach was so queasy that she couldn't imagine eating anytime in the near future. *But if I saved Philip, then it's worth it,* Michele reminded herself. Desperate to find out if it had worked, she hurried to her desk, ignoring the waves of dizziness she felt upon getting out of bed.

Her hands trembling, she went online and typed *Philip James Walker* into Google. As she frantically scanned the links popping up on the screen, she knew right away that something was wrong. None of these articles, none of these links had to do with her Philip. None of these *people* were her Philip. And if he had made a name for himself in music . . . wouldn't he be among the top searches? And even if not, if he had lived a long and fruitful life, wouldn't being part of the prominent Walker family garner him a listing on Wikipedia or some other online encyclopedia? But so far, nothing. By the time she had reached page twelve of the search results, Michele buried her head in her hands in defeat. How could she have peace of mind now, not knowing whether she had stopped his tragic end? What had *happened* to him?

Michele jumped out of her desk chair and hurried to her dressing room to throw on some clothes. School was just about the last thing she could handle right now—but she had to talk to Caissie, and it couldn't wait.

Michele ran to Caissie's locker before first period, and fortunately, she was alone. Her eyes widened when she saw Michele.

"Oh, God. Are you okay?"

"I need to talk to you," Michele burst out. "Do you think we can have lunch alone today, somewhere private?"

"Of course." Caissie peered closely at Michele. "You don't look like you're going to be able to eat a bite. . . . How about this: I'll scarf down some food during break so we can spend lunch in the library."

Michele managed a weak smile. "Thanks. I'll meet you there."

Her morning classes went by in a mindless blur, her body present but her spirit a hundred years away. At last the bell rang for lunch, and she hurried to the library. She and Caissie found a private table in the back, and the moment they sat down, Michele poured out the whole story, tears welling up in her eyes as she spoke.

"So . . . what do you think happened?" Michele asked after she had finished.

"I—I honestly don't know," Caissie said slowly. "But . . . I have an idea for how you might be able to find out."

"What?" Michele asked intently.

"Do you think you can go back to the 1920s, before the time Judy said he—he died? She said it was in 1927, right? If you can get to him sometime before that, then you can find out firsthand if he's okay, and if he's not . . . then you have a chance to try to fix this."

Michele stared at Caissie. "That is a good idea. Only I don't have anything like Clara's diary to send me back to the twenties."

"Can you go digging around the house after school?" Caissie suggested. "I mean, there's got to be something there."

"Wait a minute!" Michele exclaimed as a memory dawned on her. "I do have something. It's from 1925, though."

"That's close enough!" Caissie's eyes lit up. "Oh, my God. You get to see the Roaring Twenties!"

The second Michele got home, she raced up to her room two steps at a time. She pulled open her desk drawer, where Lily Windsor's composition book was still nestled—the book she had found during her trip to the attic weeks earlier and forgotten all about.

"Please let this work," Michele whispered.

With one hand she clutched the key around her neck; with the other she opened the composition book to the first page of lyrics. As she read the song title, "Born for It," written in Lily's messy hand, Michele found herself sinking into the book pages, just as she had with Clara's diary. And then she felt Time taking hold of her body, and she was spinning through the air so fast she felt as if her face could fly off at any moment. *This must be what Caissie meant by going faster than the speed of light,* Michele thought. And then she was dropped. Falling through the tunnel of time, she let out a bloodcurdling scream.

"*Horsefeathers!* Who are you and *where* did you come from?"

Michele looked up and there she was: her great-grandmother, the famous singer—before she was a star. Her auburn hair was styled in the wavy bob from the portrait in Michele's room, and she wore a knee-length pleated dress. Without the heavy makeup she wore in her portrait, Lily looked youthful, maybe even younger than Michele.

Michele gave her an awestruck smile, momentarily distracted from all her troubles. Never in a million years could she have imagined that she'd get to meet *the* Lily Windsor. And the bedroom—it could not have looked more different from Clara's, or for that matter, Michele's. The decor was all in the Art Deco style, cosmetics and accessories littered every inch of table space, and the walls were covered with posters emblazoned with names like Douglas Fairbanks Jr. and Ziegfeld Follies.

"I'm Michele," she finally said to her great-grandmother.

Then, remembering what she had told Clara, Michele cleared her throat and said awkwardly, "I'm a spirit."

"What?" Lily roared. "A *ghost*? I didn't do anything to you, get out of here!"

Okay, so clearly spirits were more highly regarded in 1910 than in the twenties.

"Uh, no," Michele said. "Not that kind of ghost. I'm a good spirit. I'm here to help you."

Lily stared at her. "Says you! Why should I believe that?"

Michele shrugged. "Do I look like a scary ghost to you?"

"Not really," Lily admitted, inspecting her closely. "In fact . . . well, you do look a bit like *me*!"

Michele grinned, feeling a little thrill at those words. As she glanced around the room, she noticed a worn copy of Shakespeare's *The Tempest* on Lily's unmade bed, and it gave her a spark of inspiration.

"You've read *The Tempest*?"

"Read it?" Lily scoffed. "It's only my favorite of Shakespeare's plays."

"Well, then you should understand what I am—a spirit just like Ariel from the play."

"Oh?" As Lily surveyed her, Michele could tell that she was pretty tempted to believe in the idea of having her very own Ariel. "Well, it *would* be like me to have something otherworldly enter my life," she sighed dramatically, a tinge of pride in her voice.

Michele tried not to laugh. "Yeah, well. It could be worse."

"As a matter of fact, I *was* looking for a solution to a terrible predicament," Lily continued. "Is that why you are here, then?"

"Um, what's the predicament?" Michele asked.

"We-ell . . ." Lily eyed her carefully for a few minutes, as if judging whether Michele looked trustworthy. "All right, I'll level with you. I need to sneak out of here and get to the big singing contest tonight at the Cotton Club."

"But why would you need a singing contest? You're—" Michele stopped herself just in time, remembering that Lily probably hadn't made it big yet. Sure enough, Lily impatiently explained, "This contest could be my big break! We have to find a way to get me there."

"Okay, but first, can you tell me something?" Michele drew in a deep breath. "Do you know anything about Philip Walker? Does he still live next door?"

Lily gave Michele a suspicious look. "Aren't spirits supposed to know everything?"

"Just tell me," Michele begged. "Please."

"Oh, all right. He doesn't live next door anymore, hasn't for years. I think I heard he's somewhere in London. And I never met the big pill. The Walkers were blacklisted from our family after he broke his engagement to my cousin Violet, back when I was a baby. Apparently he couldn't get over another girl." Lily rolled her eyes, as if to say, *Like anyone could prefer another girl to gorgeous Violet.* "Naturally we've hated those sour Walkers ever since. And now Daddy is just about killing Mr. Walker in business as payback," Lily said conspiratorially.

Michele stared at Lily, reeling from all the news. *She* was the reason for the big Windsor-Walker feud? *It makes sense. I should have realized it sooner,* Michele thought. But still, she had always assumed that the rift was caused by something else—

206

business sabotage, maybe, but not *her*! Michele felt a stab of fear at the knowledge that it was all her fault. And worse, Philip wasn't even here in New York? How could she have any chance at saving him now? *I have to draw him out somehow,* Michele realized. *I have to find a way to bring him to me here.*

"Now, how do you think we should get to the club?" Lily pressed. "It's all the way in Harlem."

"Let me think." Michele paced the room, then suddenly stopped and looked at Lily. *Wait a minute,* she thought, her mind racing. *Lily is a singer, and I know for a fact that she becomes famous. If I give her the songs I wrote with Philip and she performs them . . . then not only will he know that I'm here, but it could launch his career!* She would have to come up with some sort of alias for him, of course, since she couldn't imagine Lily doing anything to help a "sour Walker." But this could still be the big break he needed. She couldn't imagine him giving up on his life at just the time when he was finally reaching people with his music.

"Lily, I think we can help each other," she said abruptly. "I'll get you to the Cotton Club. But I need you to sing my songs."

"Ex-*cuse* me!" Lily exclaimed, giving her an affronted look. "Since when do spirits have ulterior motives and drive bargains? Plus I already have my audition song prepared."

"I don't mean tonight, but soon. And you don't have to sing them if you totally hate them," Michele assured her, feeling a little guilty for bribing her great-grandmother. "But I have a . . . a good feeling about the songs for you." She threw Lily a meaningful look. "You might want to—to trust my spirit guidance on this one."

"Oh, bother. All right," Lily said, relenting. "I'll hear them, but later. Now, what is your great plan?"

"Tell your parents you're going over to a friend's house to spend the night, but just make sure it's a friend who can cover for you if they call. Then, instead of going to your friend's, we'll walk to the Plaza Hotel, reserve a room, and take a taxi to Harlem from there." As she spoke, Michele wondered what the heck she was getting them into.

"Well, *now* you're on the trolley!" Lily said, her eyes shining. "That's a nifty plan. I have money for emergencies in my undergarments drawer, and it should be enough dough for the hotel and taxi."

"Just be sure to put on extra makeup and dress older, so they'll think you're at least eighteen when you try to book a room," Michele advised.

"Don't you worry about that. If anyone knows about costuming, it's Lily!" she said confidently.

"Oh, and one more thing," Michele added. "No one but you can see me."

Lily changed into a kimono, and Michele watched curiously as she got ready, humming and doing funny vocal exercises all the while.

"Hey, where are the . . . others? Clara and Frances and the rest?" Michele asked, wondering how it happened that Lily was now living in the mansion.

"They live at the homes of their husbands, of course. Cousin James moved to England when he married Lady Pamela, so when Uncle George died, my father inherited the mansion."

Lily sat at her vanity and began plucking her already thin eyebrows with a vengeance, until Michele had to stop her.

"Wait, you're overplucking!"

Lily wiggled her skinny eyebrows at Michele. "Oh, darling, that's the *look*." She shook her head in amusement.

Next she rimmed her eyes with black kohl and applied mascara from a tube that Michele was amazed to see read MAYBELLINE. She dusted bright powder blush on her cheeks and then carefully applied red lipstick called Cupid's Bow, giving her lips a dramatic bee-stung appearance.

"How does it look?" Lily asked.

She looked way overdone to Michele, especially with the bright spots of blush on her cheeks, but at least the smoky eyes and Cupid's Bow lips made her look significantly older. She gave Lily an approving nod.

Lily grabbed a roll of heavy tape from her vanity table, and Michele was astonished to see her tape her breasts with it, flattening her chest.

"Uh, doesn't that defeat the purpose?" Michele blurted out. "I thought you were trying to look older."

"Where have you been, darling?" Lily asked patronizingly. "Don't you know that big breasts are not in fashion? The flatter, the better!"

Michele had to laugh. Her generation would be horrified by this sentiment—but glancing down at her own less-than-huge chest, Michele knew she would have been a hit in the 1920s.

Lily hurried into her dressing room, and when she returned,

she was wearing a gorgeous sequined flapper dress. Michele's breath caught in her throat. *Mom would have loved this,* she thought. It was a sleeveless silver dress, knee-length with a dropped waist and a gathered skirt. Her wavy bob was tucked into a cloche.

"Gorgeous," Michele declared.

"Why, thank you!" Lily grabbed a black feather boa off her dresser and wrapped it around her shoulders. *And now you just overdid it,* Michele thought, but Lily looked so pleased with herself that Michele didn't have the heart to tell her to ditch the boa.

"All right, I'm going to ring the housekeeper now and tell her of the plan so she can be the one to tell my parents. If they see me dolled up like this, the jig'll be up!"

There was of course no intercom yet installed in the room, so Lily called her housekeeper on an old-fashioned cradle telephone. After explaining that she was going for a sleepover at Sally's, Lily quickly packed an overnight bag and threw on a pair of pointy-toed low heels and a boldly patterned long coat. "Let's go!"

Michele and Lily hurried into the elevator and left the mansion through the back garden, then walked the two blocks to the Plaza Hotel. Michele followed Lily into the beautiful Beaux Arts building, and once inside the Fifth Avenue lobby, with its soaring ceiling and mosaic floor, she was thrilled to be able to see the Plaza in all its 1920s glory. The pomp and grandeur of the hotel served as the perfect backdrop for the Gatsby-esque characters who flitted in and out.

Reaching the front of the reception line, Lily registered for a room under the alias of Contessa Crawford. "Could you pick *anything* less subtle?" Michele asked, rolling her eyes. Lily didn't bother responding, clearly proud of her new name. As Lily instructed the receptionist to call her a taxicab, Michele wandered around the lobby. She watched as glamorous women in extravagantly festooned mink coats sank their heels into the thick Persian carpets while the men, wearing top hats and holding elegant walking sticks, sat in the antique French chairs and settees. The chandeliers cast a dazzling glow over the swanky figures inhabiting the room.

Michele felt a hand grab hers, and she turned to see Lily smiling excitedly. "The cab is here. This is really happening!"

Michele and Lily went outside to the Plaza's front entrance, where a compact yellow Ford taxi was just pulling up. The driver stood beside his car, wearing a formal uniform with brass buttons and shiny boots. He chivalrously opened the car door for Lily and fluffed the leather backseat with a wooden paddle.

Well, this sure is different from the modern-day New York cab experience, Michele thought with a chuckle, climbing in unseen after Lily.

As they made their way uptown in the old-fashioned car, Michele pressed her face to the window. She watched in fascination as the Upper East Side's homes, shops, hotels, and restaurants faded, giving way to the many churches, brownstone apartment buildings, and juke joints of Harlem. Before long the cab was surrounded by the sounds of jazz and nightlife as they pulled up to the plantation-style building known as the Cotton

Club. Lily paid the driver and instructed him to pick her up in three hours. Then she grabbed Michele's hand and the girls jumped out of the car, the brilliant whirl of a piano and the strangely familiar blare of a jazz trumpet summoning them from inside. As they reached the line outside the door, Michele felt a jolt of nerves: everyone looked and seemed so much older than she and Lily were. How were they supposed to get in?

"Lily, I don't know about this—"

"We can leave right after the contest," Lily assured her. "We've come this far; we can't give up now!"

When they reached the front of the line, the doorman stared at Lily suspiciously, as if seeing through the layers of makeup. "What are you doing here all alone? You aren't old enough. Get out of here."

"No," Lily insisted desperately. "I promise I am old enough." But her voice sounded so childish as she said this Michele cringed.

"Identification, please," the doorman ordered.

"Oh no, I left it at home!" Lily cried, a little too frantically. The doorman gestured to a nearby police officer, and Michele and Lily looked at each other in horror. It was all over. Lily wasn't going to sing at the Cotton Club, she would be escorted home by the police, and it was all Michele's fault—

"The girl is with me."

Lily jumped as a firm hand gripped her shoulder. She turned around and looked into the eyes of a stocky cigar-smoking stranger. He was handsome in a rugged way, unshaven with sleepy dark eyes, and wearing a three-piece wool suit with a homburg hat. He gave Lily a quick, reassuring grin.

"Oh, sir, I didn't realize—all right, then. Sorry for the trouble, miss." Astonished, Lily and Michele looked at the doorman as his tone immediately transformed from gruff to friendly.

Without a word, their rescuer ushered Lily inside, and Michele followed. The world of the Cotton Club engulfed them in its haze of smoke, jazz horns, husky voices, and dancing feet. Despite Prohibition, the alcohol was practically overflowing out of glasses. Michele was surprised to see that while nearly all the performers onstage were African American, the audience was made up only of Caucasians. Michele realized that while Americans might have evolved since 1910 to appreciate the gift of black music, African Americans were still unfortunately treated like second-class citizens in the 1920s, unable to patronize the very establishments they performed at.

The man led them to a booth close to the band, and when Michele looked up, she nearly fell over in shock at the sight of a young Louis Armstrong, the twentieth century's foremost jazz trumpeter, playing with the band. So *that* was why it had sounded so familiar!

"I can't believe I'm seeing Louis Armstrong live!" Michele said to Lily, marveling. But Lily didn't seem too starstruck. Michele wondered if she was happening upon the beginning of his career.

"Look how close we are to Fletcher Henderson!" Lily exclaimed, gesturing to the pianist, who was playing with a furious zeal.

"So what's your name, doll?" the man asked, pulling out a fresh cigar from his pocket.

"Li—Contessa Crawford," Lily answered, her cheeks flushing. "Pleased to meet you. And you are . . . ?"

"I'm Thomas Wolfe. I produce the shows here." At that, Thomas looked over at Fletcher, who gave him a friendly nod. Lily was wide-eyed.

"Why did you help me?" she blurted out.

"Well, I couldn't help feeling sorry for you. I reckon you are too young to be here, but I couldn't stand to see a pretty dame like you turned away," he replied, flashing her a toothy grin. Lily practically swooned, but something about his smile rubbed Michele the wrong way.

"Sleazeball," she whispered to Lily.

After another couple of songs by the Fletcher Henderson Orchestra, the Cotton Club emcee announced the start of the singing contest. Michele and Lily watched attentively as all sorts of singers hit the stage, performing everything from gospel songs to the Broadway hits of the day. A beautiful, husky-voiced woman who reminded Michele of Billie Holiday sang a soulful ballad that brought half the house to tears, while a young man in a pin-striped suit and spats wowed the crowd with his acrobatic dancing in the middle of his song.

Lily was the second-to-last performer, and Michele saw a trace of hesitation cross her face as she took to the stage. But a second later it was gone, and she was singing and dancing her heart out, performing Gershwin's "Fascinatin' Rhythm" with amazing flair. Michele's mouth hung open in awe as she watched. She had always known that Lily had an incredible voice, but it was stunning to hear a sixteen-year-old belt out a song with the bluesy soul of Ella Fitzgerald, scatting and hitting impossibly high notes, while also managing to dance like Ginger Rogers. She had overpowering star quality.

When she hit the final note, the audience jumped to their feet, cheering and whistling. Lily skipped back to their booth, her face flushed with exhilaration.

"Whoa!" Michele cried. "You couldn't have been any better. Congratulations!"

Lily smiled broadly at Michele and then turned to Thomas, who was lavishing compliments on her. "Marvelous, simply marvelous! How did you manage to sing like an angel while dancing like that?"

Lily giggled. "Oh, practice, you see."

After one last song, by a so-so performer who had the misfortune of following Lily, the emcee announced that the judges would be deliberating on their choice, and he would declare the winner of the contest within the hour. Lily was a basket case as they waited, practically jumping out of her skin, while the orchestra did its best to hold the patrons' attention.

At last, the emcee returned to the stage, and silence fell over the whole club, awaiting the results.

"And the winner of a weekly singing gig at the Cotton Club is . . . Contessa Crawford!"

The audience roared their approval, and Lily jumped to her feet ecstatically. She was soon swallowed by a crowd of new fans, as well as the contest judges and members of Fletcher Henderson's orchestra. Michele watched in amazement as Lily shook hands with Louis Armstrong. *That's my great-grandma!*

Lily hurried back to the table, her eyes still dancing. "We have to go! It's been over three hours. Our cab will be waiting."

Once they were settled back in the Model T, Michele couldn't help asking, "Do you think your parents will let you play the gigs? I mean, the Cotton Club *is* a speakeasy."

"Goodness, no." Lily laughed. "A young heiress traveling to Harlem to sing jazz? That's unthinkable in my folks' society. So they just won't have to know. I'll be a proper, good society Windsor girl by day, then jazz vamp Contessa Crawford by night."

Michele shook her head, laughing. It seemed impossible that this free-spirited, independent-thinking girl could have given birth to someone as stuffy and rigid as Walter. And suddenly, she remembered one of her mother's rare comments about her family: *"Grandmother told me that my father changed when he fell in love with my mom. Of course, he had always been much more reserved than Lily, which I suppose was his natural way of asserting his independence, being the only child of a larger-than-life personality. But my mother came from a very strict, snobbish New England family, and she had an overpowering personality herself, in a different way. Dad just fell in line with Mom's thinking and beliefs. So while my grandmother found high society a bore, my parents let it rule their lives. Sometimes I think that if it hadn't been for Mom, Henry Irving might have been accepted as my fiancé."*

Michele looked at Lily, feeling a wave of sadness that her great-grandmother's spirit and spunk hadn't rubbed off on her only child.

15

Back at the Plaza that night, the girls settled into their decadent fourteenth-floor room, paid for with Lily's emergency "dough." Their guest room had two marble fireplaces, ornate chandeliers, and a Fifth Avenue view overlooking Grand Army Plaza, which was a circular courtyard in front of the hotel featuring an equestrian statue of the Civil War's General Sherman. As Michele looked around, she told herself that the next time she time traveled, she seriously *had* to remember to bring her digital camera. She was vaguely aware that she needed to get home, that she was long past her curfew—but the carefree exuberance of Lily, and Jazz Age New York, was beginning to rub off on her. Michele found herself too keyed up to pay attention to the time.

Lily ordered room service, and the two girls celebrated over chicken and ham pie, petit fours, and sparkling cider.

"Tonight we really hit on all sixes," Lily sighed happily. "I can't thank you enough."

"I have to say, I feel pretty darn pleased with myself too." Michele grinned.

"Now, I seem to recall making you a deal," Lily said grandly. "How about you sing your songs for me now?"

Michele froze. She'd been full of confidence about her plan before, but she felt completely ridiculous singing for Lily now, after having just seen her bring the house down. And what if she hated the songs? "I don't know—I'm a terrible singer—"

"Well, that's why you write instead," Lily said matter-of-factly. "Now, let me hear. I'm awfully curious to hear the type of music a spirit would bring me."

"Okay. Here goes." Michele turned to face the door so she wouldn't have to look at Lily while she sang. She decided to start with "Bring the Colors Back."

> *"Why, when you're gone*
> *The world's gray on my own*
> *You bring the colors back . . ."*

she began.

When she finished, she nervously turned to see Lily smiling at her incredulously.

"Well, you were right about your singing—but the song is

rather swell!" Lily exclaimed. "It's just the type I like to sing. I'd like to give it a jazzier blues flavor, though. Like this.

"Why, I feel numb,
I'm a sky without a sun
Just take away the lack
And bring the colors back."

Lily sang beautifully. "That does sound better! That sounds awesome!" Michele cried.

"Awesome?" Lily furrowed her brow in confusion.

"I mean, um, swell! It sounds swell," Michele said with a laugh.

"Did you write it about a chap?" Lily asked curiously. "Is he handsome?"

Michele nodded, swallowing hard. "Yes. Very."

"I've never had those feelings about any person," Lily confessed. "But that's how I feel about music and performing. That's where I find the . . . the colors in my world." She smiled wryly. Michele smiled back, thrilled that Lily had identified with her lyrics.

"Let me hear the other one." Lily looked at her expectantly.

"Okay. Try to imagine this one with a ragtime feel." Michele sang "Chasing Time," a little more sure of herself now, so she didn't feel the need to sing with her back to Lily.

"Why, that's aces!" Lily said excitedly. "The lyrics are quite intriguing, and just right for a vamp like me. Ragtime's gotten passé, but there is a new similar style that's gaining favor, that would suit this song. It's called big band. Have you heard of it?"

"Yeah, I love it!" Michele said enthusiastically. "So . . . what do you say? Will you perform the songs?"

"I will," Lily agreed. "And I must say, you are a rather good songwriter."

Michele's cheeks warmed with pride. *If only Mom could hear the great Lily Windsor praising me!*

"I only did the lyrics," she said modestly. "My cowriter composed the music."

"Well, the lyrics are quite special," Lily said. "Now, enjoy this, as it might not happen again. I don't praise others very often, you see."

"Thanks!" Michele beamed. "Thank you so much."

Michele awoke the next morning in an unfamiliar, yet deliciously cozy, double bed. She glanced at the tall grandfather clock across the room and sat up with a start. It was ten o'clock. *Oh, my God. I fell asleep here. I'm going to be so dead when I get back to my time.* She did her best to push the thought away, focusing on Lily instead. She had to get Lily back home before her parents got suspicious and uncovered the truth. She hurried out of bed and gently shook Lily awake. "Lily, we have to go."

Lily jumped out of bed and quickly scrubbed off the makeup she had been too tired to take off the night before. She changed into a conservative sweater-skirt combo and a wide-brim hat that covered half her face. Once Michele had assured her that she was perfectly presentable for her parents, the girls hurried down to the hotel lobby to check out.

When they returned to the Windsor Mansion, a tall, formally dressed butler greeted them at the door. "Good morning, Lily. You're home just in time for brunch."

"I've got to go," Michele murmured apologetically to Lily.

"Oh, not just yet," Lily insisted when they were out of the butler's earshot. "Stay at least till after brunch."

"Well . . . okay." Michele followed her into the dining room, figuring that an hour probably wouldn't make much difference at that point.

"Hello, Mother, Father," Lily called out, going around to their chairs to give them each a kiss on the cheek before settling into her seat across from them. Michele slipped into the empty chair next to her.

"Good morning, dear," Mr. Windsor answered, digging into his grapefruit while scanning the *New York Times* headlines. Even though it was a Saturday morning, he looked dressed for the office, in a short suit jacket, a double-breasted vest, and wide-leg trousers.

"How was the sleepover?" Mrs. Windsor asked in the melodic, old-fashioned tone of voice heard in black-and-white movies. She had auburn hair like Lily's, but she wore it in shoulder-length waves and parted on the side. She was dressed in a long wool sweater over an ankle-length pleated skirt, with a long knotted string of pearls dangling from her neck.

"Oh, it was good fun," Lily said breezily. "Who's in the papers today, Daddy? Any of our friends?"

"Unfortunately, yes. John Singer Sargent has died of heart failure," Mr. Windsor replied sadly.

"Oh no!" Lily cried. "That's so awful. And to think he so

recently painted my portrait—I had no idea it was the last time I'd ever see him. . . ."

Michele's jaw dropped. So the portrait of Lily Windsor hanging in her sitting room was by John Singer Sargent? He was one of the most famous American painters; Michele had seen his work in museums since she was a little girl. Michele wondered if Clara's portrait was also by Sargent.

"We'll be at the funeral, of course," Mrs. Windsor told Lily.

As the brunch conversation drifted on, Michele sat back and listened with fascination to the talk of current events of eighty-five years earlier. Lily fidgeted with boredom when the topic shifted to politics, but Michele listened attentively. She learned that the current president was Calvin Coolidge, who Mr. and Mrs. Windsor seemed to adore for his tax cuts, and the first woman governor in the United States had just been elected in Wyoming. Mr. Windsor spoke worriedly about Italy's new dictator, Benito Mussolini, and Michele shuddered at the name, recognizing him as one of the Axis villains of the upcoming World War II.

The conversation turned to books, and Mr. Windsor commented that Fitzgerald's new tome, *The Great Gatsby*, wasn't selling as well as his previous books. "Have you read it, girls?"

"I positively loathed it," Mrs. Windsor answered, just as Lily gushed, "It's simply swell!" Lily laughed, but Mrs. Windsor gave her an irritated look.

"Really, dear, I don't understand how you could enjoy a trashy novel like that, all about silly flappers making a mockery of society. I trust you don't behave that way when we're not around?"

"No, Mother," Lily said in a grudging tone that let Michele know they'd had many variations of this conversation before.

"That's what I like to hear, that my daughter is a proper young lady. Speaking of which, the Vanderbilts and Whitneys are hosting an art gala next month and they've invited you to sing! Your father and I were thinking you could do Madame Butterfly's aria."

Lily's face fell. "No, Mother, I don't sing classical. You know that! Please, let me sing what I'm good at—"

"Those Harlem songs?" Mr. Windsor broke in. "Absolutely not, Lily. You know that would be highly inappropriate."

"It's only jazz. There's nothing wrong with it," Lily argued. "Just think, this would be the perfect opportunity for your society to see what a talent I am—"

"It is out of the question," Mrs. Windsor said firmly. "You'll perform an art song or nothing at all. Now, let's change the subject."

Lily gave Michele a despairing look. *What is it with these people?* Michele wondered. First Philip was denied the music he loved, and now Lily?

After brunch, Michele gestured for Lily to follow her outside. Once they were on the front steps and out of earshot of Lily's parents and staff, Michele said, "I really do have to go now, but I'll be back soon."

"Do you promise?" Lily's eyes were suddenly anxious. "And don't forget, you need to bring me the sheet music for the songs."

"I know. I'll bring them with me next time. I'll see you soon." Michele gave Lily a hug and waited for her to run inside, then clutched her key necklace. *Time, I'm ready for you to send me back now.*

Suddenly, the front gate swung open and an older gentleman entered the garden. Michele froze in her tracks.

He wore a business suit and leaned on a silver-topped cane, a briefcase hanging from his other arm. His gray hair was parted in the middle, and the dark eyes beneath his wiry spectacles looked oddly familiar to Michele. Then she realized who he was.

"Irving Henry," she breathed. He looked like an aged version of the photo she had seen in the old Windsor album.

To her astonishment, Irving looked up. "Yes, miss?"

Michele covered her mouth with her hand. "Oh, my God," she whispered. "You can see me?"

Irving's fair skin seemed to turn a whole shade paler. He came closer, and as he peered at Michele, his eyes focused on the key around her neck. His body began to shake, his cane barely able to hold him upright.

"Are you okay?" Michele hurried forward to steady him, but as her hand grasped his arm, she felt a force push her back, and the familiar spinning of Time enveloped her. She looked at Irving Henry as she whirled away from him, and saw that he was staring at her, his mouth open in shock, and his eyes inexplicably brimming with tears.

"So you've decided to come home now?"

Michele looked up to find that she was back in 2010, nearly colliding with Annaleigh on the front steps.

"Oh," she replied, catching her breath. She was so consumed with thoughts of Irving Henry that for a moment she could barely speak. "Um, I've—I was at Caissie's. Didn't I tell you I was going?"

"No, *you* didn't," Annaleigh said humorlessly. "But thankfully when I called the Harts, Caissie answered and told us you were there. Otherwise your grandparents would have called the police. Why do you insist on going out without telling us, and leaving your cell phone at home? Come in. Your grandparents want a word."

"I'm really sorry," Michele said, reluctantly following Annaleigh inside. Her grandparents were seated in the Grand Hall and they both looked up sharply at the sound of Annaleigh's and Michele's footsteps.

"She's home," Annaleigh announced.

"Thank you, Annaleigh. That will be all," Dorothy said, dismissing her. She fixed Michele with a plaintive look, and Michele instantly felt a wave of shame for worrying them, especially after Dorothy had been kind to her the other night. Once Annaleigh had left, Walter laid into Michele.

"Young lady, what will it *take* for you to learn the rules here? It's very simple: you *have* to let us know when you are leaving the house. There should be no need for poor Annaleigh to have to call and track you down. And for heaven's sake, take your phone with you! One more occasion like this, and you'll be grounded for a full month."

"I'm sorry," she mumbled. "It won't happen again." *It better not,* she thought. She didn't know what she would do if she had to be stuck in 2010 for a full month!

As soon as she was in her room, she grabbed her cell and called Caissie.

"Thank you, *thank you* for covering for me," she said as soon as Caissie picked up. "You won't believe where I was!"

Caissie listened with rapt attention as Michele told her all about her adventure with Lily. The only part of the story Michele left out was her meeting Irving Henry. She didn't feel ready to talk about it yet. She was beginning to have an idea of who Irving Henry might be, and the thought was too incredible, too unthinkable, to share with anyone just yet.

When Michele had finished filling her in, Caissie said with an amazed laugh, "Wow. Only you could manage to find true love *and* launch a songwriting career in the past."

"Well, it's not for me. I mean, it's not like I can claim the songs as my own here in our time," Michele reminded her. "It's the only way I can think of to help Philip."

"It really is a great idea," Caissie said. "So shouldn't you be going back with the sheet music now?"

"Believe me, I want to, but I'm afraid to leave again so soon and risk getting into even more trouble with my grandparents. The last thing I can afford right now is to get grounded. I'll go tomorrow right after school," Michele decided. "Will you be my alibi again? I think I'll tell my grandparents we're working on some major, time-intensive project, to explain why I'm gone for these chunks of time."

"Yeah, good plan," Caissie agreed. "Good luck!"

Between classes the next day, as Michele was exchanging books at her locker, she heard a familiar voice behind her. "Hey there."

She turned to flash Ben Archer a quick grin. "Hey, what's up?"

"Need any help with those?" He nodded at her books.

"Nah, I'm good. Thanks, though." She shut her locker and fell into step beside Ben as they walked to their science class. Just as she was beginning to wonder what he wanted, she heard him clear his throat nervously.

"So, um . . . this Autumn Ball thing . . . ," he began.

Michele felt her face freeze. Oh no. Was he going to ask her on a date? How could she stomach going on a date with another guy when she was still so preoccupied with Philip? But how could she say no? She liked him as a friend. She didn't want to hurt his feelings—

"I was thinking, you know, since you're new and all, you might not have anyone to go with," he continued, then reddened as he seemed to realize how that must have sounded. "I mean, not that you *shouldn't* have other offers—"

Oh, boy. She'd almost forgotten about the lack of game possessed by most guys her age in 2010. Philip, with all his eloquence and elegance, had officially spoiled her. Though this conversation was starting to depress her, Michele forced a laugh, wanting to put Ben at ease. "It's okay. I know what you meant."

"Cool. Well, anyway, want to go with me? To the dance?"

Michele studied the floor, wondering how to respond. *You're technically not with Philip anymore,* Michele reminded herself, the thought causing her heart to constrict painfully. *You can't stay away from other guys the rest of your life.* But it was tempting.

"Um, yeah," Michele finally answered, giving him a smile. "Thanks, Ben. The only thing is, uh, I'm in a sort of complicated . . . long-distance situation with someone. But I'd love to go with you as friends, if that's cool."

Ben's face fell for a moment, but he quickly recovered. "No worries. Going as friends is totally cool," he said smoothly.

"Awesome." Michele looked up to see that they'd reached their classroom. "Well, talk to you later, then. And . . . it should be fun."

"For real." Ben grinned. "See you later."

As soon as she reached the Windsor Mansion and alerted Annaleigh that she'd be working on a school assignment at Caissie's, Michele gathered the sheet music Philip had written and tucked it carefully into her shoulder bag. She picked up Lily's composition book to go back to 1925, but a loose paper fell out of the book—a program from one of her Cotton Club gigs. As Michele bent down to retrieve it, she was sent flying backward. . . .

She returned to the Cotton Club to find that two weeks had passed since Lily had won the contest. Michele spotted her ensconced in the smoky scene, cozied up in a booth with the producer, Thomas. When Lily spotted Michele, she beamed and jumped up. "I'll be right back," she told Thomas, and turned quickly toward the women's restroom. Michele followed her, and once Lily had checked that no one else was in the bathroom, she let out a little squeal.

"Spirit girl! You're back!" She teetered in her heels. "I was wondering when you'd return."

"Are you drunk?" Michele asked, noticing Lily's glazed expression.

"I've only had a little giggle water today," Lily replied with a sly smile.

"Why was that Thomas guy practically feeling you up? He's so old. Have you not noticed the receding hairline?" Michele made a face.

"Don't be such a bluenose," Lily snapped, but Michele could tell she had hit a nerve. "I have to go warm up backstage. My show is about to start."

"Okay. Good luck," Michele called out as Lily flounced off.

Michele wandered back into the audience. The Fletcher Henderson Orchestra was playing again, and that night Louis Armstrong was singing as well as playing the trumpet. Michele swayed dreamily as she listened to his signature gravelly voice. This was too incredible!

On all sides of her were couples dancing 1920s dances, from the Charleston to the turkey trot, their legs and arms flying. The women were loud and boisterous, wearing dresses with plunging necklines and puffing on cigarettes, a stunning contrast to the proper, buttoned-up ladies Michele had encountered in 1910. Most of the men were dapper in their pin-striped suits and top hats, but Michele noticed a handful of menacing-looking characters. She wondered if they were mobsters or bootleggers—or both?

Suddenly, amid the buzz of conversation, Michele heard a familiar name: "Mr. and Mrs. Windsor just arrived, did you hear?" "Came to see the new singer everyone's been raving about, our own Contessa!"

Michele froze. They couldn't be talking about Lily's parents—could they? Michele followed the craned necks and whispers to the Cotton Club's entrance. And sure enough, there they were, striding in—and looking furious. They had obviously found out about Lily. Harried-looking footmen flanked the couple, shielding the Windsors from the club-goers pressing in on all sides.

Michele raced through the club, anxiously looking for the entrance to the backstage area. Once she found it, she spotted Lily waiting in the wings.

"Bad news," Michele said immediately. "Your parents are here. It looks like they know."

The color drained from Lily's face. "Oh, my God. We have to get out of here! Help me out of this dress, please!" She started urgently pulling at her costume.

Michele began to help with her buttons, but then stopped suddenly.

"No," she said, realizing something. "You have to go on."

"*What?* Are you off your nuts?" Lily demanded.

"Your only choice is to do the best singing and performing of your life tonight. The truth is out whether you do the gig or not, but this way, your parents can see with their own eyes how good you are," Michele insisted. "And who knows . . . maybe they'll be impressed enough to let you continue."

"Do you really think that's likely?" Lily asked skeptically.

"It's your best shot," Michele said encouragingly. "You can't back out now."

Lily sat down nervously. "I don't know if I can do this. . . ."

Michele grabbed her hand and pulled her back up. "Yes, you can! You have nothing to worry about. Come on. I have a feeling about this."

Lily took a deep, shaky breath. "All right. . . . Wish me luck."

As Michele watched from the wings, Lily stepped onstage and began her first song, a cover of Fanny Brice's "My Man."

"It cost me a lot, but there's one thing that I've got, it's my man . . ."

The audience was instantly riveted, engrossed in this tale of soul-crushing love, as Lily's mature, bluesy voice made them forget that they were watching someone too young to have lived through it. But one couple was far from entertained—Lily's parents, Mr. and Mrs. Windsor, who were sitting stiffly at a front table, their faces lined with fury. Lily swallowed hard and continued, throwing herself into the performance.

"Two or three girls has he that he likes as well as me, but I love him . . ."

Lily ended the song to a standing ovation. But in the midst of the excitement, as Lily curtsied and the audience cheered, Lily's father jostled his way through the crowd, his wife right behind him, until they were in front of the stage.

"Daddy," Lily gasped, her face pale.

Without a word, Mr. Windsor marched forward and plucked his daughter off the stage. The applause and cheers died as a shocked murmur rippled through the audience.

"Hey!" the club owner, Gene, roared. He ran over to Lily and Mr. Windsor, Thomas right behind him. "What do you think you're doing with my singer?"

"Oh, crap," Michele groaned, hurrying to join Lily. This was hardly the reaction she'd been hoping for when she'd urged Lily to go onstage.

By the time Michele reached the main floor of the club, the crowd had gathered in a circle around Lily, her parents, Gene, and Thomas, watching with equal parts glee and horror as "Contessa Crawford" was outed as sixteen-year-old heiress Lily Windsor.

"Sixteen?" Thomas gasped, turning red. "You told me twenty-two!"

Gene's face was a mask of fury. "Are you trying to shut me down, little girl? You know I could lose the club if they found out I was hiring underage performers!"

As Lily looked pleadingly from one angry face to the next, Michele saw her as a completely different person from the confident, defiant flapper she had been before. Now Lily just seemed like a scared, defeated teenager.

"I—I suppose I wasn't thinking," Lily answered in a small voice. "I just wanted so much to be a singer, to make it and be heard—"

"Well, now that's the end of that," Lily's father told her firmly. He turned his attention to Gene. "I cannot apologize enough for my daughter's despicable actions. I'll have my accountant ring you to settle a financial sum for any inconvenience caused by her behavior and the termination of her contract."

Gene's expression brightened considerably at the words "financial sum," but Lily was now in tears. "Termination of my contract?" she repeated, her voice choked.

"There's also the matter of Lily's audition with Florenz Ziegfeld," Thomas said, avoiding looking at Lily. "Am I to understand that is being canceled?"

"Florenz Ziegfeld?" Lily's mother echoed. Michele could have sworn she saw a look of pride briefly cross her face. "Of the Ziegfeld Follies?"

"That's the one," Thomas answered grimly. "He'll be none too happy with me when I tell him that the girl I was raving about won't be showing."

"Oh, Father, please!" Lily flung herself at Mr. Windsor. "Please don't make me cancel."

Mr. Windsor hesitated for a split second, then scowled and shook his head. "I think you've had enough show business. We're out of here."

Back home in Lily's bedroom, Lily was a wreck. "What am I going to do?" she wailed, flinging herself onto the bed. "I've lost it all!"

Michele didn't want to admit it, but she felt just as hopeless as Lily. So much for her plan to rescue Philip through the release of their songs. And then she felt a cold wash of fear come over her as she thought, *What if I changed history and stopped Lily's career from happening? What if she was never supposed to get involved in the Cotton Club, and by helping her I ruined her chances?*

"I'm so sorry, Lily," Michele whispered. "I was only trying to help. . . ."

"It's not your fault," Lily replied, wiping her mascara-smudged eyes.

"Can I—can I ask you something? Why do you want this so bad? Is it just that you want to be a big star?" Michele asked.

"No!" Lily sat up, momentarily distracted from her crisis. "Of course it's not just that. It's about the way I *feel* when I perform, like I've come alive. Like that song of yours—well, music is what gives *my* world color. Everything's so gray without it, I'm just bored and muddling through. But then, when I get onstage . . . magic happens," Lily explained, a faraway look in her eyes. "And then, the music of jazz and blues, I love how it's like a *bridge* between people and races and nationalities; it brings everyone together. I love that the most."

Just like Philip, Michele thought. She felt a fresh surge of admiration for both him and Lily. That they both inhabited worlds rife with prejudice and racism yet had no understanding of or tolerance for it showed Michele how special they were.

Michele smiled at Lily. "I know just what you mean. And I

think if you explain it the way you just put it to me, your parents will find it in them to understand. Maybe they just need you to promise that the show biz will stay onstage, know what I mean?" She thought for a moment. "They see you performing in a speakeasy, and I guess it makes sense that they'd freak out, more because of what goes on in those places than the music you're singing. So show them that they don't have to worry about you becoming an alcoholic or a 'fallen woman' or whatever it is they're afraid of. Show them that you want to do good things with your talent." She suddenly remembered Lily's composition book. "Show them, write a song conveying everything you just told me."

"But you're the songwriter, not me," Lily said, frowning.

"You can do it too," Michele said encouragingly. "Just sit down and try writing something like those jazz songs you like so much, and you'll see that you're a songwriter. Trust me, I know."

Lily impulsively threw her arms around Michele. "I don't know how I can thank you for everything you've done for me. Especially when I was such a brat most of the time."

Michele grinned. "Well, it's been exciting for me too. Most of the time, at least!"

"If I do succeed in convincing my parents to let me continue, I promise to perform your songs too," Lily said. "I know it means a great deal to you and it's the least I can do. And they are very good songs, besides."

"Thank you. And that reminds me!" Michele pulled the sheet music out of her bag and handed it to Lily.

"'Music by PW and lyrics by MW,'" Lily read. "What the dilly? No real names? And who is PW?"

"No one you know," Michele replied breezily. "And that's just how we prefer to be credited. Nice and . . . simple."

"All right," Lily said dubiously. "If that's how you want it."

Michele pulled Lily into another hug, suddenly feeling emotional. "Good luck, Lily. I'll be pulling for you."

"Thank you. I'll do my best, spirit." Lily smiled at Michele.

In 2010 the next day, Annaleigh was full of excitement when Michele returned home from school.

"Your grandparents are taking you out tonight!" she exclaimed with the enthusiasm of someone who'd just won a huge shopping spree. "Isn't that wonderful? It will be so great for the three of you to have a fun night out together."

"Where are we going?" Michele asked. She was pleased that her grandparents wanted to do something nice for her, but she had to admit she was a little nervous about spending a whole evening with them.

"I booked the three of you tickets for *Mary Poppins* on Broadway, and then dinner at Chez Josephine."

"Mary Poppins?" Michele giggled. "Isn't that a kids' show?"

"A family show," Annaleigh said, correcting her, but she looked a little worried. "I hope I didn't make the wrong decision. Your grandparents asked me to choose the show, after all. I thought a musical was the best bet, but so many of them are just so modern, with rock music and all, and I knew Mr. and

Mrs. Windsor wouldn't appreciate that. So when the ticket operator said *Mary Poppins,* I thought, 'Well, that sounds like the right show'—"

"It sounds great." Michele interrupted her with a smile. "Don't worry. I'm sure we'll love it."

Since it was her first Broadway show, Michele decided to dress up a little. She wore a knee-length black dress with heels, adding Marion's Van Cleef butterfly necklace as the finishing touch. When she met her grandparents downstairs that evening, she saw that they had dressed up too, Dorothy in a navy blue chiffon dress and Walter in a crisp suit and tie.

"Michele, you look beautiful!" Dorothy exclaimed when she appeared on the staircase. Dorothy's eyes warmed as she took in Marion's butterfly necklace.

"Thanks." Michele smiled. "And thank you for planning this."

"Oh, Annaleigh deserves the credit for doing the planning. But we wanted to show you a good time in the city tonight. We know you've been going through a tough time," Dorothy said.

"And . . . well . . . we're sorry we haven't been better companions," Walter finished with an awkward smile. "It's hard for us—but we want to try."

Michele looked at them, touched. She was especially surprised by Walter's softening, and she wondered if Dorothy had filled him in on her emotional meltdown after the Newport trip. "I really appreciate all this. And I'm sorry too, about the other night. I should have respected your rules more. I will from now on."

"Good," Dorothy said warmly. "Now, we'd better hurry if we want to make curtain."

Fritz drove them across Midtown to Forty-second Street in the heart of Times Square, the boisterous, bright "thoroughfare of the world." The SUV passed dozens of Broadway theaters, their marquees big and bold enough to be seen from miles away, as well as New York City landmarks such as the MTV studios and Hard Rock Cafe. Fritz pulled up to the New Amsterdam Theater, which had a gigantic *Mary Poppins* poster emblazoned over the theater's exterior walls.

As they entered the lobby, Michele gasped in amazement. The New Amsterdam Theater, disguised amid the kitsch of Times Square, was a veritable palace inside. It was an Art Nouveau dream, painted and designed in lustrous shades of mauve, green, and gold. The lobby was decorated with Shakespearean wall reliefs and ornate carvings, and framed black-and-white posters of old-fashioned showgirls and actresses lined the walls. After they'd handed over their tickets, Walter led Michele toward one of the posters near the staircase leading to the mezzanine level.

"There's my mother!" he said proudly.

With a gasp of excitement, Michele gazed at the poster. There was the ambitious teenage Lily, perched on a stool in front of an antique French tapestry, wearing a lacy dress and her dancing shoes. Her head was turned to the side to face the camera, and her eyes had a knowing look, as if to say, *Of course I'm here. Where else would I be?*

"So she did it!" Michele blurted out, nearly limp with relief at the knowledge that her rewriting of history hadn't ruined Lily's career after all. "She really made it!"

Her grandparents looked at her quizzically, no doubt wondering why that was suddenly such a surprise to her.

"I just realized I've never asked you," Michele said, turning to Walter, "why you and Lily kept her maiden name. I mean, what about . . . your dad?"

"I never knew him," Walter said, his eyes focused on Lily's photo. "My mother was very . . . modern. She didn't believe that a star like herself should have to take a man's name." He gave Michele a knowing look. "And she also fully believed in divorcing a philandering husband."

"Oh. Wow." Michele stared at her grandfather. "I didn't know." And suddenly, a piece of the puzzle fell into place. Walter had grown up fatherless, just like Michele. He'd watched Lily experience betrayal by the man she trusted. It was no wonder he had been so strict with his own daughter, so suspicious of Henry Irving and his motives. *It wasn't just about his lack of money and social standing,* Michele realized. He had been genuinely worried about Marion. And in that moment, Michele felt sure that whatever Walter and Dorothy might still be hiding, they hadn't paid Henry to leave.

"I'm sorry," Michele told Walter.

"Don't be," he said with a half smile. "My mother always said that no man made her feel the way her music did. I have a feeling she didn't much miss my birth father—especially with all the beaus who kept calling, even when she was past middle age. She was very . . . unusual, my mother. But she was happy."

Michele grinned. "Unusual" sounded about right.

An usher led them to their seats, and as they waited for the show to begin, Michele's mind raced with the question of whether Lily had ended up performing the songs she and Philip had written. She didn't dare ask her grandparents, in case it was now information she should readily know, but she couldn't wait to get home and check online.

But to her surprise, once the curtain opened and the show began, Michele found her thoughts disappearing as she was transfixed by the story of the magical nanny. The catchy songs, incredible Broadway voices, and awe-inspiring special effects and stage design had her captivated. As she glanced at her grandparents, she was glad to see that they looked the same. The show reminded her of watching the movie with her mom when she was little, and she remembered that *her* mom had watched the movie with her parents as a little girl too. There was something special about that, and on impulse Michele squeezed her grandmother's hand. Dorothy turned to smile at her.

As the finale song, "Anything Can Happen If You Let It," began, Michele thought that her travels through time had definitely proven the song's message. The stage turned dark as Mary Poppins and the Banks family were transported to the stars, and in that instant, something incredible happened. A dark, shadowy pall came over the theater, and then it was suddenly lifted, and Michele jumped out of her seat, crying out in amazement at what she saw.

Her grandparents were gone; all the *Mary Poppins* audience members had disappeared, replaced by women with bobbed hair and dropped-waist dresses and men with top hats and walking sticks. And on that grand stage above was the young Lily

Windsor, standing in an enormous spotlight and wearing a long, slinky white sleeveless dress, a fur stole draped around her shoulders. Her voice was hauntingly beautiful and brimming with soul as she sang.

"Why, I feel numb,
I'm a sky without a sun
Just take away the lack
And bring the colors back."

"Oh, my God!" Michele shrieked. She spun around to look at the audience, and to her amazement, they were singing along. They *knew* the song!

She ran up to the front row aisle, tears welling up in her eyes as she mouthed the words, and Lily caught her eye. She did a double take and then beamed at Michele, but didn't miss a beat in her singing. As soon as the song ended, Michele ran up the staircase leading to the stage and raced backstage, floating invisibly past leggy chorus girls, until she spotted Lily.

"Lily!" Michele cried.

"Follow me," Lily whispered, and Michele hurried alongside her into a dressing room with a gold star pinned on the door.

Once inside the dressing room, the girls squealed and hugged, jumping up and down.

"You did it, Lily! You convinced your parents; you made it into the Follies! It's all upward from here."

"You did it too. 'Bring the Colors Back' is a hit. The phonograph record is selling like hotcakes! And I'm introducing

'Chasing Time' in the new Follies beginning next month. Ziggy—that's what we call Ziegfeld—well, he loves both songs, thinks they're rather new and fresh," Lily said excitedly.

"Oh—my—God! Thank you!" *So this is what success feels like,* Michele thought as a warm glow spread throughout every inch of her.

"And that reminds me. A very handsome dapper Dan dropped by the stage door two weeks ago and asked me if I knew a Michele—someone no one could see but me."

Michele's heart nearly stopped. *Philip.*

"I was frightened by that, frightened that he knew our secret, so I asked what he meant. He said he wanted to see you," Lily continued. "I told him you weren't here, and then he handed over a package and said to give it to you—and then he just left! I kept it here in my dressing table, just in case. Would you like to see it?"

Michele could barely breathe. "Yes," she whispered.

Lily opened a drawer in her dressing table and pulled out a small package. As Lily handed it to her, Michele was too overcome to speak.

"Who is he?" Lily asked as Michele stared at the package without opening it.

"He's . . ." Michele swallowed hard. "He's the one I wrote the song about."

"I wondered that," Lily said with a smile. "Is he a . . . spirit, like you?"

Michele shook her head. Lily was surprised into silence, and she sat at her dressing table while Michele studied the package. Her heart pounding furiously, Michele opened the envelope and a letter fluttered to the ground. She picked it up and read it hungrily.

June 16, 1926

My dearest Michele,

How unbearably long it has been since you were last in my arms, since I last heard your sweet voice and kissed those perfect lips. Since you left, each day seemed to run meaninglessly into the next. That is how it's been for fifteen long years. I left home as planned, but the emptiness followed me to London, even while I played piano for the London Symphony Orchestra.

And then, two weeks ago, it all changed. I was at a dinner party held in honor of songwriters George and Ira Gershwin, who are at work here on a new show, when George sat at the piano, as he always does when there's a party. But the surprise was that he wasn't playing his own music—he was playing ours. Our very own "Bring the Colors Back"! You can imagine my shock and amazement, and the joy I felt at knowing that you had returned! You had to be back. I found out everything from the Gershwins, that your relation Lily Windsor had made the song a hit with the Follies, and I immediately gave notice to the London Symphony and booked passage to New York. I'm writing you now from the ship.

Is it possible that you might have reconsidered

*your stance, after all these years? I can't help hoping,
though I am afraid to. A part of me knows that if
you had, you would have come to me instead of Lily.
But regardless of whether I see you again, I hold as a
treasure your return and what you have done for our
song. It is the sign I've been aching for, the sign that
you still love me as I never stopped loving you.*

*I must confess that I did not pursue my
composing in London the way we would have
expected. You always believed in me, and now it is
time that I believe in me in the same way. The
public's reaction to "Bring the Colors Back" has given
me the desire to return to New York for good and try
to make it as a composer. Thank you—thank you for
returning to me the strong sense of purpose I once
felt, when you were in my life. Michele, I promise to
find you again—no matter what. And enclosed in
this package is a symbol of that promise: my family
ring. I've also enclosed the address of the hotel where I
am living now, the Waldorf-Astoria, in the hopes you
might be able to reach me.*

I love you.
Philip

Michele's eyes were streaming with tears by the time she
reached the end of Philip's letter. Every sentence seemed to twist
her heart in such a way that she felt both broken and whole.
She was vaguely aware of Lily's hurrying to her side and trying
to comfort her, but her mind was miles away, as she thought of

what could have been if only she and Philip had lived in the same lifetime. Why had Time made such a mistake with the two of them?

She remembered his mention of the ring, and she reached further into the envelope. Buried inside, wrapped in tissue paper, was a gold signet ring, carved with a raised ornamental *W.*

"Aces!" Lily exclaimed, her eyes as wide as saucers as she stared at the ring. "Are you *engaged*?"

"In my heart I am," Michele said with a smile. She gazed at the ring, feeling like her heart was so full it could burst at any moment. She slid the ring onto her finger, loving how it looked. But she knew what she must do.

"Lily, do you have any stationery here that I can use?"

"Of course." As Lily rifled through her things, Michele held Philip's letter close. If she closed her eyes and imagined hard enough, she could almost hear his voice whispering the words he had written. Michele was suddenly reminded of the Portuguese word her mom had taught her on their last day together: *sodade.* A feeling of nostalgia so intense there was no English translation. That was just how Michele felt now.

"Here you go." Lily handed her a pen, a pad of paper, and an envelope. "You can use my dressing table to write."

"Thanks, Lily." Michele sat down and began to write.

Dear Philip,
I love you just the way you love me. I'll even
admit that sometimes I wonder if I love you more.
No matter what happens in my future, you will
always be the one.

I can't thank you enough for the beautiful ring.
It means so much to me, and I love being able to
wear something every day that belonged to you.

I wish I could say that I had found a way for us
to be together, but I haven't. I still don't fully exist in
any time other than my own. But I came back to
show you all that you have left to live for. Please—
I need for you to move on, have a family, and of
course, keep composing. I couldn't stand the pain of
knowing I caused you a lonely life or stopped you
from reaching your full potential. But always
remember that I still feel the way I did during our
days and nights together in 1910. I'll always consider
you my true family. I hope you will too.

I love you forever.
Michele

Her eyes were blurry from tears by the time she finished the letter. She addressed the envelope PW, so as not to arouse any outrage from Lily over her corresponding with a Walker, and then turned to her great-grandmother. "Lily, can you do me a huge favor? Can you please have this delivered to the Waldorf-Astoria tomorrow morning?"

Lily nodded and took the letter. "PW—the composer of your songs," she said slowly, revelation dawning on her.

Michele nodded but didn't say more.

"You're—you're not just a spirit, are you?" Lily blurted out.

Michele looked at her and found that she couldn't lie anymore. "No, I'm not," she confessed. "The truth is . . . I'm from the future. From the year 2010. And . . . I'm your great-granddaughter."

Lily's jaw dropped, and she stared at Michele in astonishment. That was when Michele felt Time calling her back, as Lily and the dressing room became hazy, and the ground began to shake. But just before 1926 vanished, Michele caught a glimpse of Lily smiling in wonderment as she watched Michele—the girl who Lily now knew as her future great-granddaughter—fading back to her own time.

"Go and chase your dreams, you won't regret it. Anything can happen if you let it."

Michele landed jarringly in her seat beside her grandparents at the New Amsterdam in 2010 only to find that everyone was on their feet, clapping to the rhythm and cheering. *It's the curtain call,* Michele realized. *Was I only gone for one song? How is that possible?* She staggered into a standing position.

Dorothy gave her a relieved look. "There you are! Where did you go?"

"Oh . . . I had to go to the bathroom," Michele improvised. "I snuck out during the song."

As the curtain fell, Michele glanced down at her ring finger and sucked in her breath. There it was—the signet ring from Philip!

On the way home after dinner, Michele suggested to her grand-parents that they listen to one of Lily Windsor's records together before bed. "Seeing her poster up in the theater just made me want to hear her again."

"That's a great idea, Michele," Walter said, looking pleased. Once they reached Windsor Mansion, he led the way to the drawing room, where the vintage record player was kept. He rummaged through the stack of records until he chose *Lily Windsor at Carnegie Hall, May 1935*. After setting the dial on the record player, Walter plopped into his easy chair by the window, and Dorothy and Michele shared the couch.

The first song on the album was the one from Lily's

composition book, "Born for It." Michele closed her eyes and listened to the vintage sound of old-time jazz filling the room.

> *"Make them feel, make them fly*
> *Send their stories to the sky*
> *I'm singin' it*
> *Ooh, I was born for it*

> *"When that trumpet starts to play*
> *All the world's cares fade away*
> *I'm livin' it*
> *I was born for it."*

"This was actually the first song she ever wrote," Walter remarked. "She was just your age."

Michele smiled, overcome with emotion. "I thought so."

As the second song began, Michele froze; it sounded just like Philip's piano intro to their song "Chasing Time." Sure enough, Lily's bluesy voice began to sing the chorus.

> *"I can't live in the normal world,*
> *I'm just chasing time. . ."*

The orchestra joined in, and it was too much. This all went beyond Michele's wildest dreams. *Mom would never believe this—Lily Windsor singing one of* my *songs at Carnegie Hall!* she thought with an incredulous laugh.

"Michele! Why are you crying?" Dorothy asked in alarm.

"Oh, it's just . . . I love this song," she said, now half crying and half laughing. "Sorry, I'm a little . . . sensitive."

It seemed unfathomable that her travels back in time could have affected history so much—others' histories as well as her own—but they had. In fact, it was beginning to feel like all time periods were happening at once, in layers, like the layers of a cake. Below her were previous time periods, playing and replaying themselves, and above her was the future. And somehow, for some inexplicable reason, *she* had been chosen to live between the layers.

She wiped her eyes, listening alertly to the piano. "Who is that playing, do you know?"

"Of course. That's Phoenix Warren. This was quite a star-studded show," Walter said proudly.

"Phoenix Warren! You know my mom named me after his composition, 'Michele,' right?"

"No. No, we didn't know that," Walter said, looking down. Dorothy's face was pained.

"You miss her . . . like I do," Michele realized, after a beat.

"Of course we do," Walter said, his voice quietly intense.

"I'm sorry for—for always assuming . . ." Michele's voice trailed off. She was unsure how to phrase what she meant. But her grandparents seemed to understand.

"Thank you, dear," Dorothy said kindly.

Walter glanced at the mantel clock. "It's getting late. We'd better head up to bed. You have school in the morning."

Michele nodded. "Okay. Thanks again for tonight. I had a really great time."

Her grandparents smiled at her, and Michele was glad to see that their smiles reached their eyes.

That night brought a series of dreams, vignettes unfolding one after another. . . .

Michele was alone in a cold, silent graveyard. She didn't know how she had gotten there and she was desperate to get away, but she felt herself being pushed forward, toward something she didn't want to see. She moved, trancelike, until her shoe touched a hard surface. She jumped back and saw that she was standing before a simple white headstone. IRVING HENRY, it read. 1869–1944.

Suddenly, the scene changed, followed by far calmer dreams of turn-of-the-century cotillion dances, jazz clubs, and the sea in Newport. And then she saw Philip.

He was standing by the fire in an elegant hotel room—and he was reading her letter. Now in his thirties, Philip was even more handsome than before. He had grown taller and stronger; his face was more defined; his intense eyes were somehow even deeper and bluer than before. He reminded Michele of those movie stars from the golden age of Hollywood—Clark Gable and Errol Flynn.

"I'll do what you ask, Michele," he said to himself. "I will move on, for you. But no matter what, I will find a way back to you. I promise."

Michele woke with a lump in her throat. She had never longed to reach out and touch Philip, hold him, more than she did now. She was tempted to take back her words, to try to go back to him for just one more night. But she knew that she couldn't. Before meeting Philip, Michele had never really understood when people talked of being so in love that they would put the other person ahead of themselves. But now

Michele understood. She would give up all her own chances at happiness for him, to protect him.

The frightening dream about the graveyard flooded back to Michele, and she shuddered. It was clear that Irving Henry was trying to tell her something. But was she ready to hear it?

❧❦

"*Oh,* my God!" Caissie grabbed Michele's hand and stared at the ring the next morning in front of her locker. Michele had just finished filling Caissie in on her latest adventures in time. "And you're wearing it on your wedding finger, I see!"

Michele pulled her hand away, blushing. "Yeah, well . . ."

"How in the world are your future boyfriends going to measure up to this whole affair?" Caissie wondered as they started walking to class. "Like, say, Ben Archer, for example?"

"Excuse me?" Michele stopped to give Caissie a look.

"I overheard one of the cheerleaders talking about how he's taking you to Autumn Ball," Caissie admitted. "Why didn't you tell me?"

"Because we're just going as friends. It's so not a big deal," Michele told her. "Honestly, I'd rather not go at all. I just think he's a cool, nice guy and I didn't want to hurt his feelings, so . . ."

"Hold up." Caissie stared at Michele, hands on her hips. "Are you saying Philip is it for you? You're not going to give anyone else a chance, you're just going to live the life of a nun from now on?"

"No, I just . . . You don't understand. I feel like he's . . . like he's waiting for me," Michele said sheepishly.

"Michele, he's not even *alive*!"

"You don't need to remind me," Michele said hotly. "And I didn't mean it like that—I don't know what I mean."

"You're the one who encouraged Philip to move on," Caissie pointed out. "So you should too. You can't exactly settle down with a 118-year-old ghost, can you?"

"Says the girl who still hasn't asked Aaron out yet," Michele retorted.

Caissie's mouth fell open. "What?"

"Come on, you know you can be honest with me," Michele said in a gentler tone. "I've seen the way you guys act around each other. It's so obvious you're into each other, but too nervous to admit it."

Caissie's face had turned red. "I'm not so sure he would agree with that. . . . You swear you won't say anything?"

"I swear," Michele said. "But I just know he feels the same way."

"Come on. We're going to be late," Caissie said, in an obvious bid to change the subject. "Let's take the shortcut."

As they cut through the administration office to class, Michele stopped short in astonishment. Someone who looked like the teenage *Philip* was studying a school map.

"Caissie!" she cried.

Caissie, who was in the middle of sending a text message, looked up a second too late. He had turned the corner, and as he walked past, Michele saw that it wasn't her Philip at all. He didn't have that purposeful stride that Philip always had when he walked. In fact, how could it have been Philip? *I'm the time traveler, not him,* Michele reminded herself.

254

"What?" Caissie asked, following her gaze. "What are you looking at?"

Michele bit her lip. "Nothing, I thought . . . well, never mind."

Michele sat at her computer that afternoon, frozen in shock. Wikipedia and every other online source she had just checked still had no listing or information about Philip Walker. There was no triumphant body of work from the composer of "Bring the Colors Back." There were no news articles about him, no records, nothing—as if his life had never been. *What happened?* she wondered, feeling dizzy. *I saved him—he had all these plans— how could there be no trace of him now? What* became *of him?*

Michele got up, desperate to talk to Caissie. There had to be something she could do or some kind of scientific explanation Caissie might come up with. She raced downstairs, but as she headed toward the door, something caught her eye: an odd, hazy glow coming from the library.

"Annaleigh?" Michele called out uneasily. There was no answer.

She walked tentatively into the library. As she stepped into the room, she saw that she was alone, and yet she felt another presence there. She nervously tried to back out, but she felt herself being pushed forward, as if by an invisible hand. She saw a book lying on a reading table, the strange glow coming from the ceiling above it. Without warning, the book snapped open on its own. Michele gasped and tried to run, but she was frozen with fear, stuck in place. She watched in terror as the pages flipped back and forth, then came to rest. Michele felt herself being nudged toward the book, and as she moved closer, she saw that it was a photo album. And it was opened to the old photo of Irving Henry, circa 1900.

Michele shakily reached for the album, and suddenly her legs felt paralyzed, her hands glued to the album, as she was flung back in time with the stunning realization *It's happening again.*

"Walter! Hurry up, dear. We're going to be late."

Michele jumped, the photo album falling from her hands. She was alone in the library, but the female voice she heard was familiar. Anxiously, she ventured out to the Grand Hall. A middle-aged couple was waiting by the door: a dark-haired man in a black suit and hat and a red-haired woman in a black three-quarter length skirt and sweater set. As Michele looked more closely at the woman, she felt a jolt of recognition.

"Clara!" she cried, overcome with emotion at seeing her all grown up. But to her surprise, Clara didn't react as though she had heard anything. She simply looked straight through Michele, as if she weren't there. *She can't see me anymore,* Michele realized with a pang of sadness.

A boy of about eight or nine came barreling down the stairs in a little black suit of his own. Michele drew in her breath in shock as he came closer. There was no mistaking those eyes. It was her grandfather, Walter!

"But I don't *want* to go to a funeral for some old stranger," he whined as Clara grasped his hand.

"Now, Walter, that's no way to speak of the dead," Clara admonished. "Mr. Henry was a very nice man who worked for the family for years. We have to pay our respects. And besides, we're meeting your mommy there."

Mr. Henry. Michele gulped. *They're going to Irving Henry's funeral.*

"And I *don't* see why Mommy and Stella went out without me either," little Walter said, pouting.

"Darling, your cousin is an engaged young lady and sometimes she needs girl time with her auntie," Clara explained. "You'll understand when you're older and you have a young lady of your own."

Walter grimaced. "Blech!"

As Michele looked around, she noticed that something was very different. The Windsor opulence was far less on display, with the mansion missing many of its luxurious decorative touches. Instead, American flags of different shapes, sizes, and textures were hung throughout the house. So far she hadn't spotted any member of the normally sizable Windsor staff. A cream flag bearing a blue star and a gold star was hung on the front door. *A blue star means someone in the family is in the army . . . and a gold star means someone's been killed in action,* Michele remembered from history class. And that was when the dates on Irving Henry's headstone from her dream flashed back to her. Was it really . . . 1944? A cold feeling ran down Michele's spine as she realized that this was the middle of World War II.

"Let's go, Sam, Walter," Clara said.

Clara's husband, Sam, opened the door and the three of them trooped outside and into the black Chrysler two-door car that was parked in the driveway. On impulse Michele

257

followed them, slipping unseen into the backseat next to little Walter. As Sam drove uptown, Michele was distracted from their conversation by the sights of 1940s Manhattan. Posters for the war effort were emblazoned on every commercial building. RUMORS COST US LIVES! cried one, with a grim illustration of a man whispering war secrets. BUY WAR BONDS! urged signs on every street. But the most common picture in the posters was the smiling, determined, and grandfatherly face of the wartime president Franklin Delano Roosevelt.

Bookstore windows advertised titles such as *The Officer's Guide* and *So Your Husband's Gone to War!* Department store windows busily promoted a plethora of war relief materials, from blackout drapes to Mickey Mouse gas masks for children. Michele shuddered. *What a terrifying time to be alive,* she thought. The New Yorkers walking briskly past were all wearing similar plain cotton clothing, nothing like the formal ball gowns and tuxes of 1910 or the dazzling flapper dresses of the twenties. Michele saw the same anxious yet determined expression on many of their faces.

Sam pulled into the Trinity Church Cemetery and Mausoleum, which was surrounded by elm and oak trees and grassy lawns and overlooked the Hudson River. Michele followed as they headed toward a group of people surrounding a hole in the ground, where the coffin was being lowered. She stood slightly behind Clara, Sam, and Walter, thinking how surreal and insane it was that she was not only back in the 1940s, but there with the grandfather she lived with in 2010—who had no idea that his future granddaughter was in his midst.

"Mommy!" he called out suddenly, waving.

"Hi, darling," a familiar voice cooed.

"Lily," Michele whispered, nearly overwhelmed with emotion at being with them all together. Lily was now a woman in her midthirties, and she still looked dazzlingly glamorous, even in a black funeral dress. Her hair was no longer in her twenties bob; she now had shoulder-length pin curls under a wide-brim hat. A girl about Michele's age was with her, dressed in a billowy black blouse and a matching formfitting skirt, white socks, and saddle shoes. Her wavy dark hair and sandy brown eyes were familiar to Michele, and she realized that this was Stella, the girl from the portrait in Michele's sitting room. *She must be Clara's daughter!*

As Lily and Stella headed toward the rest of the family, Stella suddenly froze. Her eyes locked with Michele's. *She can see me,* Michele realized in amazement. *But why her? Why not the others?*

Lily scooped up Walter in a hug, and Clara and Sam gestured to Stella to join them, but she stayed rooted to her spot. "Who is that?" she blurted out. "That girl behind you. The one in those tattered trousers."

Michele glanced down. Oh, yeah. She was wearing her Abercrombie jeans with the strategic rips.

Lily looked up sharply at Stella's words, and Clara's eyes darted around the area. For a moment Clara and Lily met each other's gaze, then quickly looked away. And Michele knew: *They're both looking for me!*

"Sweetie, there's no one of that description," Sam said.

Stella looked at her parents incredulously and pointed to Michele. "But she's right there!"

259

"We don't see anyone, dear," Clara said, making an apologetic gesture.

The color drained from Stella's face and she looked from Michele to her parents, clearly stunned that she was invisible to them. Stella forced a laugh, trying to hide her panic from them.

"Never mind, then," she said shakily. "I'm just . . . hungry and I must have gotten light-headed and—and thought I saw someone."

"We'll get lunch right after the service," Sam assured her. "Come stand with us."

Stella obeyed but stood as far from Michele as possible, casting her frightened looks every few minutes.

"It's okay. I'm not going to hurt you. I can explain," Michele called out to her, trying to sound reassuring, but Stella promptly turned her head, pretending she hadn't heard.

Just then the vicar arrived. As the funeral service proceeded, Michele's mind drifted off. She wondered where Philip was now. Was he okay? Was he in New York? When would she be able to find out what had happened to him?

"My uncle Irving was a man who didn't belong in his time."

Michele's head snapped up at those words. A middle-aged blond man was speaking, glancing down at note cards in his hand.

"We all know he was a brilliant attorney. We also know that he was brilliantly eccentric." At that, a laugh rippled through the crowd. "My uncle had an obsession with time—Time with a capital *T*, as he called it. He believed in the future. That's where he said he belonged, where he said he *loved*. It was part of his imaginative eccentricity, yes. But Uncle Irving's passion for the future gives me relief, for I know that's where he is now: in his

Heaven of the Future." With a smile, the blond man stepped back and the crowd applauded, murmuring supportively.

Michele felt her heart thudding loudly in her chest. Her mind was racing, confirming the answer that seemed too unbelievable to be real. She sank onto the dirt, barely able to hear the rest of the funeral service, with the words of Irving's nephew echoing in her ears: *He believed in the future. That's where he said he belonged, where he said he loved.*

Why had Irving Henry been able to see her? Why had he stared like that at the key around her neck? Why had he looked at her as though seeing a ghost? Why had his face looked vaguely familiar to her?

Because he's my father.

Michele hugged her arms to her knees as she felt her whole body tremble, tears welling in her eyes. The young man Marion had fallen for, who went by the name Henry Irving, who seemed so different from the other boys of the 1990s . . . was none other than the man being buried that day. This meant that she was born to a father from the nineteenth century and a mother from the twentieth. It was unthinkable. *But then . . . is it any more impossible than my being here right now?*

18

Michele dazedly followed the Windsors back into the car after the funeral, her head still spinning from her discovery. Stella took one look at Michele climbing into the Chrysler and announced that she'd ride home with Aunt Lily. The Chrysler reached Windsor Mansion before Lily's car, and Michele took the opportunity to race upstairs to her—or rather, Stella's—bedroom. She was desperate to return to her own time.

As Michele swung open the bedroom door, her eyes took in all the changes. The Art Deco–style decor of Lily's room had given way to a cheerful, kitschy 1940s look. A bright red rotary phone was on the bureau, and standing in a place of honor was a large table holding both a radio and phonograph. The posters on the walls were of Frank Sinatra, Judy Garland, and the Glenn Miller Army Air Force Band. Framed photos of Stella with a cute, lanky guy in army uniform were placed throughout the room. The calendar on her desk was set to May 1944.

Michele sank onto the desk chair and was just about to take hold of her skeleton key when she heard a sharp gasp. She looked up to see Stella in the doorway, quivering with fear.

"What do you want?" Stella cried, her voice strangled. "Why are you following me?"

"I'm not! I mean—I'm not going to hurt you, don't worry—"

Should I just tell her who I really am? Michele wondered. *Then I can give her the good news that America wins the war.* But just as she was opening her mouth to tell the truth, she heard a warning in her mind. *What if her knowing ahead of time that America is to win the war changes the outcome? What if the element that caused us to win the war was the frantic attention to it, the fixation, even on the home front, on doing anything and everything possible to win?*

"You're a ghost, aren't you?" Stella whispered. "A ghost from the graveyard."

While the ghost alibi had worked well enough with Clara and Lily, Michele figured that the idea of being followed home by a graveyard ghost was hardly comforting to Stella. "No," she said quickly. "I'm . . . someone only you can see. But I'm good. You have nothing to be afraid of."

Stella stared at Michele. "Are you . . . are you saying you're all in my head? Like an—an imaginary friend?"

"No, I'm real," Michele assured her, not wanting Stella to

panic that she was going mental. "It's just that you're the only one who can see or hear me."

"Why me?" Stella pressed her.

"Well, because—because we're supposed to know each other," Michele said, improvising.

Stella stared at her, taking this in. She squeezed her eyes shut as a thought occurred to her. "Are you here because of Jack? Did something happen to him?"

"Who?"

"Jack Rosen—my fiancé," she answered, nervously biting her nail. "He's fighting overseas, and I haven't heard from him in weeks. It's not like him. . . ."

"Your fiancé? How old are you?" Michele asked in surprise.

"Seventeen."

"Wow. That's so young to get married," Michele remarked.

"Everyone's marrying young now. We don't know how long our boys have," Stella said quietly. "But he gets to go on leave next month, so we're planning to marry then. It won't be the type of grand affair typical of Windsor weddings, as we don't have the rations for a reception, or even for a nice wedding dress. But I don't care. It will be a fairy-tale wedding to me just to be married and have him home safe."

Michele smiled at her. "I'm sure it'll be great."

Suddenly the terrible, loud whine of a siren sounded. Michele jumped, but Stella didn't seem surprised.

"What's that?" Michele gasped.

"Air raid blackout drill," Stella answered briskly, hurrying out of the room. Michele followed her downstairs to the Grand Hall. Clara, Sam, Lily, and Walter soon joined them, along with two household staff members, all carrying candles. Michele watched in amazement as Sam pressed a button and the entire house was blanketed in darkness—all the lights were switched off, and heavy black curtains fell over the windows, covering every bit of light. Then they hurried out the front door, Michele running after them. Behind the house was a small shed, which Michele had never seen before. Once inside, she realized that it was an air raid shelter. The walls were protected with sandbags, and there were two bunk beds in the small space, along with a shelf holding food and first aid supplies. Michele shuddered and sat against the sandbags with her knees hugged to her chest. She knew it was only a drill, but it was still frightening. Little Walter curled up on the lower bunk, Lily cradling him in her arms, while Stella climbed up to the top bunk. Clara and Sam huddled together against the sandbags next to the invisible Michele, the staff members across from them. There was a few minutes' silence as they waited for the all-clear signal, and then Lily cleared her throat.

"Stella and I spent a couple hours at the Red Cross this morning, making care packages for the soldiers. We included your letter and gift in the package for Charles."

"Our son will soon be home safe," Sam said confidently. He looked up at Stella. "And Jack too."

The siren blared again, and Michele covered her ears. It was the most awful noise. As the others gathered their candles and prepared to leave the shelter, Michele closed her eyes, picturing 2010, and silently begged Time to send her home.

And then there she was—standing on the back lawn of the Windsor Mansion, where the air raid shelter had once stood.

Shivering in the cold evening air, Michele hurried to the front door. But as she turned the knob, she saw to her horror that her hand was bare—the ring from Philip was gone! It must have fallen off while they were running into the shelter. Michele looked desperately at her naked hand, crushed. How could she have lost something so important?

The next morning, an anguished scream jolted Michele awake. She jumped out of bed, terrified. That was when she saw that she wasn't in her bedroom—she was in Stella's. Michele raced to the desktop calendar and saw that it was June 7, 1944. For a moment she stood frozen in surprise. She had never gone back in time in her sleep before. What was *happening*?

The scream turned into a howl. Michele raced out of the room and down the stairs, praying all the way that nothing was seriously wrong, that everyone was okay. But she found Stella in a heap on the floor, screaming Jack's name over and over. An army officer stood in the doorway, his face ashen. Clara, Sam, and Lily were huddled around Stella, their faces scrunched up with grief as they tried to comfort her. Little Walter stood behind them in his pajamas, his face frozen, his tiny body shaking.

Michele watched the scene in horror, her heart in her throat. Stella dropped the telegram and Michele read the devastating opening sentence: *We regret to inform you that Private Rosen has been killed in action.*

Suddenly, Michele had never felt angrier in her life. What

was the *point* of loving when the people you loved were taken from you? When Death or Time were always looming and poised to strike, why did love even exist? She squeezed her eyes shut and Marion's and Philip's faces filled her vision. *Why must we spend so much of our lives missing people instead of being with them?* Michele wondered. Her eyes were filled with tears as she approached Stella and wrapped her in a hug.

Throughout the rest of the day, the Windsor family holed up in the drawing room, rallying around Stella. Michele sat beside her on the couch, holding her hand protectively. Clara sat on Stella's other side, stroking her daughter's hair. Lily was in the rocking chair beside the couch, holding Walter on her lap. Stella couldn't speak, but the others all talked proudly of Jack. There was much emotion when a telegram arrived from President Roosevelt himself, reporting that Jack had died in combat while fighting the Nazis in Normandy the previous day. The president would be awarding Jack a posthumous medal of honor.

Sam read aloud newspaper articles praising the success of D-day and stating that it signaled the beginning of the end for Nazi Germany. "Your fiancé died for his country, Stella, and his mission was a success," Sam said earnestly. "There's no more noble way to go."

Stella nodded slightly, her face still looking glazed and shocked.

Suddenly, the sounds of a distant parade were heard: trumpets blaring, people shouting and whistling, feet stomping. Michele looked anxiously at Stella. As the parade came closer on its route down Fifth Avenue, the music became loud and clear:

> *Over there, over there,*
> *Send the word, send the word, over there,*
> *That the Yanks are coming, the Yanks are coming,*
> *The drums drum-drumming everywhere . . .*

Stella slowly got up and moved toward the front balcony, the others following closely. She stood at the railing, watching silently. As the parade approached Windsor Mansion, with its blue and gold stars hanging in the windows, it stopped and directed the rest of the song to the family on the balcony.

> *So prepare, say a prayer,*
> *Send the word, send the word, to beware*
> *We'll be over, we're coming over,*
> *And we won't came back till it's over, over there!*

Michele watched as Stella, her eyes spilling over with tears, began to mouth the words, mustering a brave smile for the parade crowd. Stella gazed at the people, seeing the HOORAY FOR D-DAY! signs, and posters bearing blue and gold stars.

"I'm—I'm so proud of him," Stella gasped, and fell sobbing into Clara's arms.

As Michele watched the patriotic scene both inside and outside the Windsor Mansion, she realized her pride at being an American. It was the American drive for a better world, and its spirit of survival in the face of crisis, that had propelled Jack and thousands of other young men to risk their lives every day for their country and the Allies. It was that same spirit that led Stella to suddenly say, "I want to finish out Jack's mission."

"What do you mean, sweetie?" Clara asked, helping her back inside.

"I mean . . . I want to do something major to help," she said, pacing the drawing room. "We *have* to win this war. It's the only way Jack won't have died in vain."

After a few minutes, Lily spoke up. "What about a fund-raiser, or a drive? There's always a need to sell more war bonds and collect rubber and metals for the army."

Stella stared at Lily. "That's it! A fund-raiser concert—with you as the star attraction! Instead of tickets, people will have to buy war bonds and donate materials for the military."

As they discussed the idea, Michele stared at Stella in amazement. *I wasn't sent here to help her,* she realized. *I'm here to learn from her. I've lost my mom and Philip, but I need to be brave like Stella, like all the men and women who lose loved ones but keep going with life.*

Michele was suddenly overcome with pride at being a Windsor. The Windsor women had all been through tragedy and heartache, but they always held their heads high, moved forward, and never lost hope. They were the strongest, most inspiring women Michele knew, and she was stirred by them, motivated to follow their example.

Michele pulled Stella aside. "I know Jack is so proud of you right now," she said. "I'm proud just to know you."

"Thank you," Stella whispered.

The doorbell rang, and a moment later, a group of Stella's

classmates hurried inside, their faces stricken as they rushed forward to hug their friend. Michele made her way to the staircase, sensing that it was time for her to return. But before she had made it to the third floor, she felt Time pushing her forward, and she held on to the railing as she was sent flying. . . .

She landed on the mezzanine, still clinging to the staircase railing for dear life. Through the glass door she saw Walter in his office, writing behind his desk. His head was bent low and he didn't see Michele. As she watched her gray-haired grandfather, all she could see was the little boy he had been, his small body shaking, his face terrified, at the horrors of war. She felt a sudden rush of affection for him—and sadness. She was beginning to realize what a tragedy it was that Marion and her parents had never repaired their relationship.

Michele remembered Irving Henry's funeral service and shivered. So Walter had seen him buried in the ground nearly fifty years before his relationship with Marion began. How was that even *possible*? She wondered what her grandparents knew about him, how *much* they knew. But as she glanced back at Walter's office, she knew she wasn't ready to ask just yet.

The next afternoon, Michele slowly walked into the library, seeking out the old photo album. She needed to see the photo of Irving Henry again. *My dad,* she reminded herself. It still didn't feel real.

Opening the photo album, she saw an inscription in the

front cover: *Merry Christmas, Mother & Father! I hope you enjoy the photos as much as I do. With love from Stella, 1940.*

Just as it dawned on Michele that Stella was the one who had put together the fateful photo album, she felt Time's choreography take hold, sending her back. . . .

"Why, it's you!"

Michele jumped back in surprise. Stella was standing in front of her, wearing a dark evening dress, purse in hand, and looking as though she was just about to leave the house.

"You're back!" Stella exclaimed, her eyes bugging out.

"Yeah, I guess I am," Michele said, looking around her. "How are you? Are you okay?"

"Yes. We're actually just about to leave for the fund-raiser concert Aunt Lily and I organized. Would you like to see it?"

"Of course I would!" Michele followed Stella outside, where Clara and Sam were waiting for her in the Chrysler, the two of them in evening wear. As Sam drove into Times Square, Michele noticed that the thoroughfare's famously bright, animated signs were all dimmed, making the area seem like a ghost of itself. But the Square was packed, and the Chrysler sat in a traffic jam of cars and cabs.

"This is the most crowded I've seen any New York street since the gas ration and dimouts began," Sam commented. He caught Stella's eye in the rearview mirror. "They're all coming for you, sweetie."

"They're coming for Lily and to support the war effort," Stella corrected him, but she looked proud all the same.

As they walked toward the Palace Theater on Broadway, Michele drew in her breath at the scene in front of her. Outside the theater was a long line of people handing bags of precious war materials—rubber, tinfoil, paper, nylon, and silk—to two volunteers standing in front of huge boxes labeled VICTORY SCRAP DRIVE. Sam carried their own scrap bag, and Michele followed the family into line. Once they'd handed in their war materials, they moved into the lobby, where two tables were set up with volunteers selling war bonds. After they had bought three bonds, which acted as tickets, they made their way to their reserved seats in the center orchestra.

And what a show it was! Michele stood in the aisle next to Stella's seat, watching in amazement as Lily emceed the star-studded V for Victory concert. The show began with Lily leading a chorus of soldiers in a rousing rendition of "Over There." Then the Andrews Sisters, the famous harmonizing trio of the day, performed their hit swing number "Boogie Woogie Bugle Boy" as the audience stood up and danced in front of their seats. Louis Armstrong came onstage to massive cheers, and he and Lily performed the wistful ballad "The White Cliffs of Dover," a song symbolizing England's optimistic hope for a return to peace. Lily, Louis, and the Andrews Sisters performed several other patriotic songs, from "Remember Pearl Harbor" to "Praise the Lord and Pass the Ammunition!" As they reached the end of the show, Lily stepped up to the microphone and announced, "This last song is dedicated to my cousin Stella's brave fiancé, Private Jack Rosen, who died fighting for our country on D-day. He is a hero and he will be greatly missed."

The audience erupted in applause and cheers for Jack, and when Michele turned to Stella, she saw that she had tears in her eyes. Michele squeezed her hand.

"I have a special guest star on this song," Lily continued. "Everyone, please welcome Phoenix Warren."

The audience once again burst into cheers and whistles, and Michele leaned forward, eager to catch a glimpse of the famed man whose composition had inspired her name.

He stepped onstage amid the massive applause, and Michele stared at him. He stood tall and proud in his navy suit adorned with a V for Victory pin, and even with salt-and-pepper hair, he was the type of man who looked handsome and debonair in middle age. As he smiled at the audience, Michele felt a jolt of familiarity. Where had she seen that grin before?

Phoenix strode purposefully to the piano, and that was when Michele saw his deep blue eyes. For a moment, she couldn't breathe. Phoenix Warren was really *Philip Walker*!

As Michele was reeling, Lily began to sing to Philip's accompaniment, their two instruments echoing together beautifully inside the theater.

> *"I'll be seeing you*
> *In all the old familiar places*
> *That this heart of mine embraces*
> *All day through.*
> *In that small café*
> *The park across the way*
> *The children's carousel*
> *The chestnut tree, the wishing well . . ."*

273

As Michele stared dizzyingly up at Philip and Lily onstage, she realized how true these lyrics were. *None of these people are alive in my lifetime—but I can still see them, still find them.* If her time travels had shown her anything, it was that 2010 was not the only present time. *Other time periods are all around us, and the spirits of those we've loved and lost still surround us. We just have to be able to see them and feel them.*

Michele hurried down the aisle to the edge of the stage, but Philip's eyes were closed, as they always were when he played.

> *I'll find you in the morning sun*
> *And when the night is new*
> *I'll be looking at the moon,*
> *But I'll be seeing you.*

Philip opened his eyes. She watched as his face registered astonishment at the sight of her, and then those beautiful blue eyes filled with tears.

As Lily and Philip took their bows, Michele hoisted herself up onto the side of the stage and waited for him in the wings. He dashed offstage after a quick bow and seized her hand, pulling her into an empty corridor backstage. They were near each other at last, but as they stood nervously facing each other, it was clear that something was different now. Philip was all grown up.

"So you're—you're Phoenix Warren," Michele stammered. "Would you believe that I was named after your composition?"

" 'Michele,' " Philip said softly. "I wrote that for you."

And with that, Michele threw her arms around him and

they shared a long embrace. But something was still different. She had last seen him when they were both teenagers and lovers—but the passage of time for him had waved its wand and now they could only be friends. Friends who had forever, irrevocably changed each other's lives.

As she pulled away, Michele said, "So you kept your promise to me, then. I had thought—well, I didn't know what happened to you. . . ."

"When I read in the paper back in '27 that Uncle and Mother believed me to be dead, I realized . . . perhaps it was a divine mistake," Philip said. "They were so determined that no Walker heir should be a performer, and did everything they could to wreck my career and life, even by proxy when I was in London. So I realized that I had lost everything that mattered to me but my music. And I decided that Philip James Walker would be no more, and be reborn as someone new—just as a phoenix rises from the ashes."

"*Wow . . .*" Michele clasped his hand. "I can't tell you how thrilled I am to know that you're all right, better than all right—that you're living your dream."

Philip smiled. "I had to. I couldn't break my promise to you. And now . . . will you make me the same promise? To always move forward with life, pursue your writing, and have a family?"

"I thought you promised you'd come back to me," Michele couldn't help saying as tears stung her eyes.

Philip gently wiped away her tear. "I will," he said. "Somehow. It just might not be in the way you expect."

Before Michele had a chance to ask what he meant by that, she heard the sound of footsteps backstage. She turned to see a smartly dressed woman in her forties, with strawberry-blond hair and sandy brown eyes.

"Darling, you were wonderful!" the woman exclaimed, hurrying to Philip's side and wrapping her arms possessively around his neck. Michele shrank back, feeling as if she had just been punched in the stomach.

Philip turned to give Michele an apologetic look, but Michele shook her head and said through her tears, "It's okay. I'm glad you're not alone."

And with that, she ran onto the stage and down the steps to the audience, and there was Stella, looking for someone.

"There you are," she said when she saw Michele. "Are you all right? Why are you crying?"

Be brave like Stella, Michele reminded herself. "I'm okay. Congratulations, Stella, you did a wonderful thing tonight."

Stella gave her a small smile. "Thanks. I just wish Jack had seen it."

"I know he did," Michele assured her.

Stella took her hand. "Come on. We're going home."

On the drive back to the Windsor Mansion, Michele somehow instinctively knew that she was going home to her own time—to stay. Sure enough, when she climbed out of the 1940s Chrysler, she found that she was suddenly alone. She turned back to see where Stella and her parents were, but they had vanished, along with the vintage car. She was back in 2010.

That night, Michele dreamt of her mother. . . .

Michele was heading upstairs, smiling contentedly. She stopped in shock when she saw the vision at the top of the staircase—Marion, surrounded by a hazy white glow.

"Mom!" Michele cried, running into her mother's outstretched arms.

"You did very well, sweetheart," Marion said, beaming at her daughter.

"Mom! It's so good to see you." She buried her face in Marion's shoulder, breathing in her mom's comfortingly familiar scent. She looked up excitedly. "I've thought of something—by going back in

time, I was able to change history. I'm going to find a way to go back to that day and save you!"

Marion shook her head slowly. "No, sweetie, you can't. It was my time to go. When it's your time, there is nothing any of us can do to change that."

Michele looked down, her eyes brimming with tears. "But why—why was it your time? How can it be, when you were still so young? And I need you, so much."

Marion held Michele's face in her hands.

"But I'm always here with you, just as Philip is. And I've already fulfilled my purpose on this earth."

"What was it?" Michele asked, wiping her eyes.

"Bringing you into the world, of course," Marion answered, smiling. "Because you are a girl with the potential to change the world."

Marion threw her arms around her daughter, and the two of them shared a tight, tearful embrace.

"Mom—I found out the truth about him," Michele blurted out. "My dad."

Marion smiled tearfully. "I know. It's such a shock—and yet it makes sense in a way. It explains so much."

"Have you seen him?" Michele asked breathlessly. "I mean, now that you're both—"

Marion shook her head, her eyes pained. "No. And I have this feeling that—that he hasn't left the earth, not really. That he's still traveling, still looking for . . . something."

"I'm going to find him," Michele declared, her heartbeat quickening with anticipation. "I don't know when or how—but I know I'm going to find him. For both of us."

Marion nodded, smoothing her daughter's hair and giving her a tender smile.

"It's time for me to go now, my sweet Michele," she said softly. "Please know that I will love you always."

"I love you too, Mom. Forever," Michele whispered.

"I'll be seeing you," Marion said with a smile, just before vanishing.

The next morning, Michele walked up the front steps to school, a spring in her step. For the first time since her arrival in New York, she was ready to live—*truly* live—in her own time again. She finally felt ready to surrender to the present.

As she was digging in her bag for her homework assignment, she heard the sound of a late student skidding into the room just as the final bell rang.

"Class, we have another new transfer student," Mr. Lewis announced. "Everyone, meet Philip Walker."

Michele's head snapped up in shock.

Oh—my—God.

She was too stunned to move a muscle as she locked eyes with the spitting image of a young Philip Walker. Michele realized with a jolt that *this* was who she had seen by the school office that day when she'd thought she had seen her Philip.

The new student continued to look at her with those intense sapphire eyes, even as the teacher handed him a folder of class materials. As he reached for the folder, Michele saw it on his finger—the gold signet ring that Philip had given her. The very ring she had lost.

Michele smiled at him in amazement as Philip's words echoed in her ears: *"I will find a way back to you. No matter what, I promise."*

TO BE CONTINUED

AUTHOR'S NOTE

While the story of *Timeless* is fictional, the world in which the characters live is based in reality. One of the greatest joys for me in writing this book was researching the eras that Michele visits. As I threw myself into studying the Gilded Age, the Roaring Twenties, and the World War II years, I felt almost as if I'd been there, thanks to the amazing resources I had.

NEW YORK

I consider New York City the principal player of *Timeless*, as it is both the backbone of the story and an ever-changing, complex character. My greatest tool in researching the history of this incredible city was simply spending time there, walking the streets where so many walked before me, and visiting the landmarks that are like living tributes to bygone eras. If you too are fascinated by New York history, I highly recommend visiting the New-York Historical Society and the Museum of the City of New York. Additionally, Big Onion Walking Tours offers historical tours of many areas of the city. I took Big Onion's historical tour of Central Park, which proved valuable to me when it came time to describe the park circa 1910.

Below are some of the materials I used in my research:

At the Plaza: An Illustrated History of the World's Most Famous Hotel, by Curtis Gathje; *Central Park,* by Edward J. Levine; *Inside the Plaza: An Intimate Portrayal of the Ultimate Hotel,* by Ward Morehouse III; *Gotham Comes of Age: New York Through the Lens of the Byron Company, 1892–1942,* by Peter Simmons; *On Fifth Avenue: Highlights of Architecture and Cultural History,* by Charles J. Ziga and Robin Langley Sommer; *The New Amsterdam: The Biography of a Broadway Theater,* by Mary C. Henderson; the website for the Drive to Protect the Ladies' Mile District, www.preserve2.org/ladiesmile/; the official Central Park website, www.centralpark.com; and the great PBS series *New York: A Documentary Film,* directed by Ric Burns.

THE WINDSOR MANSION

Thanks to the incredible Preservation Society of Newport County, we can see just how the New York Four Hundred lived during the Gilded Age. While the Fifth Avenue mansions of Old New York have all sadly been demolished or converted into office buildings, hotels, condos, etc., the spectacular homes owned by these same New York families (the Astors and the Vanderbilts, for example) are fully preserved in Newport, Rhode Island. In fact, the trip that Michele's class takes to visit the Newport Mansions is based on the trip I took while researching *Timeless*. I even stayed in the same hotel as Michele and her class, the Hotel Viking.

I absolutely recommend visiting beautiful Newport and touring these homes, which are unlike anything you'll find elsewhere in America. The Windsor Mansion is based on two different Vanderbilt mansions in Newport: Alva Vanderbilt's Marble House and Alice Vanderbilt's The Breakers. (The homes were usually attributed to the wives of the family, since they generally ruled society and the home in those days.) Both Marble House and The Breakers were designed by the foremost architect of the late nineteenth century, Richard Morris Hunt. If you decide to visit Newport, stop in at The Breakers to view the inspiration for the Windsors' Grand Hall, and visit Marble House to see what the impressive exterior of the Windsor Mansion looked like. If you can't get to Newport anytime soon, the Preservation Society of Newport County (www.newportmansions.org) offers books with wonderful photographs and descriptions of the houses, along with a DVD that takes you into the homes for a glimpse. A&E's *America's Castles* DVD series also includes an excellent episode on the Newport Mansions and the families who owned them.

Other books that helped me build the Windsor Mansion include *Gilded Mansions: Grand Architecture and High Society*, by Wayne Craven, and *Great Houses of New York: 1880–1930*, by Michael C. Kathrens.

THE NEW YORK FOUR HUNDRED
AND THE GILDED AGE

The book that was most helpful to my understanding of the New York Four Hundred and the reign of Caroline Astor (as described in Chapter Four of *Timeless*) was *A Season of Splendor: The Court of Mrs. Astor in Gilded Age New York,* by Greg King. It's a must-read if you're interested in this period. I also highly recommend the addictively entertaining and informative biographies and autobiographies of the Four Hundred family members, including: *Consuelo and Alva Vanderbilt: The Story of a Daughter and a Mother in the Gilded Age,* by Amanda Mackenzie Stuart; *Fortune's Children: The Fall of the House of Vanderbilt,* by Arthur T. Vanderbilt II; *King Lehr and the Gilded Age,* by Lady Decies; and *Sara and Eleanor: The Story of Sara Delano Roosevelt and Her Daughter-in-Law, Eleanor Roosevelt,* by Jan Pottker.

Other books I consulted include *Dawn of the Century: 1900–1910,* part of the Time-Life *Our American Century* series, and the novels of Edith Wharton, especially *The House of Mirth* and *The Custom of the Country.*

THE JAZZ AGE AND THE ROARING TWENTIES

The history of jazz, and how it evolved from ragtime and later developed into rhythm and blues, is a subject I am passionate about. The geniuses involved in creating this music and the fantastic songs they wrote and performed are, in my mind, one of the greatest gifts American history has given us. *Jazz,* the comprehensive PBS series directed by Ken Burns, gives a full overview of the music and its origins. And simply listening to the greats of the day, such as Bessie Smith, Louis Armstrong, George Gershwin, Duke Ellington, Billie Holiday, Count Basie, and Cab Calloway, will send you into that Harlem Renaissance atmosphere.

Some of the books I recommend to help you immerse yourself in the 1920s are *Anything Goes: A Biography of the Roaring Twenties,* by Lucy Moore; *The Jazz Age: The '20s,* part of Time-Life's *Our American Century* series; and the novels of F. Scott Fitzgerald, especially *The Great Gatsby.* There are also fantastic films that bring this edgy world to life, particularly Francis Ford Coppola's *The Cotton Club,* Alan Rudolph's *Mrs. Parker and the Vicious Circle,* and Robert Z. Leonard's *The Great Ziegfeld.*

AMERICA AT WAR

The most emotional parts of the *Timeless* process for me were researching World War II and writing about the Windsors' experiences in 1944. It was simultaneously humbling, heartbreaking, and inspiring to read about the sacrifices and strength of Americans back then. Visiting Springwood, Franklin Delano Roosevelt's home in Hyde Park, New York, I felt as if I had been transplanted into the middle of those turbulent years. The incredible Franklin D. Roosevelt Presidential Library and Museum houses exhibits and artifacts that bring FDR and the war years to life.

I also recommend the following books:

Decade of Triumph: The '40s, another Time-Life *Our American Century* volume; *New York in the Forties,* by Andreas

Feininger (photographs) and John von Hartz (text); *Over Here! New York City During World War II,* by Lorraine B. Diehl; and *Summer at Tiffany,* by Marjorie Hart.

There are countless beautiful films set during World War II, but I want to especially recommend John Cromwell's wonderful homage to the homefront, *Since You Went Away.* Another excellent pick is "FDR," from PBS's *American Experience* series.

TIME-TRAVEL THEORIES

As Caissie tells Michele, Albert Einstein did indeed believe that time travel was possible. In fact, he proved that one could feasibly travel to the future! For more information on this thrilling topic, see this page from PBS's *Nova* website: pbs.org/wgbh/nova/time/think.html.

Most books on Einstein discuss his theories pertaining to time. From among the many, I recommend *Einstein 1905: The Standard of Greatness,* by John S. Rigden. Who knows—maybe within the next hundred years, time travelers like Michele will walk among us. ☺

For more notes and recommendations, please visit my website at alexandramonir.com.

ACKNOWLEDGMENTS

This project has been a true labor of love, and I have many people I wish to thank.

First, to the Delacorte Press editor who believed in my story and gave me the opportunity of a lifetime: Stephanie Lane Elliott, I am so grateful to you! You and Krista Vitola are the dream team. Many thanks to you both for making this such a wonderful experience.

To my incredible agent, Andy McNicol at William Morris Endeavor, who encouraged me to write *Timeless* back when I first came up with the idea: This wouldn't have happened without you, and I thank you so much!

Thank you to my publisher, Beverly Horowitz. It's an honor

to be one of your authors! And to the brilliant copyeditor Jennifer Black, thank you so much.

Many thanks to Brooke and Howard Kaufman, my management team at HK. Howard, I'm so grateful for your guidance and support over the years. Brooke, thank you for being my honorary big sister, manager, and great friend all wrapped into one!

Seth Jaret, I feel so lucky to be represented by you. Thank you for believing in me from the start, and for helping me navigate the biz.

Michael Bearden, thank you for bringing your incredible musicianship to the *Timeless* songs. Working with you is a thrill and an honor!

Charlie Walk, you've been an amazing mentor to me. Thank you for pushing my writing, and for sending me to William Morris.

Heather Holley and Rob Hoffman, I'm grateful to you both for collaborating with me on songs that have led to many opportunities. Heather, thank you for your amazing musicianship that always brings out the best in me, and for your wonderful friendship.

Many thanks to the New York Public Library for letting me use the Frederick Lewis Allen Room for my writing and research.

Thank you to Chad Michael Ward and Angela Carlino for the beautiful cover art. Neal Preston, thank you for lending your art to my author photo.

Special thanks to Eric Reid and Laurie Pozmantier at WME, Chad Christopher at SMGSB, and everyone at Random House who is involved with *Timeless*.

I'd also like to acknowledge my incredible circle of family and friends, who have all cheered on this project. First and foremost to my father, Shon: You've had the biggest impact on my life, and I am both humbled and inspired by you. Your support and belief in me is what gave my dream wings, and I thank you, with all my heart, for everything.

To my mother, ZaZa: You're my best friend in the world and it's our relationship that inspired the closeness between Michele and the women in her family. I can't thank you enough for all you've given me.

Arian, thank you for your valuable feedback on this project, and for your love and support. I'm so lucky to be your sister!

Papa, thank you for all the imaginative stories you told us as kids. They made me want to become a storyteller myself. ☺

Many thanks to Stacie Surabian and Marise Freitas for helping with my projects over the years and for being like family to me. Thank you to my incredible mentors and friends Maury Yeston, Karen McCullah-Lutz & Kirsten Smith, and Greg Brill.

Mia Antonelli, thank you for being the most wonderful friend a girl could ask for, and for always being there for me. Chris Robertiello, thank you for all the laughter and inspiring moments.

Gratitude and love to my grandparents, aunts and uncles in Southern and Northern California and my close friends Roxane Cohanim, Ami McCartt, Adriana Ameri, Kirsten Guenther, Sai Mokhtari and Rita J. King. And I can't forget little Honey, my special companion during the long hours of writing!

To the memory of an incredible woman: my grandmother

and namesake, Monir Vakili. I always wished I could have met her, and it was this desire that led me to write about Michele meeting her relatives from the past.

And of course, thank you to the readers! I hope you enjoyed *Timeless.* ☺

ABOUT THE AUTHOR

A singer/songwriter and first-time novelist, ALEXANDRA MONIR divides her time between Los Angeles and New York. For the original music, news, and more on *Timeless,* visit her website at alexandramonir.com.

HEAR THE ORIGINAL SONGS FROM

Timeless

DOWNLOAD THE ORIGINAL SONGS FEATURED
IN THE BOOK!
VISIT **ALEXANDRAMONIR.COM** FOR DETAILS,
THEN ENJOY LISTENING WHILE YOU READ FOR
THE COMPLETE *TIMELESS* EXPERIENCE!